Thomas P. Roberts

Memoirs of John Bannister Gibson

Late chief justice of Pennsylvania. With Hon. Jeremiah S. Black's Eulogy, notes from

Hon. William A. Porter's essay upon his life and character, etc.

Thomas P. Roberts

Memoirs of John Bannister Gibson
*Late chief justice of Pennsylvania. With Hon. Jeremiah S. Black's Eulogy, notes from Hon.
William A. Porter's essay upon his life and character, etc.*

ISBN/EAN: 9783337424091

Printed in Europe, USA, Canada, Australia, Japan

Cover: Foto ©Raphael Reischuk / pixelio.de

More available books at **www.hansebooks.com**

MEMOIRS

OF

JOHN BANNISTER GIBSON,

LATE CHIEF JUSTICE OF PENNSYLVANIA.

WITH

HON. JEREMIAH S. BLACK'S EULOGY,
NOTES FROM HON. WILLIAM A. PORTER'S ESSAY
UPON HIS LIFE AND CHARACTER,
ETC., ETC.

BY

THOMAS P. ROBERTS.

PITTSBURGH:
JOS. EICHBAUM & CO. 48 FIFTH AVENUE.
1890.

INTRODUCTION.

The opinion of those acquainted with Judge Gibson's writings, so far as I can learn, is, that his genius was *sui generis*, and that he came to exercise it at the formative period, the period which witnessed the firm establishment of republican government in America, upon which the war of 1812 set its seal, and in the quarter of the century that witnessed the inception of canals and railroads which hastened wonderfully the settlement and civilization of the continent.

In the determination of the new and perplexing problems governing these new species of corporations, which arose during the period in question, the courts of no State took a more conspicuous part than those of Pennsylvania; and from 1816 to 1853, a period of thirty-seven years, Judge Gibson sat on the Bench of her Supreme Court.

But whatever his merits, I do not feel qualified, being only a layman, to speak of him as a jurist, and have, therefore, attempted only the humble task of gathering together the incidents of his private life and the history of his ancestors. I felt impelled to this duty by reason of the fact that but little is known by the public concerning his personal history; for, as was aptly said in a public address, "In our 'American Encyclopædia,' which purports to give in its sixteen big volumes, biographical sketches of all eminent Americans, there is no mention whatever of John Bannister Gibson."*

The Hon. Wm. A. Porter published in 1855, two years after Judge Gibson's death, an essay on his life, character and writings; aside from this, and Judge Black's beautiful eulogy, nothing has been written which merits even the title of a review of his life as a judge, while no one has heretofore attempted to sketch his personal history beyond the extent of a few paragraphs.

Regarding the private history of a man about whom his own friends know so little, the task, after a period of a third of a century has elapsed since his death, of producing a connected and entertaining sketch is a difficult one. I will feel satisfied, under the circumstances, if this effort will lessen the labors of the historian in the future who is destined to appear, as Judge Porter says, to write the history of the judiciary of Pennsylvania. My aim has been to make this not only a personal sketch, but a compilation of the published matter concerning the part taken in that history by Judge Gibson. Judge Porter's essay has long been out of print, and readers will doubtless be pleased to see reproduced a very large portion of that writer's selections from Judge Gibson's opinions, with his own interesting and able comments thereon. This feature, at least, will be recognized as not the work of a novice or a layman.

To the family and relatives of Judge Gibson I am indebted for much useful material; also to ex-Chief Justice Agnew; Hon. James T. Mitchell and Hon. Henry W. Williams, of the Supreme Court; Hon. William G. Hawkins, of Pittsburgh; Thomas J. Keenan, Esq., and William

---

* Hon. Thos. J. Keenan, at the Pittsburgh Bar meeting in memory of the late Hon. Jeremiah S. Black.

B. Rodgers, Esq., of the Pittsburgh bar; Hon. Charles H. Smiley, of Perry county; Boyd Crumrine, Esq., Reporter of the Supreme Court; Hon. John Stewart, of Chambersburg, and the Rev. J. A. Murray, of Carlisle, from whom many valued suggestions and contributions were received.

T. P. R.

PITTSBURGH, PA., July, 1890.

CONTENTS.

JOHN BANNISTER GIBSON,

LATE CHIEF JUSTICE OF PENNSYLVANIA.

PART FIRST.

ANCESTRY AND PERSONAL HISTORY.

CHAPTER I.

EARLY RECORDS OF THE FAMILY — MILITARY SERVICES OF
JUDGE GIBSON'S FATHER — AND NOTICES OF HIS UNCLE,
GENERAL JOHN GIBSON.

THE lineage of persons of note, besides being of interest
to the general reader, possesses value to the physiologist, and,
indirectly from him, it is to be hoped, the lessons it teaches
will prove of benefit to mankind in general. But for most
Americans the task of tracing a pedigree on direct lines, beyond a few generations, is a difficult one. This difficulty is
probably due to the frequency of marriages between representatives of different races, of different language, and religions,
the sundering of national ties, and the consequent loss of
interest in such things. However, when it comes to genealogy
simply, which admits the lines of maternal ancestry, almost
any American can, with the help this double chance affords,

2

reach back to Penn, or to the Mayflower, and having once crossed the ocean with a single syllable of a name, shortly find a great-grand parent among the " honorables," and if he pursues it still further, prove himself to have sprung from the loins of some villainous duke. They were mostly of that stripe, for on one point all history is agreed, viz., that the strongest villains became the greatest dukes.

Vested with the proud distinction of citizenship, the American who has thus threaded his way back to the ducal, or, perchance, kingly, ermine, can complacently congratulate himself on the fact that, after all, it was not a descent, but rather an ascent, step by step, which marked his family history from its dark days of blood to these blessed years of enlightened peace.

In the case of John Bannister Gibson, it seems profitless to attempt to trace his lineage to the shores of Europe. We can get him there among the numberless grand and great-grandfathers and mothers of his maternal line, but the name of Gibson, in this immediate family, seems to be American, " native and to the manner born," though such, obviously, could not be the fact.

The established tradition is that the family is of Scotch-Irish descent, and Judge William A. Porter, in his essay on Judge Gibson, says the name in Scotland was Gilbertson. The earliest record of the family shows that in the year 1730 Governor Hamilton was instructed by the Proprietors (the Penns) to lay out the city of Lancaster at or near the tavern of George Gibson, who was the grandfather of the subject of this sketch.

In the Pennsylvania Historical Collections, page 397, the following interesting mention is made concerning this event and place :

"Governor Hamilton, at the request of the Proprietors, laid out Lancaster in 1730, at a place where George Gibson then kept a tavern with the sign of the 'Hickory Tree,' on the public road by the side of a fine spring. A swamp lay in front of Gibson's, another of some extent lay to the north. Near the spring there once stood a tall hickory tree which, tradition says, was the center of a little hamlet of a tribe called the Hickory Indians. The swamp north of Gibson's is supposed to have extended from the center of the square bounded by Duke, Queen, Chestnut and Orange streets, to the swamp along the run, now Water street. Gibson's pasture, afterwards Sanderson's, was leased at an early period to Adam Reigart. Gibson's original tavern is said to have been situated where Slaymaker's hotel now is (1843), and the spring was nearly opposite."

The late General George Gibson, U. S. A. (brother of John Bannister), said, in speaking of this Lancaster ancestor, that he lived until 1786, and was buried in Carlisle.

"Like all the Gibsons," the general continued, "he was a man of gigantic strength and size, measuring six feet and eight inches in height."* When asked who was his great-grandfather, the general replied he did not know his Christian name, but was certain of the fact that he also was born in this country. General Gibson was born at about the date of the inception of the Revolutionary war, and in 1861, shortly before his death, when the above conversation took place, his memory of his grandfather was perfect.

The family most probably came to America about the

---

* In 1856 or 1857, when the workmen were excavating for the broad foundation of Judge Gibson's monument, they disclosed the remains of this ancestor. The coffin had almost disappeared in dust, but the length of a thigh bone, which was accidentally exhumed, astonished the workmen and made a permanent impression on the writer, who was a witness of their proceedings.

time of the Penns' settlement, or earlier. They were num-
bered among the English who descended in 1674 from New
York (then New Amsterdam) to drive the Dutch from the
lower Delaware. If a Gibson arrived with Penn, he evidently came, as did Miles Standish with the Puritans, carrying a flint lock to keep order in meeting. The country
west of Lancaster, to the Susquehanna, was debatable ground
with the Indians even after 1730, and Gibson's tavern was
no doubt a shelter or stockade for the incoming tide of
settlers. The Gibsons have been on the frontier "debating
with the Indians" almost continuously from that date.
Colonel George Gibson, son of Judge Gibson, for many years
in command of the Fifth United States Infantry, died at
his post in New Mexico in 1888.

George Gibson, of Lancaster,* had two sons, George and
John, and two daughters, one of whom married Captain Jacob
Slow of the Continental army, and the other a Mr.
Read, of Middlesex, Cumberland county, Pa. One of Captain
Slow's daughters became the wife of Robert Calender, whose
son Robert was appointed commissary general of the army
by President James Monroe. Another of his daughters was
married to Simon Snyder, one of the governors of the
commonwealth of Pennsylvania.

Just how long the Gibsons remained in Lancaster is unknown, but it is believed that George, the father of Judge
Gibson, moved to Silver Spring, Cumberland county, in 1770,
where he became the owner of Silver Spring mills. He

---

* He was married to Elizabeth De Vinez, the daughter of a French count,
a Huguenot, who, after the revocation of the edict of Nantes, took refuge in
Ireland. The late general, Judge Gibson's brother, recollected his grandmother
Elizabeth very well. He describes her as a highly refined and accomplished
lady, "particularly attentive to the etiquette of the table," and it was from her
the older boys received the groundwork of their knowledge of the French and
Spanish languages. She died whilst Bannister was young.

was married two years later to Ann, daughter of Francis West. The year 1770 is probably the date of the permanent settlement of the family in the Cumberland Valley, but the elder George (and most likely the son also) had to frequently visit Carlisle about the period of its settlement, and later. In one of the accounts of Braddock's expedition, a courier taking the news of the dire disaster of July 9th, 1755, was directed to proceed as far as Carlisle and meet George Gibson, who would forward the report to Benjamin Franklin, who, more than any other Pennsylvanian, was assisting the English by furnishing supplies of horses and wagons for their use, and of which, particularly the wagons, neither Virginia nor Maryland could furnish nearly enough. No doubt but Gibson was an agent in this work in obedience to Franklin's proclamation.* The town of Carlisle by this time was secure, and the country about it being rapidly settled by the Dutch from the Delaware and from Holland.

Before the opening of the Revolution, the father became too old for effective military service, but his two sons, George and John, figured extensively in the history of those exciting times. History says but little of the Continental patriots who spent their lives on the frontiers, holding the savages by the throat, while their brethren fought the red-coats. Occasionally a monograph appears, but so far none upon the Gibsons and their share of the work, yet such a sketch could be woven into an interesting romance founded on fact.

Something is due to them, and it is appropriate that a brief statement be made, not only to illustrate the character of these men, but to unqualifiedly contradict the aspersion of the character of Judge Gibson's father by Townsend Ward, author of "The Western Insurrection."

---

* "History of Braddock's Expedition," Penna. Hist. Soc., p. 164.

In April, 1782, shortly after the massacre of the Moravian (Christian) Indians on the Muskingum river, no less than ninety having been wantonly murdered, even in their churches, by rabid frontiersmen from Fort Pitt, Wheeling and Beaver (Fort McIntosh), General William Irvine, in command at Fort Pitt, wrote to his wife at Carlisle, mentioning the above incidents, and stating that these militia were also highly incensed against Colonel Gibson, "and sent him word they would scalp him, also. A thousand lies are propagated all over the country against him, poor fellow. I am informed the whole is occasioned by his unhappy connection with a certain tribe, which leads people to imagine for that reason that. he has an attachment to Indians in general."*

To this extract from General Irvine's letter, Mr. Ward appends the following note:

"The latter part of this extract, no doubt, relates to Colonel Gibson's living, as he did for several years, with an Indian woman, who, like Pocahontas, impelled by love, had saved him from a cruel death at the hands of her tribe. He subsequently left her, and marrying, became the father of John Bannister Gibson, Chief Justice of Pennsylvania. The first love was constant in her feelings, and years afterwards spoke of Colonel Gibson with great affection."†

Had Mr. Ward read more from the voluminous published letters of General Irvine, he would have certainly known that it was John, and not George Gibson, to whom he (Irvine) referred. George at this time was at York, Pa., as elsewhere related, and is nowhere mentioned about this

---

* "Contributions to American History," Penna. Historical Society, p. 149; published 1858.

† "Rea's Incidents," published in a Beaver newspaper.

date as being at Fort Pitt with his brother, although he had frequently been at that place before the Revolution.

Colonel John Gibson had had temporary command of Fort Pitt in 1779, during Colonel Brodhead's absence, and after charges of speculating with public funds had been preferred against that officer, was formally 'placed in command at that post in September, 1781, by the authority of no less a commander than General Washington, as the following letter will show :*

HEAD OF ELK, Sept. 6th, 1781.

SIR:—Colonel Brodhead having been directed in my letter to him of this date to resign his command of Fort Pitt, during the dependence of his trial, on sundry accusations brought against him whilst in command, you will immediately upon the receipt of this assume the like command at the post of Fort Pitt and its dependences, as has been committed to Colonel Brodhead.

*   *   *   *   *   *   *

I am, dear sir, your most

obedient servant,

GEO. WASHINGTON.

To Col. JOHN GIBSON,
          Fort Pitt.

General Irvine came as a stranger to Fort Pitt before the close of the Revolution, in November, 1781, relieving John Gibson of the command. Although his family had before that time settled in Carlisle (Irvine was of Irish birth), John Gibson and Irvine appear not to have been personally acquainted.

Colonel John, as well as his brother George, having been well educated, and with a genius for language, easily acquired a knowledge of the Indian dialects. Whether or not

---

* "Washington-Irvine Correspondence," Butterfield, p. 62.

it was for his pursuit of this knowledge among them, the Indians gave the *nom de guerre* of "Horse Head" to John, is unknown; but probably no white men on the frontier equalled them in this respect. John Gibson has left a lasting memorial of his abilities as a translator of the Indian language in the speech, or message, of Logan,* the Mingo chief, "Who is there to mourn for Logan," etc., delivered at the close of Lord Dunmore's war in 1774, on the banks of the Scioto river. We are left in doubt whether to admire most the pathos of the savage orator, or the genius of the man who could interpret its fiery grunts into English deemed graceful enough to be placed in the school books. Doubts exist in the minds of some commentators on American history, as to whether such a speech was really ever delivered. Sir William Johnston, Thomas Jefferson, who brought it into notoriety, and others, have had its authorship attributed to them, but the testimony of the earliest writers agree that it was a real message, and delivered to Gibson.†

John Gibson remained at Fort Pitt as its commander for many years after the Revolution, and finally became a permanent resident of Braddock's Field, Allegheny county, where he died in 1822. Thrown into constant contact with acquaintances, friends and relatives from the Cumberland Valley, it seems strange that none of them in their correspondence allude to any Indian wife and child. He afterwards became an intimate friend of Irvine's family, and the statement of General Irvine was made according to hearsay, after a short acquaintance. Gibson's numerous enemies among

---

* Logan came originally from the Juniata river valley, and it is not unlikely that his tribe and himself, before they moved to Yellow Creek, Ohio, were known to the Gibsons, and hence the friendship between them so frequently alluded to. At least this conclusion appears to be a reasonable one.

† A succinct sketch of John Gibson's life, including Logan's message, will be found in the Appendix (A).

the insurrectionists during the great Whiskey Rebellion of
1794, in which he took a prominent part on the side of
the government, would most likely have ventilated his record on this score, had the story been credited at that date.
Everything betokens that the story originated from the tales
of ignorant men, who attributed his charity and kindliness
of heart for oppressed Indians to a vile motive.

He appears to have been a fearless man. Thus contrast
General Irvine's letter to his wife (a part of the same letter
previously mentioned) with one on the same subject from
Gibson to the Moravian bishop. Irvine says: "Many children were killed in their wretched mothers' arms. Whether
this was right or wrong I do not pretend to say. * * *
Whatever your private opinion of these matters may be, I
conjure you, by all the ties of affection, * * * not to
express any sentiment for or against these deeds, as it may
be alleged the sentiments you express come from me or be
mine. No man knows whether I approve or disapprove of
killing the Moravians."

Not so profoundly cautious in regard to his opinion, and
he, of all men, most in danger of the cutthroat Indian
haters and escaped convicts who formed a large proportion
of the population of Fort Pitt at that period, was Colonel
Gibson in his answer to the letter from Bishop Siedel (the
Moravian bishop of Bethlehem, Pa.) He says, under date
of May 9th, 1782, from Fort Pitt: "Mr. Schebosh will be
able to give you a particular account of the late horrible
massacre perpetrated at the towns on Muskingum, by a set
of men, the most savage miscreants that ever degraded
human nature. Had I known of their intention before it
was too late, I should have prevented it by informing the
poor sufferers of it."*

* "W.-I. Correspondence," p. 362.

3

Irvine probably told the truth when he wrote of Gibson: "A thousand lies are propagated all over the country against him, poor fellow," and then he proceeded to assist in the propagation of the most contemptible one.* A man who was afraid to express his opinion of the perpetrators of one of the foulest crimes which have stained the pages of the history of the frontier, was certainly capable of this.

In calling attention to a weak point in his character, no offense is intended to the memory of General Irvine, whose name is engraved on the tablets of history as one of the bravest and most distinguished of soldiers who fought during the Revolution. He was born at Fermanagh, Ire-

---

* The following is an extract from John Sappington's deposition (testimony in the examination of the Mingo massacre), see p. 268, New Ed. "Jefferson's Notes," 1853: "I was intimately acquainted with General (John) Gibson, and served under him during the late war, and I have a discharge from him now lying in the land office at Richmond, to which I refer any person for my character, who might be disposed to scruple my veracity. I do not believe that Logan had any relations killed, except his brother (at the killing of the Mingoes, June 30th, 1774, at Baker's Bottom, opposite the mouth of Yellow Creek, near Wellsville, Ohio). Neither of the squaws who were killed was his wife. Two of them were old women, and the third, with her child which was saved, I have the best reasons in the world to believe was the wife and child of General Gibson. I know he educated the child and took care of it as if it had been his own."

Also this apparently corroborative testimony, from the " Record of Upland, and Denny's Journal," p. 490, being an extract from the recollections of Lieutenant Murphy, related in 1849, when he was 97 years old, to Dr. William H. Denny: "I was well acquainted with John Gibson—served under him when he was Colonel of the 13th (Virginia) Regiment—have seen his Indian wife Betty."

These men were apparently unaware of the fact that he owed these Indians a debt of gratitude for having spared his life several years previous to this time. John Gibson, when not fighting Indians, was attending strictly to business, and it is difficult to conceive that he would maintain a wife in a distant Indian tribe. He was almost constantly surrounded by friendly Indians; why, therefore, not provide a domicile for his " Pocahontas," had he been possessed of one, near his homestead at Fort Pitt? However in the future these views may be regarded, no writer can truthfully assert that George Gibson, the father of John Bannister, was hampered with an Indian woman and a half-breed family when he married Ann West. Speaking of George Gibson's character, Dr. Denny says: " Besides being a gallant soldier, he was an accomplished gentleman, a man of wit and fine imagination." p. 489, work above mentioned.

land, November 3, 1741. Graduated at the Dublin University, and became a surgeon in the English navy. He emigrated to America in 1763, and settled in 1764 as a physician in Carlisle. Between 1774 and 1776, he was a member of the Provincial Assembly from Carlisle. He was made colonel of a regiment by Congress, and on May 12th, 1779, was appointed brigadier general. After the war he was a member of Congress, and died in Philadelphia July 29th, 1804.

Of the military services of Captain, afterwards Colonel George Gibson, father of John Bannister, we can catch only occasional glimpses. Seldom being in separate command of important posts or expeditions, his chances to make a record were not as good as those who outranked him. In Cæsar's Commentary one reads much of Cæsar and of the invincible sixth legion of which the immortal Julius was once commander. Had the more generous, and far more accurate, Thucydides lived at that period and written, the history of Cæsar's times would have been valuable beyond computation.

The families of individuals may cherish for a while the name and fame of their progenitors, but as a rule a few generations bury their deeds in oblivion; and such has almost been the fate of Gibson *pere*.

George Gibson had been with his brother John in the West, but after the close of Lord Dunmore's war in 1774 he repaired to his home in the Sherman Valley, at Westover Mills, the property of his father-in-law, and to which place he moved from Silver Springs in 1773, the year following his marriage. It is said that he was not successful in business affairs in the Cumberland Valley. It is generally conceded, however, that military life unfits most men for ordinary business, probably because in its routine the incentive to gain is missing, and no field offers for the development of business tact.

At the call to arms for the Continental army, he, hastening to Pittsburgh, early in 1776 recruited a company of one hundred men at that place for service in the army, being perhaps the first man to organize a considerable force for this purpose west of the Allegheny Mountains. The "ear piercing fife," with its mate the "spirit stirring drum," was then, as now, a necessary concomitant of the militia company. But while drummers can always be improvised on short notice, the fifer must have music in his soul. No fifer could be found in the woods, and no doubt the discontent among the men was great on the first march until their captain proved himself not only equal to the duty of commanding, but of playing the fife as well. Had this picture caught the eye of Trumbull we might have expected it to be immortalized on canvas along with others of his revolutionary scenes. A man of Gibson's genius, at such a time, would stand dignity aside for the humor of the thing.

He reported with his men to Colonel, afterwards General Hugh Mercer, who was at that time at Williamsburg, Va., recruiting and drilling a regiment for service in the North. Gibson's men were for the most part the wildest kind of frontiersmen, who had never been subjected to any species of discipline. Shortly after their arrival in camp, finding the commissariat not up to their ideas, at least as regarded quantity, they proceeded to forage on the farmers on their own account. Their captain had no end of trouble with them, for while they listened to him they obeyed neither him nor any other commander, hence they were jocularly called "Gibson's lambs." Finally, General Mercer arrested the entire lot, but instead of dealing harshly with the men, he appealed to their patriotism, no doubt promising them a liberal supply of provisions, and settled the trouble quietly. The men never again gave grounds for complaint.*

Colonel George Gibson served during the entire war, being absent from the field only when appointed by the Virginia State authorities to negotiate secretly with the Spanish government for a supply of powder and lead for the Virginia State and Continental troops, in which he was eminently successful. The knowledge of the French and Spanish languages acquired from his mother were of the greatest service to him on this important mission. On this mission he traversed the wilderness from Pittsburgh to New Orleans, sending the supplies back in flat boats after many vexatious delays.

General Washington seems to have reposed so much confidence in his executive ability that, after the surrender of the British army under Cornwallis, at Yorktown, the entire body, excepting the commissioned officers, was placed under his command when they were sent to York, Pa., as prisoners of war. A somewhat detailed account of his services will be found in the Appendix (B), in the report of a congressional committee, of which the distinguished Mr. Muhlenberg, of Pennsylvania, was chairman.

Just after the close of the war he was consulted by General Irvine at Fort Pitt, as to the best route for a projected expedition against Detroit.† He was familiar with the Ohio Valley and the Muskingum country, but north of where Columbus now stands, he was a stranger.

During the remainder of his life George Gibson was

---

* For one account of this incident, see sketch of Mercer in the "Casket," published in Philadelphia, 1833, p. 316.

† Gibson's letter from York, Pa., to General Irvine. "Washington-Irvine Correspondence," p. 353.

more at home, though for want of a congenial occupation
and an inborn restlessness, spent much of his time hunting
and in the saddle, traveling to and fro among his own and
his wife's relations in the Cumberland Valley and in Lancaster county.   His son Bannister says he had "no positive
vices."   Faint praise, perhaps, but considering the grossness
of some of his neighbors, he did well to live as a gentleman
among them.   His lively disposition and fund of anecdote
made him universally popular, and had he turned his attention to politics, he might have been returned to the
Legislature, or to Congress; but there can be no certainty
regarding this supposition, for his claims would have been
contested by lawyers of signal ability, in the neighboring
town of Carlisle, who were far more adept than he in
shaping the "will of the people."   •

Early in 1791, Congress having voted that a levy of
two thousand soldiers, in two regiments, from Virginia and
Pennsylvania, be made to assist General Arthur St. Clair
in an expedition against the British, Indians and renegades,
who made Detroit their base of operations against the settlers of the Ohio Valley, George Gibson was appointed
lieutenant colonel and field commander of the "Second
Regiment of Levies."   These men were enlisted for the
term of six months only, and before they had fairly started
out from Fort Washington (Cincinnati) the time of many
had expired, and they became clamorous for their discharges,
while many others deserted.

St. Clair's expedition was the first considerable military
undertaking which engaged the attention of the young United
States,* and it was made before the departments of ord-

---

*The Indians who began to steal their horses as soon as they were landed at
Fort "Washington opposite the Licking," enjoyed the distinction of capturing
the first animals branded U. S.   See Denny's Journal.

nance and supplies were properly organized. Men were even sent from prisons to fill the ranks. Under all the circumstances it is a wonder that St. Clair found himself able to proceed at all. He was, no doubt, entitled to the verdict of acquittal of blame which he afterwards received at the hands of a congressional committee.

The Indians were met on the banks of the Wabash, ninety miles north of Fort Washington in the midst of a swampy country, which is known to this day as the Black Swamp Region. The attack was made just after morning parade in the camp, November 4th, 1791, and before sunrise. In a few moments the army was entirely surrounded by an unnumbered host of savages. Out of 1,400 men actually engaged, thirty-seven officers and 593 privates were killed or reported missing, and thirty-one officers and 252 privates, wounded, leaving less than 500 unhurt. American troops were never so severely handled by Indians, except in the Custer massacre on the Little Big Horn, June, 1876. In many respects it was a repetition of Braddock's battle.

Of the sixty-eight officers killed and wounded in the four regiments engaged, eighteen belonged to Gibson's regiment. He was wounded in the head early in the engagement, but fought afterwards with a bandage around it, making himself a conspicuous target for the riflemen of the enemy, who lurked behind the trees. He was wounded a second time, and again by a shot through the wrist, which totally disabled him.* Major Butler, the gallant soldier from young Pittsburgh, his next in command, was also wounded. Both did their utmost to rally their men in attempts to clear the front. Nearly all the desperately wounded were left on the

---

* This is from records obtained in Ohio several years ago. Denny's Journal is the authority for the losses and the incidents, except as they refer to Gibson personally.

field.   Colonel Gibson, though mortally wounded, was safely carried by his men to Fort Jefferson, a stockade thirty miles back on the road towards Fort Washington, which place had been built by St. Clair, when on the advance and while waiting for supplies to come up.   Here Colonel Gibson died a few days afterwards, and there his body still remains.*

* The township in Mercer county, Ohio, in which the battle was fought, is named "Gibson," after Colonel George Gibson. The writer is probably the only one of his descendants who has ever visited Fort Jefferson where the colonel is buried.   No one, when he was there, could designate the spot where the veteran reposes.   In traveling along near the old trail of St. Clair's army through Preble and Darke counties, Ohio, the writer was told that it could be distinguished even in the forest, by the straggling line of sycamores, which had succeeded the oak and beech cut away by the pioneers of the army.   Other old clearings in this region are now also grown up in sycamore, but there does appear to be a "trail" of them quite marked in places.   In Pennsylvania, neglected roads or old trails through native pine forests sometimes grow up in chestnut, presenting a curious contrast to the surrounding arborescent growth.

CHAPTER II.

JUDGE GIBSON'S HOMESTEAD — THE BIRTHPLACE ALSO OF
TWO GOVERNORS — HIS EARLY EDUCATION AND COLLEGE
CLASSMATES.

In a letter written from Carlisle, under date of July
9th, 1851, to his friend John William Wallace, of Philadelphia, Judge Gibson gives the following particulars respecting his maternal ancestry:

"You ask about my maternal relations. My mother was
Anne, daughter of Francis West,* a substantial freeholder,
descended from an Irish branch of the Delaware family,
probably before it was ennobled. The peerage is an English,
and I believe an existing one. My maternal grandmother
was a Wynne. Owen Wynne, the head of the family, is,
or lately was, the first commoner in Ireland, and refused
a peerage. Through the Wynnes, we are connected with
the Coles of Enniskellen. Another connection, not so rep-
utable, was the famous Colonel Barre, the associate of
Wilkes in his politics and his vices.

---

* Francis West, after his emigration to this country, settled first either in
Lancaster or Chester county, Pa. He was a cousin of the distinguished artist,
Benjamin West. He at one period was Colonial Judge of Cumberland county,
when its territory embraced many of the present southern counties of the State.
He died in 1786, and is buried at Carlisle. He was married to Mary Lowery, and
their family consisted of two sons and three daughters. The sons were named Edward, who died in Landisburg, Perry county, in 1816, and William, who died
in Baltimore, Md. Dorothea married Michael Kingston, and settled in
Juniata County, Pa.; Mary married Ross Mitchell; the third married George
Gibson, as related. Judge West was a Tory at the opening of the Revolution,
and his feeling against his son-in-law George Gibson, who was an ardent Federalist, or Republican, was extremely bitter for a while, although they ultimately
became entirely reconciled.

4

"My mother was born at Clover Hill, near Sligo, in 1744, and came with the family to this country about 1755, She died on the 9th of February, 1809. I believe her father had been a Trinity College boy, for he spoke Latin after the fashion of his day. * * * * * I was born among the mountains of Cumberland. [Perry originally formed a part of Cumberland county.] Fox hunting, fishing, gunning, rifle shooting, swimming, wrestling and boxing with the natives of my age, were my exercises and my amusements. My mother, who, having been educated in Philadelphia, was qualified for the task, directed my reading, and put such books into my hands as were proper for me. We had from one to two hundred volumes, Burke's Annual Register included, and I read all of them so often that they are as fresh in my memory as if I had read them yesterday. My poor mother struggled with poverty during the nineteen years she lived after my father's death, and having fought up gallantly against it, till she had placed me at the bar—died. She was certainly a noble soul, but the little talent of the family came from my father's side; I should say genius, for he had no talent at all. He was celebrated as a humorist, and even a wit, but though without a positive vice, he never could advance his fortune, except in the army, for which alone he was qualified."*

---

*In a letter to the writer, Mrs. McClure, Judge Gibson's only surviving daughter, thus refers to her grandfather—letter dated Carlisle, Pa., December 29th, 1886: "Ma told me he was constantly traveling, a great lover of society, and was the life of a party, full of wit, for which he was very celebrated. When I went a bride to Pittsburgh in 1833, Mrs. Harmar Denny's mother, old Mrs. O'Hara, then very aged, asked to be told when I came to return Mrs. Denny's visit, for she was anxious to see me, as she knew and admired my grandfather so much, and told me that she met him last in Philadelphia, and that he 'would be invited to four parties of an evening, and wherever he went, the men would follow, so much was he admired,' etc. I guess the stupidity of Perry county

Mrs. Gibson was left with four sons at the time of the death of her husband in 1791, and she had a daughter who died in infancy. The oldest of these boys was Francis West,* seventeen years old; George, fifteen; John Bannister, eleven years at the time of their father's death, and William Chesney, several years younger.

John Bannister Gibson was born on the Westover Mill property, in the old house still standing, but now little better than a ruin, November 8th, 1780.

There is a story connected with this old mansion which deserves to be retold, of its being the cradle spot of so many distinguished men, and it can be best related in the language of its author, the Hon. Charles H. Smiley, senator from Perry county, used in the proceedings of the Legislature of Pennsylvania, April 14th, 1881, on the occasion of the death of the Hon. William Bigler, ex-governor of this State. Speaking of Bigler, Mr. Smiley said:

"Other tongues have told to-day the story of his life, and the service he rendered the State, and I would not undertake to add to what has been so eloquently said, were it not that investigation into the local history of my native county justifies me in making a statement concerning the birth-place of the Honorable William Bigler, different from what has been generally adopted by the country.

"On the banks of Sherman's creek, in Perry county, less than fifty miles from this chamber, towards the setting

must have been unendurable to such a man. I have heard both Pa and Uncle George speak of their mother as being a well educated woman. She went to a boarding school in Philadelphia, and had quite a library of well selected books for those times, which Pa read so often that he could repeat pages of them. Her boys certainly owed everything to her. Old Mrs. Duncan, Judge Duncan's wife, told me she was a devourer of books, would read by moonlight and while knitting her sons' stockings. There is evidently where Uncle Frank and Pa's fondness of reading came from."

* Frank was born March 27th, 1774—died March 18th, 1856.

sun, there stands an old building strongly marked by dilapidation and decay. This building is well known throughout that section of country as the Gibson mansion. Four miles up the stream are the Perry county warm springs, a popular summer resort. A rifle shot below the house is a huge pile of bowlders known as Gibson's rock, and on either side of the stream immense hills are piled up toward the clouds, forming a gorge through which the stream runs to the open fields below.

"Whether to the singular beauty of the locality may be attributed the genius and the prodigies that went forth from this spot, I know not, but it was the good fortune of the old house to have one room in which were born five men who have made their mark on the times in which they lived, to wit: John Bannister Gibson, chief justice of the Supreme Court of Pennsylvania, who gathered a store of pearls for the profession from the depths of legal lore, and whose name is revered wherever the common law is known; General George Gibson, commissary general of the United States army for many years prior to the rebellion; Honorable John Bigler, who by a singular coincidence was made governor of California at the same time that his brother became governor of Pennsylvania; Honorable William Bigler, the subject of this sketch; and Honorable John Bernheisel, who in after years adopted the Mormon faith and became the representative of the polygamists in Congress. It was from this retired spot that William Bigler, the miller's son, started out on a career of almost three score and ten years."*

---

*Under date of November 4th, 1886, Mr. Smiley, in a letter to the writer, says: "The statement I made in connection with the old Gibson mansion as the birthplace of the Biglers, etc., provoked quite a newspaper controversy in this section of the State and resulted in the development of facts which I think fully sustain my assertion. William Bigler was born in December, 1813.

BIRTHPLACE OF JUDGE GIBSON.

The fact that the Biglers were born in the old mansion has always been known in the Gibson family. For some years after his mother's death in 1809, Francis Gibson resided in Carlisle, and the father of the Biglers leased the mill and homestead during his absence. Francis afterwards returned to the old place, where he died March 18th, 1856, at the advanced age of eighty-two years. He was a kind hearted old gentleman, venerated by his friends and neighbors, and dearly beloved by his family. Like his brothers George and Bannister, he was very tall and had been a powerful man physically in his younger days. He had considerable taste for music and excelled as a violinist. His health remained perfect to the last.

We do not wish to have it inferred that Francis Gibson ever became a great performer, but both he and his brother Bannister possessed decided genius for music. Bannister far surpassed his brother as a performer because of his superior opportunities in the musical world. It was not with Bannister, however, a controlling passion, though seldom, indeed, where the talent for music is developed so much as in his case, that its subject does not become a votary.

The widow's property consisted of about seventy-eight acres, including the mill on Sherman's creek, a log structure with only "one run of stone." As the country about the place was sparsely populated, the business of the mill returned her a very scanty means of subsistence. The government was neither so rich nor so generous as it is now to the widows of its fallen soldiers, for neither she nor her children ever received a cent in the way of a pension. Her position was assuredly a forlorn one. Left as she was, in a mountain wilderness in which there were no schools of any kind, there appeared no hope that she would be able to educate her sons. Neither did employment of any kind present itself near her home where she could have apprenticed her boys to useful trades. The country was so mountainous that even agriculture was confined to very limited spots along the creek bottom.

With the determination not to permit her sons to degenerate, Mrs. Gibson built a school-house near the homestead, where she taught the boys, herself. That she was a successful teacher is proved by the fact that before her son George was twenty years old she had secured for him a place in the counting house of Alexander McDonald, a distinguished importer in Baltimore, who, while a resident of Carlisle, had been an intimate friend of her husband.

Soon after entering Mr. McDonald's service, George was made supercargo of a vessel in the East India trade, and was able to be of some assistance in the education of his younger brothers. In after years he remarked that aside from the schooling he received at home from his mother, his education "had not cost two shillings."*

William at an early period adopted commercial pursuits, and like his brother George, eventually became supercargo of a vessel in the foreign trade from Baltimore. He died at the old home about the age of thirty. He was convalescing from an attack of yellow fever that he had contracted abroad, and brought on a relapse by exposure during a hunting expedition.

Being probably the most studious of the boys, as we may infer from the letter already given, Bannister seems to have been reserved by his mother to enter the legal profession. Who knows but this noble woman often dreamed of the fame destined for this chosen son? She must have had

---

* For a sketch of George's life see Appendix.

high hopes concerning him. But she did not live to real-
ize her fond anticipations, for in the language of the son,
which almost breathes a sigh, "having placed me at the
bar, she died."

She was a devout member of the Church of England
(Episcopal), and seldom failed to attend the Sunday services
of St. John's church at Carlisle, across the Blue mountains,
and fifteen miles distant from her home. One amusing
story is told of her. Happening upon one occasion to be
in Carlisle, she unexpectedly met Bishop White of Christ
church, Philadelphia (the celebrated divine and Washington's
pastor), and she prevailed upon him to accompany her to
Perry county, that he might baptize one or more of the
boys who had not yet been christened.

It so happened that all four of the boys were off on a
hunt that day in the mountains, and as they did not return until late, the household, with its distinguished visitor,
was sound asleep before they came in; the baptism was
necessarily postponed until the morrow. The boys knew
nothing of this arrangement, and as game tracked best in
the early morning, they started before day-break to conclude
the chase abandoned the evening before. Just how the old
lady explained matters to the bishop at "coffee and muf-
fins" that morning, and the boys absent from the table, is
not told, but it is very easy to imagine that as he rode
away without having performed his duty, he believed that
Perry county required more wide-awake missionaries than
the church usually sends to the heathen in other lands.

Judge Gibson was named "Bannister" after a distinguished Virginia gentleman and lawyer of that name in
Richmond, who had probably formed his father's acquaintance in some of the Virginia campaigns.

Concerning the name Bannister, about which there have been some queries, Judge James T. Mitchell of the Supreme Court writes as follows:

"Regarding his name Bannister, I have always wondered whether his father, having a taste for dramatic art, as he had himself, had called him after the distinguished English comedian John Bannister, or whether he was named after the Virginia soldier and statesman. Your memoir solves the doubt. Colonel John Banister was a member of the Continental Congress, a signer of the Articles of Confederation, and an officer in the Virginia line during the Revolution. It was doubtless there that Colonel George Gibson knew him and for him he named his son. Colonel Banister died in 1787. The spelling, Banister, with one "n" is correct, as the Chief Justice wrote it in his earlier days. His writing it Bannister in the register at a later date was probably an inadvertence from long disuse of the name in full."

That the tracing of names is not entirely devoid of amusement the following will show. Mr. F. W. Gibson, a nephew of Judge Gibson, having written that many years ago he saw a copy of the will of Colonel George Gibson, the original of which is recorded in Cincinnati, in which the father, referring to the son, mentions him as Hiram John Bannister, an attempt was made to verify the statement. Judge Gibson never in his life to any of his family spoke of such a proposed name as Hiram. The following reply came from the Probate Court of Hamilton county, Ohio, dated October 6th, 1887: "I have examined the will of George Gibson, deceased, and find his sons' names are Francis West Gibson, George Patrick Henry Gibson, William Chesney Gibson and Matthias John Bannister Gibson." (Signed), Charles H. Fox, chief deputy clerk. The will was made, no doubt, before the name of this son was finally determined upon. As a matter of fact Judge Gibson was not baptized until after his marriage, and neither Hiram nor Matthias entered into its final make-up.

Bannister went to Carlisle to attend Dickinson College in 1795 or 1796, and graduated, it is generally believed, in 1800.

Whether he was an actual graduate, as stated by Judge Porter and many others, and also as to the year given by most of them (1800) for that event, there are grounds for serious doubt. Quite recently the Rev. J. A. Murray, a Presbyterian minister of Carlisle, addressed to his friend, the Rev. J. I. Brownson, of Washington, Pa., a letter containing interesting notices of Judge Gibson's classmates and a reference to these very matters. The letter having been shown to Boyd Crumrine, Esq., of the Washington bar and reporter of the Supreme Court, was in turn sent by him to the writer. Mr. Murray is an authority on the alumni of Dickinson College, whose pleasant campus and venerable front faces his home. Mr. Murray became a student of Dickinson in 1834, but in the following year he entered the Western University at Pittsburgh, from which he graduated in 1837, to enter immediately the Theological Seminary in Allegheny city, as a classmate of Mr. J. I. Brownson, graduating finally in 1840.

The alumni record prepared in recent years by Prof. Super, assisted by Mr. Murray and others, and from which the date is taken, assigns Judge Gibson to the class of 1798. He was four years, or nearly four years, at least, at college, and joined the Union Philosophical Society in 1797, and probably not later than his sophomore year.

5

Some of the accounts state that before entering college he had been a year or more in the grammar school. To have graduated in 1798, he must have entered college at the age of fourteen, and if the class matriculated in 1794 his classmate Alexander was then only twelve years old, and Metzger and McGinley thirteen and fourteen years old respectively. The United States Law Magazine, in a sketch of Judge Gibson, published several years before his death, places the date of his graduation in the year 1800. Mr. Murray says in reply to a letter, that he can furnish no more information on these points than the records show, nor explain how these particular records were obtained, and thus the matter must rest with the college records in conflict with tradition and the established belief of some of Judge Gibson's personal friends.

Mr. Murray's letter to Mr. Brownson will show that Judge Gibson's class contains the honored names of the sires of many well known families existing to this day— he says:

"I have several publications, each containing a sketch of Judge Gibson and all representing him as having *graduated* at Dickinson College. But I am very sure this is a mistake. He never graduated in the proper sense of that word. He was a student of the college, and afterwards, from 1816 to 1829, he was a member of the board of trustees.

In the catalogue of the Union Philosophical Society of the college his name appears in the year 1797. But in the recently published record of the students of the college his name appears as belonging to the class of 1798.

He was what we would call an irregular student, and had quite a number of irregular students as classmates, a few of whom became somewhat prominent in subsequent life, among whom were:

Elias Ellmaker, Pa. (See Biographical History of Lancaster County, p. 191.)

John C. Floyd, Va. (Afterwards governor of that State.)

Alfred M. Grayson, Ky.

William N. Irvine, Pa. (A lawyer, colonel in the army, president judge of York and Adams district, etc. See Pennsylvania Genealogies by Dr. Egle, 1886, p. 238. Colonel Irvine's wife was a sister of Judge Gibson's wife. *Ibid*, p. 233.)

William King, Pa. (An M. D. of Cumberland county.)

Ralph Martin, of Cumberland county.

George Metzger,* Pa. (A prominent lawyer of Carlisle; member of the Legislature, wealthy and generous; a trustee of our Second Presbyterian church; a bachelor, and died here in 1879, in his 98th year. By his will he founded and endowed among us what is known as the ' Metzger Institute,' a flourishing seminary for young ladies.)

John More, Pa. Thompson More, Pa. George W. Morrow. James Richards. William Ritchie. (Possibly ' Father Ritchie,' of the *Richmond Enquirer*.) Thomas Stockton, N. J. William Watson, M. D.

To these fourteen irregular students John Bannister Gibson belonged, and was the most celebrated. But belonging to the same class and who graduated were twenty-four others:

James Adair. (Licensed by the Carlisle Presbytery in 1803. Pastor of Paxton and Denny churches. Died same year, aged thirty-two years.)

Samuel Agnew, M. D. (A surgeon in the army during

---

* Mr. Murray wrote a sketch of his life.

the war of 1812-1815.   Afterwards a practicing physician in Harrisburg.   A Christian gentleman, quite prominent in social and professional life.   He died in Pittsburgh, November 23d, 1849, aged seventy-two years.   He was the father of the Rev. Dr. J. Holmes Agnew, a Presbyterian minister, professor in Washington College, Pa., in Newark College, Del., in Marion College, Mo., in the University of Michigan, etc.   Also editor of the 'Electric Magazine,' and of 'Knickerbocker,' N. Y., etc.   See 'Men of Mark' of Cumberland county, pp. 270, 394, and also the 'Presbyterian Encyclopædia.')

Joseph Brady. (A member and pastor of the Carlisle Presbytery, who died in 1821, aged forty-seven years; and was an uncle of my present wife.)

Andrew Buchanan. (Lawyer and member of the Legislature, and of Congress, etc.)

Levi Bull, D. D. (A prominent minister of the Episcopal Church in Chester county, Pa., and who had been ordained by Bishop White. He died August 2, 1859, aged about eighty years.)

John Cooper. (Principal of Hopewell Academy, near Shippensburg, founded by his father, Rev. Dr. Robert Cooper.   His son, too, was justly called a 'prince among educators.')

William Downey, M. D. James D. Greason, Esq. (Died a farmer, where he was born, near Carlisle.)

James Gustine, M. D. (Born and practiced medicine in Carlisle. A trustee of Dickinson College from 1808 to 1820. Finally removed to Natchez, Miss., where he died. See History of Cumberland County, Pa., p. 182.)

James Guthrie. (A Presbyterian minister.) George Hayes, M. D. Thompson Holmes, M. D. (Born near Carlisle, December 16th, 1780. Practiced medicine and farmed in Virginia; removed to Philadelphia in 1844, and there died in June of 1855. He was social and agreeable, and the maternal grandfather of 'Fanny Lear,' who died at Nice, in May of 1886.)

Robert Haston, M. D. Joshua Knight. (A Presbyterian minister.)

Amos A. McGinley, D. D. (He was an honored member of the Carlisle Presbytery, and for a half century was the amiable, beloved and useful pastor of but one charge, among whom he died, May 1st, 1856, aged 78 years.

William F. Mitchell, Pa. Alexander Monteith. (A Presbyterian minister.)

Robert Proudfit, D. D. (A Presbyterian minister; born in York county, Pa., June 6th, 1777. For many years a pastor in the State of New York. Then professor of ancient languages in Union College from 1818 to 1849; then emeritus professor until he died, in Schenectady, N. Y., February 11th, 1860, in his 84th year.)

William H. Rainey, V. D. M. Thomas Stockton, New Jersey. (Name occurs in both lists in the college catalogue.) John Waugh.

Henry R. Wilson, D. D. (Licensed to preach by the Carlisle Presbytery; professor of languages in Dickinson College. The faithful and useful pastor of several churches, etc. Died in Philadelphia, March 22d, 1848, nearly 70. See 'Men of Mark,' and 'Presbyterian Encyclopædia.' The Rev. Dr. H. R. Wilson, Jr., a foreign missionary, teacher, and for many years the very able corresponding secretary of the Presbyterian board of church erection, was his son.)

John Wright. (A Presbyterian minister; born February 17th, 1777, in Pennsylvania. Pastor of several churches. Died in Indiana, at Delphi, 1854.)

John Byers Alexander.* (Belonged to a patriotic family in Carlisle, where he was born, April 21st, 1782. He became a distinguished lawyer in Western Pennsylvania, and something of a military enthusiast. He was in the war of 1812 with Great Britain, and served creditably under General Harrison. He lived in Greensburg, the chief place of his forensic efforts and triumphs, and there died, May 28th, 1840.)"

---

* Concerning General Alexander, Mr. Murray further states: "My most distinct recollection of him was in or about the year 1833. There was a military encampment on the commons at the foot of Seminary hill, Allegheny. General Alexander was in command of it. It was the only time I ever saw Mr. Harmar Denny in uniform, and one day he had Alexander to dine with him. He, Mr. Denny, then lived at Kilbuck Hall, now the residence of his daughter, Mrs. Robert McKnight. I was standing on the porch, near Mrs. Denny, as the two military officers approached together. She pleasantly received Alexander, and then addressing her husband, smilingly remarked, 'Mr. Denny, you look well in military dress.' (I thought he was the better looking of the two, as he was taller and more slender.) Instantly Alexander elongated his person, expanded his chest, and with an assumed commanding tone, exclaimed, 'Madame, why don't you tell me that *I look well in mine?*' 'General, you *always* look well,' was her quick response." Mr. Murray then refers to an extended and interesting sketch of General Alexander in "Albert's History of Westmoreland County," p. 311, etc.

CHAPTER III.

JUDGE GIBSON'S EARLY FRIENDS — HIS MARRIAGE — SERVICES
IN THE LEGISLATURE — APPOINTED A COMMON PLEAS
JUDGE — HIS HOME IN CARLISLE.

Hon. Boyd Crumrine is in possession of a curious collection of Latin verses, probably exercises, of Judge Gibson,
written by him when a student. They are brief sentences,
devoted to mythological subjects, axioms, etc., each, as a rule, occupying a page of a diminutive pamphlet which young Gibson
improvised by cutting and folding the sheets and stitching
them together with brown thread. Each of its thirty pages
is signed in his unmistakable handwriting. Several are dated,
and probably all were written, during the month of January,
1800. He had not apparently at that time determined upon
a signature, for we find him writing variously, John B.,
J. B., John Banister, Jno. Ban'r, etc. The name Bannister
he then wrote with one "n," but in the registry of his
family, the only place to be found where in later years he
gives it in full, he spells it with two "n's." The early or-
thography employed by him was the correct one, as elsewhere
referred to. Throughout the exercises the infrequency with
which he dots the "i's" is noticeable, a habit which became
confirmed in after years. Mr. Crumrine obtained the papers
about twenty years ago from Mr. D. L. Wilson, of Sewickley,
Allegheny county, now retired from the law. Judge Gibson
possibly left them in Beaver in 1804, or what is more
probable, his son Bannister carried them to Jefferson College,
Washington county, which institution he attended in 1836–8.

The following examples of the Latin verses are presented with their recent free translations:

"Esse ebrium est alienum a dignitate generosi hominis quem decet esse immunem vitia." To be intoxicated is foreign to the dignity of a generous man whom it behooves to be free from vice.

"Quis philosophorum sciver sciveunt omnia?" What philosopher has learned everything?

"Sapientissime hominum possunt errare, ut stultiessimi hominum interdum recte sentiunt." The wisest of men can err, just as the most foolish are sometimes of correct opinion.

"Panci sunt semper similes sui impius est tam dissimilis Dei quam similis diaboli." Few men are always true to themselves; the impious man is unlike God as he resembles the devil.

"Ille cujus sacculi sunt vacui nummia habet domum inanem amicorum et tunicam plenam fissurarum." He whose pockets contain no money has a house without friends and a cloak full of rents.

"Homo est praeditus coelesti animo; qui captus pravis libidinibus nunquam est contenus vera felicitate." Man is endowed with a divine mind; he is a slave to base passions, is never contented with true happiness.

"Diabolus iste hostis humain generis est primens ad malum; gaudet invenire animum proclivem ad impietatem." The devil is that enemy of the human race that incites it to evil; he delights to find a mind prone to evil.

"Stulti qui sunt pertinaces suae sententiae non erunt participes mei consilii." Fools strongly attached to their opinions shall not partake of my deliberations.

Roger B. Taney of Maryland, afterwards chief justice of the United States, graduated from this institution (1795) only a year or two before Gibson was matriculated, while the name of James Buchanan was borne on the rolls only a few years later, graduating in 1809.

An anonymous writer, in a brief sketch of Gibson (Carlisle *Sentinel*, July 3d, 1886), mentions that Judge Hugh H. Brackenridge "took notice of the country boy attending college, invited him to his house, and opened to him the treasures of the finest library here at that day. The delights of this association he mentioned often in his family, and spoke of Brackenridge with tenderness to the end of his days."

The fact that his preceptor Duncan, his friend Brackenridge, and himself were to occupy seats on the bench of the Supreme Court of the State is one of those strange coincidences forming a happy episode in the history of the Pennsylvania judiciary. All three did not sit together, however, Gibson's appointment coming immediately after Brackenridge's death, but he preceded Judge Duncan several years. It has been alleged that it was largely, if not chiefly the influence of Judge Gibson with the governor that secured Duncan the appointment.

It is seen, therefore, that in the outstart of his professional life Gibson was given a helping hand by men occupying high positions. There must have been something meritorious in his case, otherwise these gentlemen would hardly have been so kindly disposed towards him.

Judge Gibson left no diary or convenient autobiographic paper or memoranda of any description which would enable one to trace his history in detail. Such a sketch would probably not be desirable even if it could be drawn, for outside of the routine of his duties, his life was that of a simple citizen, and for the most part it was uneventful. The lives of all judges who remain long on the bench are, in this respect, much the same. The whirl of business enterprise and the excitement of politics does not disturb them or engage their attention, except when clashing interests which, if left unchecked, would lead to anarchy, are quieted by their decrees. As a rule, therefore, the longer they live the less are they popularly known, and the more dependent on their real friends — the lawyers — for their advancement, or continuance, in office.

When, in 1851, the judiciary in Pennsylvania became elective, had it not been for the influence of the legal profession, actively exerted, Judge Gibson would neither have

6

been nominated nor elected to the bench of the Supreme Court. The fitness of candidates for judicial honors in Pennsylvania is determined in the great majority of cases by the lawyers who, in effect, carry the proxies of the people. If this view be correct, the evils which Judge Gibson feared, and Judge Porter and others have predicted, would result from the change from the appointment to the elective system are not likely to be realized.

The following reference to the personality of judges, which is taken from a notice of Judge Gibson in the New York "Democratic Review" (May, 1853), is interesting in connection with the point just alluded to:

"No judge can become extensively popular with the masses; the very nature of his duties forbids it. His labors are all in the desk. His most important functions are to be silent and listen. When the populace see him, it is shrouded with power and begirt with officers. If he acquires reputation, it is with the few, chiefly lawyers, who are paid to read his opinions, and to measure the length and breadth of his mind. Hence it is very rare that a judge, who has held no other place but a seat on the bench, ever attains to more than a limited popularity. It is highly probable that we of this age know Coke, Hale and Holt as well as did their respective cotemporaries. Judges live in the books of reports — not in the huzzas of the crowd, or in the bulletins of battles. There their labors are consecrated and there posterity meets them face to face. When the sound of the orator's voice is hushed and forgotten, when the thunders of battle have died away and we only learn the name of the victor from the pages of some neglected historian, and when the toils and cares of the statesman are laid to rest in his grave, then will the laborious struggles of the judge with intri-

cacies, subtleties and contradictions, in the retirement of his
study, still survive, and transmit to succeeding times his fame,
which was scarcely appreciated during that in which they
lived. *   *   *   *   Who would exchange the glory of
Solon, Lycurgus and Numa for that of all the butchers of
their fellow men?

'From Macedonia's madman to the Swede.'

To the same class of men Judge Gibson belonged; and if
he did not originate any of the great precepts, maxims and
principles of jurisprudence, he comprehended, expounded and
applied them with as much ability and success as any judge
of his time."

Judges need be neither pretentious nor conceited, and
probably few of them are, though the anonymous writer before quoted thought he saw something of this in Judge
Gibson, as he quoted the opening sentence of his will in
justification of this conclusion: "I, John Bannister Gibson,
the last of the chief justices under the constitution of 1790."
Now, it may have been that this phraseology was purposely
employed, to express with the potency of "a voice from the
dead" his persistent conviction of the unwisdom of the elective system of filling that office. But the fact is, his will,
which, if he had so designed, might have been made a finished legal instrument, is generally considered to be a paper
of only ordinary literary merit. It is scarcely probable, therefore, that he had the remotest idea of its attracting public
attention.

Judge Gibson was married to Sarah Work Galbraith, at
the home of the latter's mother, Mrs. Barbara Galbraith,* in
Carlisle, October 8th, 1812,† in the presence of William

* Judge Black, as noticed elsewhere, was led into error as to the date of this
marriage.

† Mrs. Barbara Galbraith died November 7th, 1832.

Wilkins, John Reynolds, Samuel Parker and others, by the Rev. Henry Wilson. The Galbraith family were Presbyterians, and the Rev. Mr. Wilson was pastor of the First Presbyterian church of that town. Colonel Andrew Galbraith, father of Sarah, came from an excellent family, he and one or more of his brothers having been officers in the army during the Revolution.*

---

*From "Pennsylvania Genealogies, Scotch and Irish," by William Henry Egle, M. O. M. A., Harrisburg, 1886, the following is condensed from the history of the Galbraith family:

James Galbraith (son of John G.), born 1666 in the north of Ireland, emigrated to America 1718, settled in Connestoga (now Lancaster county, Pa.), married Rebecca Chambers, and died August 23, 1744. [Possibly George Gibson, the first, may have come "in the same ship" with the Galbraiths.]

Among their children was James Galbraith, born 1703 in Ireland; he came with his parents to Pennsylvania. James was married April 6th, 1734, in Christ church, Philadelphia, to Elizabeth Bertram. He moved to East Pennsboro township, Cumberland county, at the close of the Revolutionary war, where he died June 11, 1786. Among their children was Andrew Galbraith, born 1750, in Derry township, Lancaster county, Pa. He was married to Barbara Kyle (native of Lancaster county) in 1780.

This union was blessed by a family of eight daughters and two sons. Egle forgot to speak of the wit, beauty and fine complexion of these ladies. Having seen the life-sized portrait of Sarah, and of others of these equally once noted belles of the Cumberland Valley taken in their younger days, and knowing most of them in their latter years, the writer is prepared to believe they must have formed a bevy of beauties, equalling any family group in these latter days. Egle summarizes them in the following order :

Jean, born 1781, married Matthew Miller.

Elizabeth, born 1784, married Dr. Kelso, of Harrisburg, Pa., died April 8th, 1818.

Juliana, born 1786, married William McNeil Irvine.

Mary, born 1789, married February 13th, 1810, Michael Ege.

Sarah, born January 25th, 1791, married J. B. Gibson; died January 25th, 1861.

Barbara, born 1793, married a Mr. Gordon, of Georgia.

Dorcas, born 1795, died February 23, 1808.

Ann, born 1797, married Charles Hall, a Baltimore merchant; she was a widow in Carlisle for many years, where she died in 1858.

Their descendants are scattered throughout the country. The late Hon. Frederick Watts, of Carlisle, married a daughter of Mary and Michael Ege.

There were two sons named Andrew and James, both of whom died in infancy; Egle does not mention them.

At the time of his marriage, Mr. Gibson was a member of the Pennsylvania Legislature, and in the following year was appointed by Governor Snyder judge of the newly organized eleventh judicial district, composed of the counties of Wayne and Luzerne. Judges Hollenbach and Fell were associated with him on the bench of the latter county. Gibson succeeded Judge Chapman.

In the paper* from which the above information was obtained, there are given the following interesting particulars concerning his life in that quiet village:

"His residence was on Northampton, between Franklin and Main streets, recently occupied by Dr. Wright. Naturally affable and easy of access, he united in manners the familiar courtesy of the gentleman with the appropriate dignity of his judicial station. Hence he became a general favorite, while his patience to hear, his talent (without seeming to hurry) to accelerate business, his fairness and promptitude to decide, soon commanded universal confidence.

"In the hours of relaxation from the exercise of official duties, and his law and literary reading, he seemed to take especial pleasure in company with his scientific friend, the late Jacob Cist, visiting different portions of the valley, note its geological structure, particularly the extent and position of the anthracite coal deposit,† then, from the praiseworthy experiment of Judge Fell and its fortunate result, just beginning to emerge into importance; and also, with more than common curiosity and delight to visit the ancient Indian fortifications. In one of their excursions to examine the large fort on the plantation of Mr. James

---

*Wilkesbarre *Record of the Times*, May, 1853, containing a notice of Judge Gibson's public life, etc.

†Judge Gibson's wife often stated that the first anthracite coal fires in Wilkesbarre were in her house.

Hancock, they found the medal of King George the First, which, owing to their care, is yet happily preserved.

"As a Mason, he entered into the spirit of the society, found pleasure in attending its communications, for he met there numbers of intelligent citizens, whose localities and various pursuits could hardly have brought them elsewhere together; and we think for a year or two his honor presided as master of the lodge, 'as many a worthy brother has done before him.'

"When called to the supreme bench, his departure was regarded with emotions of mingled pleasure and regret. All were glad at the occurrence of an event so propitious to him personally, and promising increased utility to that elevated tribunal; yet all were sorry to part with him, as a judge or as a citizen. His wife was a Miss Galbraith, and during his residence, the visits of her sisters and other female friends added to the social charms in the village, less populous, and far more secluded from the busy world than now."

This agreeable chronicler, who appears to have had an intimate knowledge of Judge Gibson's social life, proceeds to relate an occurrence in society life, in Washington, D. C., bringing him out prominently in a Whig assemblage. He says:

"One of the greatest trials of Judge Gibson's life arose from his political dissonance with, yet devoted personal attachment to, Henry Clay; like Governor Cass, we will not say he idolized him, but both regarded the noble-spirited Kentuckian as a nonpareil. While Mr. Clay was lying under the vituperation of Judge Randolph's blistering tongue, Judge Gibson visited Washington. The reciprocated regard, and the eminent official and political position of the judge, rendered him an object of special attention at Mr. Secretary Clay's great party. In the midst of the persecution, the fine figure and courtly bearing of the chief justice of Pennsylvania, and a distinguished leader in her Democratic ranks, waiting on Mrs. Clay the rounds through the thronged rooms and brilliant assemblage, was at least a partial triumph; but 'discipline must be preserved;' if not in error, Judge Gibson headed the electoral ticket* for the support of General Jackson, and the consequent ouster of Mr. Clay and his friends."

Henry Clay having been mentioned, we will add an incident of Judge Gibson's meeting with Daniel Webster, which is remembered chiefly because of an amusing occurrence connected therewith. The judge happening to be in Boston upon one occasion, was invited to a banquet, and among other distinguished guests was Webster. The gentlemen having placed their hats on the hat-rack, proceeded to the dining table, where they sat long. In the midst of the feast Webster, having been suddenly reminded of an important engagement he must meet, quietly left the room. On the following day, on the street, Gibson again met Webster, who, espying his hat on the former's head, claimed the privilege of an exchange. It appears that Webster had taken the judge's brand new hat from the rack by mistake, leaving his own, which was considerably the worse from wear. Upon the adjournment of the party, the judge finding only one hat which fitted him, took it away, and probably never would have noticed the exchange, had he not been reminded of it by the more observant Webster. Both of these men had heads so remarkably large that from

---

* He did head the electoral ticket.

long experience, doubtless, neither thought such an acci-
dental exchange of hats among the probabilities.*

The reference to the fact by the Wilkesbarre writer,
above quoted, of Judge Gibson's connection with the Masonic fraternity, in answer to an inquiry directed by Judge
Mitchell, elicited the following reply from Mr. Samuel C.
Perkins, of Philadelphia, dated October 11th, 1887:

"'The late Hon. John Bannister Gibson was elected R.
W. Deputy Grand Master of the R. W. Grand Lodge of
F. and A. Masons, of Pennsylvania, St. John's Day (December 27), 1821; re-elected December 27, 1822, and elected
R. W. Grand Master December 27, 1823, and served in
that office one year. He was admitted as a Master Mason
in Lodge No. 43, at Lancaster, December 20, 1811, but a
short time afterwards withdrew. Subsequently he connected
himself with Lodge No. 61, at Wilkesbarre, and was
Worshipful Master of the Lodge for two successive terms,
from December 27th, 1814, to December 27th, 1816."

Writing from Wellsboro, Pa., under date of November
17th, 1887, Judge Henry W. Williams, the recently elected
justice of the Supreme Court, contributes some interesting
data in relation to Judge Gibson's connection in early days
with the courts of Northern Pennsylvania.

From an entry on appearance docket "A," date January 11th, 1813, Judge Williams copies the following:

"This being the day appointed by law for opening the

---

* Professor O. S. Fowler, in his "Self Instructor" (on Phrenology), mentions
the size of Judge Gibson's head as measuring twenty-four and one-fourth inches
in circumference; Daniel Webster's he gives as twenty-four; Henry Clay, twenty-
three; Napoleon Bonaparte, twenty-four inches (nearly). Of Burke and Jefferson he says, they had "very large heads," and Franklin's was over twenty-
four inches in circumference. Twenty inches is the least size given for the male
adult compatible with a "fair degree of intelligence;" twenty-two and one-third
inches he places as about the average for men.

several courts of jurisprudence for the county of Tioga, the
Honorable John B. Gibson and his associates, Hons. Ira
Kilbourne and Samuel W. Morris, appeared and took their
seats as judges of the said courts. Whereupon the Hon.
John B. Gibson produced his commission under the great
seal of the State of Pennsylvania, constituting him presiding
judge of the eleventh judicial district of the said State,
composed of the counties of Tioga, Bradford, Susquehanna
and Wayne, which commission was read in open court, together
with the oath of office thereon endorsed.

"I find Judge Gibson held the courts in this county
until September Term, 1816. His successor was Thomas
Burnside, who was afterwards with him upon the bench
of the Supreme Court. Burnside was first on the bench in
this district on the 16th September, 1816. Among the at-
torneys who practiced before Judge Gibson from 1813 to
1816 was Ellis Lewis, who afterwards sat with him on
the bench of the Supreme Court.

"The Eleventh district included this county during the
judicial services of Judges Gibson and Burnside as successive president judges of the district. The term held by
Judge Gibson in January, 1813, was the first term ever held
in this county, and was held in a log house, which for
several years thereafter accommodated the courts of the
county."

Referring to Judge Gibson's advent in the courts of
the northern part of the State the Wilkesbarre *True Democrat*, in May, 1853, says:

"He came among us while the prejudices of the State
rested heavily upon this portion of Pennsylvania, from the
long and aggravated controversy that had existed between
the Connecticut settlers and those who claimed the soil and

7

the State of Pennsylvania. Hence the appointment of Judge Gibson was to us most auspicious, as placing our destinies in the hands of one whose views soared above any low or narrow-minded prejudice." * * * "And we believe that this distinguished jurist contributed essentially in mitigating the feeling that ran in a strong current against the Connecticut settlers, and which for a season almost shut out our hopes of obtaining justice from the State authorities." * * * * "His sojourn with us has left deep and abiding impressions of respect for his commanding talents and social virtues. His domestic and social habits, aside from the able and just discharge of his official duties, were highly exemplary and amiable."

JUDGE WATTS.   JUDGE GIBSON

J. N. CORCNEY, PITTSBURGH, PA

JUDGE GIBSON'S HOUSE IN CARLISLE.

CHAPTER IV.

SOCIAL AND DOMESTIC INCIDENTS OF JUDGE GIBSON'S LIFE AT HOME AND ABROAD.

After his elevation to the Supreme Court in 1816, Judge Gibson moved his family to Carlisle, which place became their permanent abode. As for himself his duties required such constant traveling throughout the State that he could scarcely be accounted more than a frequent sojourner in the town. About the year 1820 he purchased the large brick mansion on East Main street, which remained his home until his death, which event, however, occurred in Philadelphia May 3d, 1853; and there his widow resided until her death, January 25th, 1861. The first payment on this purchase was made from his wife's means.

In this house, with its large and comfortable apartments, Judge and Mrs. Gibson gave frequent entertainments to their extensive circle of acquaintances and friends in the town; their hospitality extending, of course, to visitors and friends from a distance. Entertaining was quite the thing here, the Watts', Parker's, Biddle's, Armstrong's, Moore's, Penrose's, Blaine's,* Stevenson's, Duncan's, Ege's, Hays', Blair's, Thorn's, and others, vieing with each other in their efforts to sustain the reputation which the old town bore throughout central Pennsylvania for generous hospitality.

In her youth Mrs. Gibson was considered a remarkably

---

* James G. Blaine's ancestors were from Carlisle, and moved to Fayette county at an early period.

beautiful woman, as her portraits well testify to, and
throughout life she retained much of her fine appearance.
She was slightly over the medium in height, lithe and
graceful in movement, becoming more slender with advancing age. Her hair was a rich dark brown; eyes hazel,
while her husband's, in contrast, were light blue. Although
delicate in appearance Mrs. Gibson, as a rule, enjoyed excellent health, and was always in the best of spirits, sociable
and cordial in manner. She was an earnest Christian and
devoted mother, an excellent letter writer, maintaining a
correspondence even with her absent grandchildren. Her
household duties she managed quietly. Servants drilled
under her supervision would, in these degenerate days of
"helps," could their like be found, be esteemed of priceless value, and yet she ruled by kindness alone, for never
did a loud or angry word escape her lips, yet nothing,
from the vegetable garden to the cooking range and the
table, escaped her vigilant attention. She was just exactly
such a housekeeper as Marian Harland must have constantly in mind in her weekly chapters of instructions to
her readers. She entered with zest into every matter which
concerned her husband's welfare, and there can be no doubt
that he found in her a helpmate and counselor equal to
every emergency, for certainly their natures were in perfect
harmony.

A number of things happily conspired to make Carlisle,
in a social aspect, the most notable among the towns of
the central part of the State. First may be mentioned its
location in the midst of the Cumberland Valley, having
the Blue Mountain range in plain sight to the North, and
the South mountains (across which lies Gettysburg) equi-
distant in the opposite direction; and in a country famed

for the fertility of its soil, as well as for its salubrious climate and beautiful scenery. Next it was a "barracks town," at least so for very many years, which sufficiently explains the fact that so many officers of the army found their wives in Carlisle, and there some of them have sought retirement in their declining years. The ancient college, with its well stocked libraries, gave a turn to the literary tastes of the people, while its well-dressed undergraduates contributed to enliven the streets and add to the festivities of the younger portion of the community. The proximity of the Carlisle White Sulphur and Mt. Holly springs made the place considerable of a resort during the summer months, Baltimoreans being the more numerous visitors. Society could not do otherwise than flourish amid so many congenial surroundings, though so much cannot be said for the business energy of the place. Harrisburg, a two hours' drive distant over level roads, fast made inroads on her claims of superiority in sociability, wit, and intelligence, and long ago developed into a manufacturing city.

In a recent number of the Philadelphia *Times* (March, 1887,) the Rev. A. Nevin, D. D., contributes an interesting sketch of the life of Chief Justice Gibson, from which we make the following extract. It furnishes a pleasing picture from Mr. Nevin's recollection of Judge Gibson's personal appearance when he was in the prime of life. He says:

"We remember Judge Gibson well when as a student of law in Carlisle, 1835-7, we saw him on his frequent returns to his family during his official vacations. He was of commanding presence, tall, well proportioned, in vigorous health, with an unusually large head and penetrating eye; just such a man as would be singled out in a crowd with a desire for knowledge of his name and acquaintance with his history. There was a stateliness in his step, a dignity in his bearing, and an abstractedness in his expression, which bore the stamp of greatness and left the observer no room to doubt that he had his rank among the profoundest thinkers and ripest scholars of his age.

"Judge Gibson's preference, religiously, was for the Episcopal Church. Whilst at home he was a regular attendant upon the ministry of the church of that denomination in the place. Often have we seen him in his pew taking part in the liturgical services, and listening with interested attention to the discourses of the rector. He had, no doubt, been reared in a Christian family, and the influences and impressions of his early training clung to him with increasing tenacity and moulding on the advance of life's journey. We do not know that he was a professor of religion, but we have a warrant for the conviction that he was a firm believer in Christianity."

The time 'referred to by Doctor Nevin covers the period of the construction of the Cumberland Valley railroad from Harrisburg through Carlisle to Chambersburg, one of the first roads built in this State, and in which the judge took the liveliest interest. In common with the majority of the citizens and stockholders resident in the town, the judge, against the advice of Mr. Roberts, the chief engineer of the company, and who about this time married his second daughter (January 5th, 1837), favored the construction of the line through the main street.

Railroads were such novelties at that time that those who had a track at their front doors were envied by others on the "back streets." Not long after the opening,

however, Mr. Roberts writes in his reminiscences, a loco-
motive attached to a train upon which he was a passenger,
became tediously delayed on its way up from Harrisburg,
and finally about midnight stopped for want of fuel and
water immediately in front of Judge Gibson's house. Without disturbing any of the household, Mr. Roberts, with the
trainmen, found a way to the cellar and filled the tender
with some of the judge's seasoned hickory wood (the fuel
of the period), the water supply being drawn from the
well in the meantime. Thus did the son-in-law early seek
to demonstrate that the regard the father-in-law had for
railroads at close quarters was not wholly unappreciated by
the "soulless corporation."

Judge Gibson had what would be considered in cities a
large garden in the rear of his house, in addition to an
extensive lot in the suburbs. In these, while his opportunities for horticulture were somewhat limited, he displayed
considerable ability in grafting and pruning fruit trees.*
Peaches were favorites with him, and he raised a few trees
whose fruit would have been entitled to a premium, had
fruit exhibitions been in vogue in his time. He did not
attempt to vie with his next door neighbor, and kinsman
by marriage, Hon. Frederick Watts, in these respects (Judge
Watts was the first president of the State Agricultural Society, and later, under General Grant's administration, Commissioner of Agriculture, and was distinguished as a scientific agriculturist), but Judge Gibson did enough to indicate

---

*In a letter from Philadelphia to his wife, he writes: "On Friday I ordered
one peach, one pear and two plum trees, and two hundred and fifty asparagus
roots. To-morrow I will order another pear and two peach trees, and call at the
house on Broad street to expedite them. I thought you had two beds of asparagus. If more should be needed, I shall add them, and send directions how to
plant the roots."

that if the Supreme Court was ever abolished, he could from mother earth find congenial employment, and from her bosom draw a generous livelihood.

It would be difficult to say to what his tastes, outside of his profession, were most inclined. Judge Porter says, quoting from Wood, the late celebrated actor: "Chief Justice Gibson's sensibilities and tastes in the whole range of the fine arts, music, architecture, painting, statuary and the drama were hardly inferior to his uncommon intellectual parts." There are many reasons for thinking had he not chosen the law, that he would have been a physician.

Were an attempt made to draw a parallel between him and others, I would mention the Emperor Dom Pedro II of Brazil, whom I knew quite well by reason of a protracted residence in his dominions, as more like Gibson in versatility of knowledge than any other person I have ever seen. This does not merely refer to a general knowledge of things which many acquire by reading, observation or travel, but to the understanding of the men; · they had various and sometimes opposite aptitudes, or tendencies of. disposition. The emperor delights equally in the work of a chemical laboratory, or listening and taking part in geological or archæological discussions. Prof. Agassiz remarked to my father, after meeting the Emperor of Brazil in 1864, that his (the emperor's) knowledge of ichthyology, ornithology, zoology, geology, botany, and other departments of natural history, astonished him. Even among the faculty of specialists in the Rio University, he said he had not met his equal. Agassiz might have added architecture, language and numerous other accomplishments without going amiss. The emperor's habit of mind was such that in almost any department of research he could be content to become a specialist and have few regrets for the past.*

We need not extend these observations, except to remark that in his various tastes or aptitudes, Judge Gibson was a conspicuous example of the capacity of human beings to master general knowledge, and take equal delight in many departments of information. He read French and Italian easily, while through life he maintained the hold on the classics which he acquired at college.

He was a dextrous mechanic, and constantly kept a set of light tools at hand, with which he would undertake the ordinary repairs needed about his house and garden, and whatever of this he commenced, he finished in a neat and substantial manner, as would become a skilled workman.

A lady friend of his, meeting him in Philadelphia at her own house, had occasion to notice his perfect teeth. He was at the time quite seventy years old, while she was much younger. Her teeth were giving her a great deal of trouble, and she was considering the advisability of having a false set made. "Judge," she finally remarked, "may I take the liberty of asking the name of the dentist who furnished your teeth? They are so natural in appearance that I don't mind telling you in strict privacy that I would like to have him make me a set, for I require them badly." To this the judge replied; "Well, my dear madam, you are mistaken in regard to my teeth. They are my own, and have been used by me since I was a boy." No doubt he made compensation for the surprise and chagrin he caused his friend, by relating the facts concerning his teeth, which are somewhat curious and interesting.

---

* Since the above was written his crown has been removed, but the emperor has "few regrets for the past," for he has expressed his willingness to become a private citizen.

8

It is not uncommon with persons possessing good digestion to retain their teeth until old age. In such cases they loosen from their sockets, one after another, and actually drop out and often become lost. At the period Judge Gibson's first tooth loosened, he fastened it by means of a clamp of fine wire to its neighbors. But as one tooth followed another in loosening, he was for a long time constantly tinkering up coupling attachments, until at last the entire upper set was held in place solely by the eye teeth, which remained secure longer than the others. Finally when these also loosened, he was nonplussed, and for the first time consulted a dentist in Philadelphia, who told him that nothing could be done but to have a false set made. He was determined, however, never to use false teeth whilst he had in his pocket such a perfect set, the gift of nature. Returning to Carlisle he called upon Dr. George Hendel, a dentist of that place, noted for his inventive resources and mechanical skill. Hendel could propose no way to use the natural teeth, but the judge, not to be discouraged, started to work himself, in the dentist's office, and with the latter's appliances and assistance, in a few days' time adapted a peculiar plate to his own teeth, which he wore with comfort to the end of his days. Dr. Hendel, some years afterwards, at a meeting of dentists in Philadelphia, mentioned this feat of Judge Gibson's as a triumph of ingenuity unheard of in the dental profession.

After this performance the judge secured a complete set of dentist's tools, including a small vise which could be adjusted to his writing table. For want of human subjects he contented himself with experimental fillings in the teeth of various kinds of animals, and occasionally the teeth of some of Dr. Hendel's patients. This light, but intricate, mechanical work, seemed to afford him all the recreation he desired in the long period of his study hours.

CHAPTER V.

JUDGE GIBSON'S FONDNESS OF THE DRAMA—MUSICAL AND
ARTISTIC ABILITIES.

Judge Porter in his essay refers to Judge Gibson's occasionally quoting from Shakespeare in his official opinions. The judge was a student and admirer of the great poet; fond, also, of music and the drama. From what we know of his father we can readily believe that he, also, was a "patron of the drama" in the early days of theatricals in Philadelphia. Judge Gibson was not only an admirer, but also a critic, of no mean order, of the dramatic art as portrayed in his time. Traveling so much, he would naturally, at the hotels, make the acquaintance of the stars who at this period traveled frequently alone.

For the elder Joseph Jefferson, father of the present inimitable "Rip Van Winkle," he appears to have had a very special regard. Concerning this friendship Mr. Wood, in his "Personal Recollections of the Stage," refers at some length, quoting also a letter from the chief justice, who had written to him for information to aid in writing the epitaph for the tomb of Jefferson at Harrisburg, which he and Judge Rogers then designed erecting. (See Appendix D.)

This unostentatious act of two of the judges of the Supreme Court of Pennsylvania would never have been known to the world but for Mr. Wood's publication. Under date of April 30th, 1887, a correspondent of the Cincinnati *Commercial-Gazette*, writing from Harrisburg, thus feelingly describes a visit by Jefferson to the tomb of his distinguished father:

"The figure of a man familiar to Harrisburg theater-goers, and to every theater-goer in the country, strolled about the labyrinthine walks of Mt. Kalmia cemetery a few days ago when the sun was brightest and warmest, and the birds and flowers seemed pleased in the presence of spring. He wandered from grave to grave, closely scanning the inscriptions on the marble slabs, until he came to a lowly tomb that stands between twin oaks so tall that they seem to pierce the sky.

"'Here it is,' he said to a companion. 'The surroundings have been somewhat changed, but here is the same iron fence, and there (pointing to the inscription on the slab that covered the tomb) is the epitaph, one of the grandest compositions in the English language.' The speaker was Joe Jefferson, the actor, visiting the grave of his father, who is remembered by the old inhabitants of the country, and whose funeral here more than half a century ago was attended by the most prominent men in the State. The grave of this once famous actor is covered with a plain marble slab, on which is the epitaph, composed by John Bannister Gibson, at that time the chief justice of the Supreme Court of Pennsylvania.

*   *   *   *   *   *   *   *

"In 1882 Jefferson saw the grave of his father for the first time. He was filling an engagement here, and the day was bitter cold. With a hatchet and chisel he removed the ice from the slab, and with tears in his eyes read the beautiful lines which Justice Gibson wrote. Since then the grave has been kept neat, and is frequently visited by prominent actors and those who remember the illustrious man."

Reference has already been made to the fact that Judge Gibson was a violinist, and various stories have been told of the troubles his "fiddle" got him into in various parts of the State while holding court, but these, for the greater part, are innocent fictions. Judge Porter, his ardent friend and admirer, makes allusions to the fact and evidently considered it not exactly a blot or blemish on an otherwise "fair character," though he seems to have felt sorry he could not enter a denial of the impeachment, and reluctantly admitted the guilt of his client. So also does Judge Agnew, in his anecdotal letter, which elsewhere appears, confirm at least one of these stories. The fact is, he was a superior violinist. While it was rarely that he could be prevailed upon to give an exhibition of his powers in company or away from home, he frequently accompanied his daughters, particularly Mrs. McClure, on the piano, playing the most intricate and difficult pieces with ease. His preference, however, was for solos, and with these he would sometimes beguile himself in the privacy of his library.

He would often suddenly cease his work upon an opinion and while wooing the muses with his violin continue his meditations on a law point, and when that was definitely formulated as suddenly lay it aside and return to his writing. Those gifted with marked ability seem able to call into being, by the aid of harmonious sounds, a spirit with which they can commune. Many whose ears are susceptible to such influences have been carried by Ole Bull on his violin into realms where their own fancies never could have soared, so that when musicians speak of "inspiration" they mean exactly what they say. The same flights of imagination are experienced by the scientific cigar smoker when he lolls back in his chair to observe the rings and curling wreaths of smoke ascending from his cigar, and hence we never see them smoke in the dark, or in the open air, unless the day be calm, but to the untutored ear, or eye, as the case may be, all this is unintelligible gibberish.

That Judge Gibson was passionately fond of good music we may believe from the following extract of a letter of his to his wife: "It is supposed Jenny Lind will visit Philadelphia some time in the spring, but not in time for me to hear her. The disappointment would kill me." *

A grandson of the judge writes: "I remember quite distinctly that grandfather was an excellent piano tuner. Now real excellence in this particular is rarely attained. The whole business is complex, and a correct and discriminating ear is a first requisite, and this he had to perfection. I use the above terms advisedly, because in tuning a piano the "fifths" are tuned a little out of tune, the object of which I will not take time to explain. But here a discriminating ear comes in, and just how much to tune these fifths out of tune, so that the "thirds," "sixths," etc., and octaves come correctly from first hearings is the art of tuning to a nicety. I have seen his large form bending over a piano by the hour, and wondered how he could possibly stand the fatigue, and also wondered how such a big man could hit the little bits of high notes so nicely when tuning."†

---

* Dated 23 March, 1851.

† The above is from W. Milnor Roberts, of Cumberland, Maryland. He was fifteen years old at the time of his grandfather's death, but even then gave token of his own skill as a violinist, having been under the instruction of teachers from the age of eight years, his grandfather taking especial interest in the "family prodigy." Following the above, Mr. R. says: "Once when the Supreme Court was being held in Pittsburgh and most of the judges made the Monongahela House their home, mother happened to be stopping at the same hotel. I was sitting in grandfather's room, No. 19 (old style), as I very well remember, watching

Almost every school-boy essays at some time to become an artist or perchance a poet, and fills the blank leaves of his books with sketches or rhymes as he feels himself moved either by the influence of "Calliope" or "Euterpe." Young men differ in the extent to which they go, and the mode of worshipping their favorite Muse, though nearly all of them fall from grace when they find themselves fairly launched on the cold, cruel and bustling world to combat for a living. Judge Gibson formed no exception to the rule. The fact in his case is that he must have experienced a particularly strong inspiration for art during his boyhood years, for notwithstanding the straitened circumstances of the family, and the relatively high price of artists' materials, he obtained them, and finished during this period several rather pretentious oil paintings. While he never had a teacher he appears, as is rather strange to relate, to have commenced with and confined his efforts to portraits and historical scenes.

He was, no doubt, aware of the great name and reputation his Delaware county relative, Benjamin West (afterwards knighted Sir Benjamin West), acquired in England, and like him, may have used charcoal on barn doors for the exercise of his genius at its dawnings, though he

---

him in his shirt sleeves writing. Suddenly he looked up and said: 'Boy, have you got your fiddle with you?' I answered yes. 'I want to hear you play it,' he replied, and I ran after it. Being the first I ever owned, I was proud of it, and was anxious to hear his superior judgment of its qualities. After playing one of my then favorite airs, he picked it up to try it himself. He ran his fingers nimbly over the strings and then threw my cherished 'Cremona' down on the bed, exclaiming, 'Pah; I wouldn't give a shilling for a cart load of such fiddles' (his very words). Then bidding me to wait until he came back, he shortly returned from Kleber's store where he had purchased a violin and box, which he had carried through the streets himself, and presented to me. I have still in my collection both of those violins, and as you well know, grandfather's matchless and veritable Cremona, which not only as an heir-loom, but as well on account of its intrinsic merits, is of priceless value."

never displayed an inclination to emulate the career of that distinguished cousin.

Of the two Gibson paintings which still exist, one represents Pulaski mounted on horseback, believed to have been painted when a boy of about fourteen years. The sketch (which may have been a copy from some print) was possibly suggested from what he had heard his father say of the distinguished Polish count, who sacrificed his life at the siege of Savannah in 1779, where also fell Sergeant Jasper, the hero of Moultrie, in the cause of American liberty.

The other work, which was also his last painting, was made under interesting circumstances. While a law student at Carlisle, and at about the age of twenty-one or twenty-two, he took advantage of a holiday period to visit his mother at the old home on the banks of Sherman's creek, with the intention of going on a deer hunt in the mountains. It so happened, however, that it rained all the time that he was at home, so that he was kept within doors, where for amusement and pastime he painted on a poplar board his own likeness in miniature and profile.*

The Bible says, "like unto a man beholding his natural face in a glass. For he beholdeth himself, and goeth his way, and straightway forgetteth what manner of man he was."† The greatest portrait painters have acknowledged this homely truth, for many and woeful have been their attempts to paint their own likenesses. Between a look in the mirror and a glance at the canvas before them is but the briefest of periods, but in that moment memory is apt

---

* From a recent letter written in the old house by Frank W. Gibson, a nephew of the judge. Mr. Gibson, since writing the above, has forwarded Judge Gibson's two paintings, also a full sized portrait of Colonel George Gibson, Judge Gibson's father, to Pittsburgh, for presentation to the Allegheny County Law Library, where they now repose.

† James 1; V. 23, 24.

JUDGE GIBSON'S PORTRAIT OF HIMSELF.

Original now in the Allegheny County Law Library.

to fail, and the otherwise deft pencil hesitates, or goes astray. Providence may have thus designed men, with special reference to handsome or conceited artists, to keep them from mounting on the shoulders of their Cæsars, Alexanders, Napoleons or Washingtons, their own more complacent physiognomies. A few of them have succeeded, and on the above hypothesis they must have deserved success, and Judge Gibson's early friends united in saying that he had made a success in painting his own likeness, while the few in latter years, who have seen this work and whose critical knowledge entitles their opinions to respect, are agreed that as a mere specimen of art it possesses very considerable merit, displaying what some of them think a genius, not only for outline work, but in treatment of detail and coloring as well.* The photo-engraving presented is one-quarter size of the original painting.†

In after years Judge Gibson occasionally employed his abilities in rapid pen and ink sketches, and as Judge Porter says, amused his brethren on the bench sometimes with Nast-like pictures of some tiresome speaker in his most habitual or characteristic attitude. But he would have been the last of men to have employed such a talent in a malicious manner or for a vindictive purpose. The writer purposely refrains from dwelling on the attributes of heart of his subject, although memory, and knowledge acquired,

---

* Mr. John W. Beatty, a prominent artist of Pittsburgh, in the art columns of *The Bulletin*, a Pittsburgh society journal, speaking of this picture says: "It is not only a work of decided merit, but also of unusual interest because of the painter and circumstances under which it was painted. * * * The features, and especially the hair, are rendered with much delicacy and refinement."

† Chief Justice Richardson of the Massachusetts Court of Claims has in his possession what is described to be a very fine portrait of an ex-president of Yale College painted by its subject.

9

would justify him in placing the highest estimate on these characteristics of his nature.

In dismissing this topic, it is proper to say that Judge Gibson took no pride whatever in his "art work," if it may be so termed. The youthful effusions of his pencil and brush have remained, until a very recent date, in the secluded spot where they were born, and nothing from his hands was ever seen upon the walls of his home in Carlisle. There, however, he had collected a limited number of paintings and choice engravings, which indicated a discriminating judgment and cultivated taste. Financial inability, rather than lack of disposition, alone interfered to prevent his collection reaching to the importance and dignity which one naturally supposes belongs to a private gallery.

None of Judge Gibson's family were aware of the fact, if it be a fact, until after his death, that he had provoked the Muses so far in his latter days as to attempt a poem. Judge Porter, in his essay, prints the production and imputes it to him, and at intermittent periods the student of forgotten lore delving in old files of newspapers brings it to life. We have traced it to its first appearance, and there finding it accompanied with an editorial note vouching for its authorship, feel warranted in again presenting the pleasing hexameter lines which make the rounds as the accredited production of his pen. From the *Model American Courier*, 1853 or 1854.

"We were not aware that the late eminent jurist, Judge Gibson, ever 'dallied with the Muses nine,' nor does it appear that it was his frequent custom, though a fair and esteemed correspondent furnishes us with the following brief note, 'an exception to the general rule in the case:'

A. McMakin, Esq., Philadelphia:

My Dear Sir:—Enclosed you will find an autograph poem of the late Chief Justice Gibson, the only poetry he ever perpetrated, and presented to me a short time before his death. Yours respectfully,

A. R. R.

RETROSPECTION.*

On re-visiting the dilapidated birth-place of the author, after an absence of many years.

BY JOHN BANNISTER GIBSON.

(A first and last attempt.)

The home of my youth stands in silence and sadness,
  None that tasted its simple enjoyments are there;
No longer its wall rings with glee and with gladness;
  No strain of blithe melody breaks on the ear.

The infantile sport in the shade of the wildwood,
  The father who smiled at the games of the ball;
The parent still dearer who watched o'er my childhood,
  Return not again at affection's fond call.

And the garden—fit emblem of youth's fading flowers—
  No fawn-footed urchin now bounds o'er its lawn;
The young eyes that beamed on its rose-colored bowers,
  Are fled from its arbors—forever are gone.

Why memory cling thus to life's jocund morning—
  Why point to its treasures exhausted too soon,
Or tell that the buds of the heart at the dawning
  Were destined to wither and perish at noon?

On the past sadly musing, oh pause not a moment;
  Could we live o'er again but one bright sunny day,
'Twere better than ages of present enjoyment,
  In the mem'ry of scenes that have long passed away.

But time ne'er retraces the footsteps he measures—
  In fancy alone with the past can we dwell;
Then take my last blessing, lov'd scene of young pleasures,
  Dear home of my childhood—forever farewell.

---

* For further information regarding the authorship of this poem, see Appendix E.

CHAPTER VI.

A SKETCH OF GEORGE WASHINGTON — JUDGE GIBSON'S WEALTH
— FONDNESS OF HIS CHILDREN — PRESIDENT JACKSON
WANTED HIM ON THE SUPREME BENCH — REFUSED A
GOLDEN GIFT — THE HARMONY SOCIETY CASE — KEEPING
JAMES BUCHANAN AWAKE.

Perhaps the only time that Judge Gibson ever saw
Washington was in 1794, during his second term of the
presidency, when a division of the American army, 10,000
strong, was assembled at Carlisle, where it was inspected
by the president prior to its march to suppress the Whiskey Insurrection in Western Pennsylvania. Washington remained some time in Carlisle, but did not accompany that
portion of the army which finally marched to Pittsburgh.
Gibson, at this period, was a boy of but fourteen years,
but in later life he wrote the following interesting description of the scenes he had witnessed:

"The rendezvous of the northern division of the army,
by far the strongest, was at Carlisle, where the president
joined it as commander-in-chief. Passing through the town
without dismounting at the quarters proposed for him, he
proceeded at once, under an escort of New Jersey dragoons,
to the plain at the south of it, where ten thousand volunteers, the flower of the Delaware, New Jersey and Pennsylvania youth, were drawn up to be reviewed by him.
Finer looking fellows were, perhaps, never brought into
line, and their uniforms, arms and accoutrements were
splendid. But the observed of all observers was General

Washington. Taking off his small revolutionary cocked hat, and letting it fall at his side with inimitable grace, he rode slowly along the front, receiving, with a puff of military pride, the salute of the regiments with drums and colors, of the officers with swords and spontoons, and of private soldiers with presented arms. His eye appeared to fall on every man in the line, and every man in the line appeared to feel that it did so. No man ever sat so nobly in a saddle, and no man's presence was ever so dignified."

To a boy, as the writer then was, it was an impressive spectacle. (Coll. Hist. Soc. Pa. I, 349.)

In business matters Judge Gibson would hardly have been considered, according to present standards, a successful speculator. What little he managed to save from his salary in the course of many years, including also his wife's dower, with compounded interest amounted, at the time of his death, to about $21,000, besides his property in Carlisle, which would swell the total to possibly $30,000.

He had investments in "Mine Hill" and other lucrative railroad stocks, from the interest of which he increased the number of his shares from time to time. Upon one occasion General Wm. Robinson, of Allegheny City, gave a dinner party to him and Judge Rogers, and perhaps others of the Supreme Court. One of the judges had occasion to remark to the general, that leading a migratory life— "half in the stage-coach, half on the bench"—they seldom saw opportunities to make investments which would "double up" so rapidly as had some of his (the general's) and others of their friends. The general with his abiding faith in the future of his native city, in which he was the first white child born, replied that near them, right on Federal street, and opposite his own house, was

an extensive lot (later the property partially covered by the
present Girard House) then for sale, and as Allegheny was
bound to grow, why not buy it? Judges Gibson and
Rogers acted upon the hint and shortly afterwards the
property in question was transferred to them for a consideration of about $5,000.

Unfortunately soon after their purchase a flood from the
Allegheny river covered it several feet, and the barber and
other tenants demanded and obtained, a reduction of rents.
All the rest of Allegheny appreciated in value, but a fatality
seemed to hang over "the Supreme Court lot." Several
years after Judge Gibson's death his heirs obtained for his
share of this property the precise amount of his original
investment. Since the sale the property has steadily advanced
in value until to-day it is worth fully $125,000. General
Robinson was not to blame. This only goes to prove that
the successful man cannot impart the rules of his success
to others. If General Robinson had bought this property
either the flood would not have come, or he would have
sold it for a ship yard or a swimming school, and rents
would never have declined.

The case of Elias Spiedel vs. The Harmony Society at
Economy, Beaver county, Pa., recently pending in the Supreme
Court of the United States, recalls to mind a characteristic
anecdote of Judge Gibson. One Schrieber had a similar
case against the same society, which was ruled upon by
Judge Gibson in the Supreme Court of Pennsylvania. This is
the case of an expelled member of the society, after many
years through his heirs suing for services rendered and
accrued interest. In the Schrieber case Judge Gibson
decided in favor of the society.

Shortly after making the decision the judge received in

Carlisle an anonymous letter containing a hundred dollar note with thanks for services rendered. He could not imagine from whom it came, but as a precaution, he took it to the postoffice, and in the presence of his friends, Wm. Riddle and Wm. Penrose, handed it to the post-master with a disclaimer. Shortly after this presents of various kinds of wines from Economy were sent to him. It then occurred to him that all these things were coming from Mr. Rapp, the president of the Economite society, and to him he returned the wine, and no doubt saw to it that the money was also returned, with a cautionary note, explaining that no matter what might be the custom in continental countries judges in this country were bound to give their decisions without the hope of being rewarded by either side. He had feared at first that some secret enemy with a villainous purpose was designing in this way to injure his character, and it was a great relief to him to finally discover that the motive was friendly, though founded upon a lamentable ignorance of the proprieties governing the judiciary in Pennsylvania.

No one could have been more affectionate or more fond of the members of his family than was Judge Gibson. He delighted to have his children about him, and he was never austere in his behavior towards them; so, while they both loved and respected him, they manifested little of that fear of parents which many insist children should have. When his daughters Margaretta and Annie were of the mischievous age of the children described by Longfellow in his beautiful poem, "The Children's Hour," they played a trick on their respected parent which will illustrate the fear they entertained of him. He was at his library table busily engaged in writing, and, abstracted as usual, was an easy prey. With their busy needles and thread they sewed all manner shapes and sizes of colored rags to his coat tails, and even on his back, and having completed their task notified their mother that their father desired to see her. Just what then happened must be left to the imagination, but nowheres is it on record that those naughty girls were punished.

His love for his brothers Francis and George was equally tender and affectionate, and throughout their long lives this trio of brothers lived in perfect accord. General George Gibson usually went to Carlisle to spend the month of October as his holiday from his office in Washington, and whenever possible, even if it were only for a day or two, Judge Gibson would steal away from the Supreme Court and the two would drive over into Perry county to hunt and fish with their older brother Frank. George could shoot quail and pheasants on the wing until after his seventieth year and was a thorough-going sportsman both with gun and rod. The judge had been a great rifle shot in his youth but did not keep up his sportsmanship in his latter years, preferring to rest, and the society of his brothers quietly at the old homestead on the occasions of these reunions.

As noticed in the appendix, George had been an intimate friend of General Jackson, and it is a fact that so much did President Jackson admire the general's brother that he often said that he desired to make the judge chief justice of the United States. Certain "political combinations" alone overruled Jackson's determination in this matter. Had one more vacancy occurred on the U. S. Supreme bench during his term the place would have been tendered to Gibson without a doubt.

It may not be profitable to speculate on events which never came to pass, the "might have been" of men's lives, but of Judge Gibson's capacity for that "higher sphere," to which he possibly never actually aspired, the following from the same article in the *Democratic Review* of New York, may be taken as voicing the sentiment of his friends:

"Had Judge Gibson been transferred to the Supreme Court of the United States, in early life, where he would have found scope for his talents and a theater worthy of his ambition, he would have won a name and left a reputation second only to that of John Marshall. It is to be regretted that capacity such as his should have languished in comparative obscurity, and that intellectual might, able to have 'split the gnarled oak,' should have · been forced by circumstances to fritter away its energies and its powers in polishing pebbles and in pointing pins. Let not this illustration mislead our readers. We do not design to be understood to assert that all the business of the Supreme Court of a State is of this trivial nature. Though much of it is, there are cases sometimes arising which may well command the utmost grasp of thought of the first judge that ever adorned any judicial seat. On such occasions Judge Gibson was truly great, and proved beyond cavil that no legal question was too intricate or too vast for his comprehension."

General Gibson confidently relied upon the appointment being made, and he often spoke of it after the judge's death to his friends, who nightly assembled at his comfortable rooms near the War Department, in Washington City. The place was the rendezvous of the veteran officers of the war of 1812, the Creek and Seminole war, and the Mexican wars, and the writer can refer to a two weeks' visit spent

10

with the old soldier in January, 1861, shortly before his
death, as the period during which was then stamped upon
his memory a number of matters of interest he has endeavored to develop in this paper.

The general used to relate with much zest a story he
got from his brother Bannister, which, while good of itself,
illustrates a phase of Judge Gibson's character which probably might have shocked the more staid of his admirers
had they heard it during the judge's lifetime. To them it
would fit Lincoln, but never "a dignified judge," but being
undoubtedly true, it must be given.

In making the circuit of the State the Supreme Court
judges were usually accompanied by a number of lawyers
and interested parties, so that it was not uncommon that
the arrival of so many persons at one time in some of the
towns where court was to be held crowded the hotels to
the limit of their capacity.

On one of these occasions James Buchanan was traveling
with the judges, and when the party reached the hotel, was
assigned to the same room with Judge Gibson. The judge
being tired from the effect of the journey, retired early to
bed, but Buchanan having papers to prepare before the
assembling of the court next day, sat writing near the
judge's bed until a very late hour. The light prevented
the judge from sleeping, and when Buchanan finally retired,
the former gentleman was "past his sleep". In a short
time the sonorous breathing of his room-mate gave assurance that he was wrapped in the arms of Morpheus. The
judge then began to compare his ill fortune that night
with that of his more lucky room-mate, but gradually admiration for his friend's somnolence, as the weary hours
dragged towards the dawn, gave way to envy, and as mis-

ery loves company, he at last resolved to disturb the blissful dreams of "Pennsylvania's favorite son."

This was a cruel thing to do, but the learned judge was about this time in no frame of mind to weigh such a consideration. Within reach of his hand, as he lay in bed, was the cord operating the venetian blinds of one of the windows. Most people are probably aware of the fact that these venetian blinds, if drawn up and suddenly dropped several feet, produce a sound in every respect as loud and otherwise similar to an irregular volley of musketry. Cautiously he pulled up the blinds almost to their full limit, and suddenly letting go the cord, there came the expected rattling crash. Buchanan was bolt upright in bed in an instant, and though dazed and bewildered for a moment, very quickly called to the judge to know "what under heavens had broken loose." Simulating one suddenly awakened, he asked what his friend wanted, but although Buchanan endeavored to explain the nature of the sound which had so suddenly awakened him, the judge assured him that no such sound had disturbed his repose, and suggested that possibly his late supper had produced indigestion, and the sound might have been a figment of his friend's imagination. Thus assured, Buchanan again courted sleep, and proved his success in the suit very shortly with most contented snores. But again the demon curtain ascended, and again it came down with its hish! crash! bang! Buchanan, as before, jumped up, and in the grey light of the dawn the judge saw him standing in the middle of the floor. In evident great excitement he called: "Judge, did you hear that?" but no answer coming, he approached the latter's bed, and this time calling more loudly, awakened (?) the judge, who, yawning, asked what was the matter with his friend. No explanation of Buchanan's could convince him that there had been an earthquake, or that the ceiling had come down, or that burglars had forced the door. Only with the utmost difficulty could he prevent him from awakening the house, the judge assuring him that if he did so their fellow-lodgers might think his wits had deserted him. Buchanan slept no more. How he managed his case that day was not told by the general, but he unconsciously revenged himself on Judge Gibson at a later period, when he urged upon President Jackson the appointment of Roger B. Taney to the chief justiceship of the United States, at the time Jackson was meditating the appointment of Gibson to that office.

To his limited fund of anecdote ex-Chief Justice Daniel Agnew has sent the following welcome additions:

BEAVER, March 18th, 1887.

MY DEAR SIR:

I have your letter of the 16th inst. written at the suggestion, as you say, of my friend John H. Hampton, Esq.

I am sorry that my memory does not revive some of the things I have heard of the "great chief justice" John Bannister Gibson. It would give me pleasure to contribute anything interesting. * * * * *

There is not a single person now living who could recall a knowledge of Judge Gibson's short residence here in 1804–5. I came here in 1829 and even then heard but little beyond the fact of his admission to the bar here.

I remember an anecdote told of his sojourn in Beaver, but when and how I heard it I cannot recall. After Burnside came upon the supreme bench (he and Gibson had been former friends) they were speaking of their ages; Gibson stated his, Burnside said: "Gibson, you are a year older," and to prove it enumerated the place and times where and when Gibson had lived, and said, *inter alia*, "and then there was the year you were at Beaver." Gibson stopped him, saying: "My God, Burnside, don't bring that up against me, it ought not to be counted." The tradition is he spent that time fiddling in his office.

This reminds me of a story told of him when a judge in a northern district of Pennsylvania. He carried his favorite violin with him. On a Sunday, forgetful of the sacred day, he got out his instrument and was discoursing sweet sounds (for tradition is he was a good musician). Presently his landlord, a church member (in that day whiskey and religion often dwelt together), came rushing up to his room crying, "Judge! Judge! for God's sake quit that; you will ruin the reputation of my house." Gibson laid down the magic toy, saying: "Oh, forgive me; I really had forgotten this was Sunday."*

In my early practice in the Supreme Court, John R. Shannon, a very worthy gentleman, was arguing a cause. He was an involved speaker. He had spoken a long time and stopped, saying: "Now, if the court understands me ——"

---

* Judge Gibson's wife was asked by an intimate friend concerning the correctness of this very story related by Judge Agnew, and she denied its truth. It seemed something "shocking" for her to think of, and we believe it is a fact that the judge himself also denied it. But what matters that? Who would believe Washington if he lived to-day and denied the authenticity of the story of the little hatchet, for has not the hatchet itself been found and exhibited in museums? So also does Judge Gibson's fiddle still exist (though only on private exhibition). The fact that he carried such a "weapon" about him is evidence that he was prepared to use it to the injury of his fellows. No judge of the Supreme Court since his time we believe has been a fiddler; such has been the excellent influence of this story, whether true or false.

"Stop a moment, Mr. Shannon," said the chief justice; "I think we possibly understand you now, but if you continue longer I fear we shall not."

The following I heard told of my colleague the late Justice Henry W. Williams: In arguing a case before the Supreme Court he dealt in a sort of double pronged argument. Said the chief justice, who probably knew as many games at cards as some kinds of law: "Mr. Williams, that reminds me of branching in vingt-un." "What, your Honor?" "Branching in vingt-un." Williams looked amazed. "I do not understand the illustration." Judge Shaler being present rose, seeing Williams' dilemma. "If your Honors please, my friend Williams is a good lawyer, but his education in the branch of learning your Honor refers to has been sadly neglected."

A gentleman in conversation with Gibson one day said: "Mr. Chief Justice, I observe you are a good listener; this must be very encouraging to those who address the court?" "Ah," said Gibson, "that is an art, sir, an acquisition, to be able to look one right in the eye and seem to hear all, yet lost in your reflections, to hear nothing; that, sir, is the very acme of judicial ability."

An illustration was this: A lawyer addressing the court caught the eyes of the chief justice fixed upon him, and saw him now and then noting something on a paper before him. After he finished he said to a friend beside him, "I think I have the chief justice; he drank in all I said; I should like to see his notes." The court adjourned and Gibson walked off leaving the paper. The gentleman went up and looked at it, and was surprised to see no notes, but written every here and there, "Dam phool—Dam phool—Dam phool."

At the first term of the court held in Beaver, in February, 1804,* John B. Gibson was admitted to practice with about twenty other leading lawyers of Allegheny and Washington counties. Beaver was then in the same circuit, the Fifth. In a very humble volume just published on the Lands, Settlements, Titles, etc., etc., in Northwestern Pennsylvania, I have enumerated them. I am very sorry I cannot furnish you with something more worthy.

Yours,

DANIEL AGNEW.

In the paragraphs preceding the notice of Judge Gibson's marriage to Miss Galbraith, reference was made to an expression employed by him in his last will, and to the remark it called for by a newspaper writer, who is supposed to be a distinguished attorney of Carlisle, still in practice, and a sincere admirer of the deceased and friend of his family. So that in quoting him again it will be for the purpose of making an explanation, which the publicity of his article appears to demand. He says, speaking of the judge:

"One who knew him in his prime said of him, 'that his face was eminently handsome and full of intellect and benevolence, that his manners were frank and simple, and that he was free from affectation or pretension of any sort.' Those who saw him only in advanced life remember his face as strong, rather than handsome, but through the wrinkles discerned traces of the superb complexion which he transmitted to his descendants. That he was free from affectation is hardly

---

* It would appear from this that Judge Gibson's admission to the Allegheny county bar preceded his entrance to the court at Beaver. March 8th, 1803, he was admitted at Carlisle (Cumberland county); September 26th of the same year at Pittsburgh, and February, 1804, as per above, in the Beaver county court. Judge Porter makes no reference to his admission to the courts of Allegheny county. T. P. R.

reconcilable with the fact that he cut short a full head of dark brown hair and covered it with a wig after he went on the bench, and continued to wear it to the last, although he had beneath it, at his death, a full head of grey hair."

He wore the wig and had the hair as described. The reason he shaved his head was simply because of its heating to an uncomfortable degree when he was hard at work, and in order to keep it cool he resorted to a wig. Usually when alone in a room he took his wig off, never making any pretence to secrecy in this habit. Hon. Jeremiah S. Black, in his early acquaintance with Judge Gibson, and before he was aware of this fact, desiring to see the judge in a room in a hotel, was directed by the clerk to the proper number, but upon opening the door was astounded with the large bald head of the occupant of the room, and thinking he had made a mistake was about withdrawing, when Gibson called him in and explained the reason of his appearance. Judge Black, in relating this story to Col. Chas. McClure, U. S. A., Judge Gibson's oldest grandson, said: "the judge remarked that he considered hair simply an overcoat for the head, and he would not be bothered with a garment which he could not remove at will."

This place is as convenient as any to make a remark concerning Judge Black's friendship for Gibson, which, as is generally known, was for years of the strongest nature conceivable. But it was not so in the beginning of their personal acquaintance.

Judge Black met Gibson for the first time after he himself had become a distinguished lawyer, and he had occasion to note that the judge meeting him afterwards in throngs, failed to remember him, even after several introductions. To a man of Black's excellent recollection of names and faces, this action on Gibson's part was incomprehensible, and he took it as a slight. These great men were radically different in many important respects. Black, though a great leader of men, was essentially a man of the people, an orator of unsurpassable ability, and an indefatigable worker. He was emphatically one of America's "grand old men". Gibson could never have been a successful politician, was no orator, and attempted work from a sense of duty, not a love for it. He "struck fire" in communion with himself; Black struck it among his fellows. Black, like James G. Blaine,* could instantly recall the names of acquaintances even in crowds, but this faculty was weak in Judge Gibson, and no one regretted the annoyance it caused more than himself. Persons so afflicted, for it is an affliction, are thus frequently misjudged, and Black at first so misjudged Gibson, but that he forgot these erroneous impressions in his exalted admiration of Gibson in after years, reference need only be made to his eulogy of his friend.

---

* During the fall of 1886 the writer, by the merest accident, met Mr. Blaine on his farm at Lock No. 3, just above the town of Elizabeth, on the Monongahela river. Mr. B. was visiting the neighborhood after an absence of twenty-five years. Genl. J. Bowman Sweitzer, of Pittsburgh, formed one of the little party, and by him the writer was introduced to the distinguished visitor and two of his sons. Entering the old-fashioned town, where his mother once had lived, Mr. Blaine began his greetings with old acquaintances, and then followed some remarkable recognitions. The man whose face, with its strong characteristics, is known to the civilized world, seemed not familiar to many of the old burghers of this quaint western Sleepy Hollow. " Which is Mr. Blaine?" could be heard in anxious *sotto voce*, while that gentleman himself was pushing forward, as he recognized through the wrinkled visages face after face of men and women whom he had in some cases only casually known in his youth. He named every one, and inquired about many whom he was informed had long been dead. The anecdotes connected with the locality, which he recalled to the minds of his friends, surprised every one, not only with the vividness with which they were related, but the almost unerring accuracy of his memory. It becomes more wonderful when it is considered that the real home of his youth was at Brownsville, a town on the river thirty miles above Elizabeth, and that he saw but little of the latter place in those years.

11

As has been said by W. D. Moore, Esq., of Pittsburgh, "in his portraiture of Gibson, Black in several respects pictured himself." It was, perhaps, almost too grand and beautiful a picture for one life to live, but when it becomes the funeral mantle of these two sons of Pennsylvania, it undoubtedly misses or overdraws no truth.

The compiler owes his thanks to Boyd Crumrine, Esq., of the Washington county bar, for the following incident in the life of Judge Gibson. Writing under date of March 22d, 1887, he says:

"To-day I heard a characteristic anecdote of Chief Justice Gibson, which it seems to me is worthy of preservation. I got it in such a way that I am satisfied it is authentic.

In early times, when I believe Carlisle was a place where the Supreme Court sat, on one occasion the Carlisle bar got up a duck supper for Gibson. Connected with the college was a Rev. McClelland, who had quite a local celebrity as a witty man, keen and quick at repartee. They purposely had Prof. McClelland seated opposite Judge Gibson, and soon had them engaged in a battle of brains. It is said that the preacher was about a match for the great judge, and now and then got the laugh on him. After the supper was over, a lawyer asked Gibson what he thought of McClelland. 'Well, he's a bright man,' said the judge, 'and if he preach as well as he talks, he is about as bright a preacher as I have met.' 'That's so,' said his friend, 'and, by the way, he preaches for us to-morrow evening, and if you'll go, I'll call for you.' The judge assented.

The next evening the lawyer took the judge to church, and the preacher delivered a brilliant, eloquent and able sermon upon 'The Judgment Day.' It was observed that the judge was deeply interested. Passing from the church, his friend asked the judge what he thought of the sermon. 'Well, it was a grand, forcible sermon,' said Gibson. 'It was solemn and threatening, and I do not see how I could have stood it so well if I had not recollected that duck supper last night.'*

Yours truly,

BOYD CRUMRINE."

---

* Nothing, perhaps, could be better calculated than a late duck supper the preceding night to put one in a proper frame of mind for realizing the terrors of the judgment day.

CHAPTER VII.

In answer to questions concerning her father's domestic
life, Mrs. McClure writes most affectingly of his kindness
of heart to all his children and grandchildren; particularly
does she speak in the most grateful remembrance of his particular kindness to herself when, after her husband's death, in
1846, he insisted upon her living with her three small boys
permanently at the "old home." *   Upon an average, Mrs.

---

*To the same effect writes Mrs. McClure's oldest son, Col. Chas. McClure,
U. S. A., as herewith appended:

"NEWPORT BARRACKS, KY., January 20th, 1887.

I am in receipt of your note of the 14th instant.

Upon the sudden death of my father at Pittsburgh in January, 1846, my
grandfather, Chief Justice Gibson, wrote mother an affectionate letter urging her
to come with her children and to make his home her home.   I was then but eight
years of age.   I can never recall the ten happy years spent under his roof without emotions of the deepest gratitude.   No more considerate and delicate hospitality was ever shown orphan children.   Grandfather and grandmother, from
the day we entered their house, made us feel that we were their children.   Never
by a word, look, or act, did we feel that everything in the house was not our own.
Our boyhood was made joyous by the sunshine and warmth of grandmother's
most noble, generous and affectionate of hearts.   He was at home but little.   The
sessions of the Supreme Court required his presence nearly all of the time at
Philadelphia, Harrisburg, Pittsburgh and Sunbury.   If he could have afforded
it he would have probably made his home at Philadelphia, where he could have
spent more time with his family.   He practiced economy in his personal expend-
itures in the hope of laying up something so that his family might not be left
destitute.

When he came home for a few weeks or days, he spent the time in his library,
writing his opinions, and the evenings were passed with the family in the parlor,
where he sometimes played the violin for our entertainment, accompanied with
the piano by my mother.

McClure says, her father was not at home during more than six weeks of the year. A statement like this will give our readers an idea of the hardships and fatigue the judges of the Supreme Court underwent in the performance of their duties in the "good old times (?)" traveling by stage-coach and canal, and in the latter days of Judge Gibson's time, occasionally on railroads. With Mrs. McClure he kept up his early and easily acquired knowledge of the French language, and generally when returning from Philadelphia or Pittsburgh brought home French books on interesting subjects. He enjoyed the duets in singing of his daughters, Mrs. Roberts and Mrs. Anderson, the latter of whom had a superb soprano voice, and then his violin accompaniments, as elsewhere referred to, with Mrs. McClure at the piano. He was a master of the intricacies of music, and his advice did much to develop the taste and talent of all three of his daughters in the same direction, so that when in the cities he was a frequenter of music and book stores on their account, as some of his letters show.

Referring to the French, under the date of October 27th,

In his library, surrounded with large piles of papers and law books, he sat for hours so absorbed in his work that he was generally unconscious of my entrance. Whenever I had a difficult sentence to translate from the classics, or a chemical formula to find, I would slip in and ask his assistance, and he treated the interruptions amiably, and took pains to aid me. He had a remarkable memory, and I referred to him as to an encyclopædia. His answers and explanations won for me higher standing in my studies than I deserved.

Once some sentence recalled a long Latin poem which, to my surprise, he repeated from memory throughout. Probably he had not seen it since he was a student of the classics.

You remember, as we all do, his drawer of tools in the library, and his work at the repair of his teeth. Grandfather was generally absent-minded, and I have spoken to him in passing in the street and he did not recognize me.

He was kind and sympathetic by nature, and no beggar ever left him empty-handed. To his children and to his grandchildren his heart ever went out. Their sickness always caused him the keenest solicitude and anxiety, and their sorrows he treated as his own, and they called forth his tenderest sympathy."

1850, from Pittsburgh, he writes to his daughter Margaretta (Mrs. McClure) as follows :

" It would be impossible for me to answer your letter in French, such as you have written, and I will not attempt it. The 'tournoure' of the sentences makes me suspect that the hand of a master * gave the finishing touch. It is all pure and graceful French, nothing English in it. I have been filling up the gaps between the hours of my employment in reading Chateaubrian's 'Memoires d'outre Tomb,' a book that abounds with beautiful thoughts and poetic sentiment. In my estimation he would have been a poet of the first force (to use a French idiom), even had he never written couplets. If I can procure his 'Gené du Christianesmé' I will read it next winter."

As for his knowledge of medicine, Mrs. McClure states that in Philadelphia, Sunbury and other places, he was often taken by regular practitioners into consultation in obscure cases, and of his abilities to diagnose a case she says: "I heard Dr. Jackson, of Philadelphia, say that it was a wonderful acquirement with him, and that several times he had been called upon for an opinion where the doctors disagreed among themselves, and that his decision never failed to be the right one, as was proved where his proposed line of treatment was adopted." The orthodox in the profession of to-day may doubt the orthodoxy of Dr. Jackson and the physicians referred to for doing such a terrible thing as consulting with a layman, but as those doctors are doubtless long ago in their graves, they cannot be injured by the relation of the fact. Speaking

---

* Here he guessed aright. M. Value, the distinguished French educational writer, was at this time in Carlisle and had a large class. Mrs. McClure had endeavored to play an innocent trick on her father with the assistance of her preceptor.

further to this point, Mrs. McClure says: "He often regretted that he never found time to pursue his studies of medicine in a regular manner at some college, for he said his greatest talent was for that, and that his love of reading on the subject never left him. He paid special attention to obscure nervous disorders."*

At the close of her letter, Mrs. McClure adds: "He also paid special attention to the subject of mineralogy, and contributed articles to *Silliman's Journal*, etc." In regard to one of these articles, see note appended to a page from Porter's essay, which follows this.

The subject of the great majority of his letters home was chiefly the health of the several members of his family, and abound with excellent suggestions in this regard. Several of them would suggest the idea that the writer was a physician "prescribing by letter." Towards the end of his life his own health caused him much anxiety and suffering, particularly after his severe attack of cholera, which he contracted at Sunbury, Penna., in 1852. The illness and death of Judges Coulter and Burnside while he was enfeebled himself, seems to have further distressed him.

Under date of 23d March, 1851, from Philadelphia, he thus refers to Judge Burnside's illness:

"Judge Burnside is about as he was three weeks ago. He complains of much pain in the lower bowels, which is the only indication of the particular seat of his disease. The doctors don't know what to do for

---

* His reliance on his own judgment and course of treatment led in his last illness to his taking certain medicine without the knowledge or consent of his physician, and Mrs. Roberts mentions in a letter that the effect of one of these doses greatly prostrated him and may have been the cause of hastening his death. The best of physicians will often fail to diagnose their own cases when they are sick.

him. He is certainly weaker and thinner than he was, but his voice is good; he had no fever and his pulse is natural. James* has been at home for a few days and returned on Thursday. Judge Bell and I went out to Germantown on Wednesday, and the judge conversed a good deal with us. He is not well satisfied with his physicians, though he is resigned to die."

Up to the very last, however, Judge Gibson indicated in his letters the warm sociability of his nature. Both in Philadelphia and Pittsburgh he had an extensive circle of friends upon whom he regularly called, and when any of these gave large entertainments he always wrote his wife pleasant descriptions, and though not particularly observant of " small talk happenings," he was the faithful chronicler of the weddings, deaths and other prominent events in the families of his old friends. He thus seemed instinctively to know what would be interesting items of news to his wife and daughters. Had he been writing to grown up sons or brothers, their subject matter would, as a matter of course, have been differently chosen.

In one letter (without date) there is a point which, for the benefit of lawyers, may be worth quoting:

" The court will continue through the present week, and probably for a day or two in the next one, to finish a cause lasting over Sunday on some business of very pressing emergency. Lawyers are slack in bringing on their business at the beginning of the court, but unpleasantly urgent near the close of it. We have already dispatched more business than ever was done in Philadelphia in the same time."

---

*James here referred to was a son of Judge Burnside who afterwards became judge of Centre county, Pa., and was killed July 3d, 1859, in Bellefonte, by being thrown out of a buggy.

The epidemic of cholera which visited Pittsburgh in 1849, and again in 1850, evidently caused much alarm in the judge's family, who feared he might contract the disease while attending court in that city. As a matter of interest to many persons in Pittsburgh some points connected with its appearance there from Judge Gibson's letters may prove valuable.

Under date of September 19th, 1849, he remarks in a letter to his wife: "We did not arrive here till Monday at three o'clock in consequence of having reached Hollidaysburg too late in the evening to cross the Portage railroad that night. We slept at Hollidaysburg and consequently lost the time we had gained by the railroad from Harrisburg. We traveled from that place to Lewistown, a distance of sixty-five miles, in less than three hours. We had but few passengers till we reached Johnstown, at the foot of the mountains, on this side, where a parcel of dirty emigrants came on board (canal boat) of us. They had stopped over the preceding night, but certainly not to wash their shirts. They looked as much like food for cholera as you can imagine, but they did us no harm. There is no cholera here, either in Pittsburgh or the towns about. It had entirely established itself in Birmingham, and there never were more than half a dozen cases of it in the city proper. On Monday a drunken member of Congress was brought up the river in a state of collapse, and died on the boat at the wharf, but his body was immediately taken away and buried privately, I presume, for we have since heard nothing about him. The taverns here are nearly empty, for the dreaded epidemic has prevented traveling

12

everywhere. The Monongahela House has not more than one-fifth part of its usual custom."

Sunday, July —, 1850, he writes:

"Yesterday I sent you a telegraphic dispatch; yet we had been on the point of decamping on Thursday. The cholera had disappeared both in Pittsburgh and Allegheny before our arrival, but on Wednesday morning it reappeared on the high ground half a mile east of the court house, in the family of Mr. Metcalf, who had a small Episcopal party the previous evening, and Mr. Metcalf and his brother-in-law (Mr. Knapp) died the same day, in the afternoon, leaving his wife, son and daughter ill of the disease, but they are recovering. Mr. Metcalf was a lawyer of great respectability, and was in court the day previous. It is singular that the disease reappeared on the original infected spot, comprising not more than an acre, in which it first broke out. It was brought there by a Mr. Lang (also a lawyer) from Cincinnati, who died of it, with his whole family, and all the mortality was confined to that narrow space. There has not been a death from it in the flat part of the lower city, excepting that of Doctor Green, who contracted the disease while attending the sick in the infected district. A laborer in it, who had lived in Allegheny along the marshy bank of the canal, took it home with him, and it was confined to a narrow space there, but traveled to a village two miles further up, and disappeared, after causing two deaths. This is a true statement of the case, and you need be under no apprehension from it. No one here thinks of it."

Two weeks later he writes:

"On Thursday young Metcalf died of congestive fever,

the secondary form of cholera, under which he labored for twelve days. No new cases originated after the blow which fell upon the Metcalf family, and which carried off the father, son and brother-in-law, and I believe a servant in the family. Mrs. Metcalf and her daughter recovered from the disease. This family was remarkable for their temperance and regularity both in eating and drinking. They were pious members of the Episcopal Church. It is considered that the disease has taken its final leave of the place."

No private letters of Judge Gibson of a date prior to 1841 are known to have been preserved, and the very last one which the writer has seen is dated March 17th, 1853. It is quite probable that this is the last letter he ever wrote home, where he remained until he, in a greatly enfeebled condition, and against the advice of the members of his family and of his physicians, made his last trip to attend the meeting of the Supreme Court in Philadelphia, and to which place his family was shortly summoned by telegraph to attend his dying bedside. He says:

"Scarcely had I got rid of the cold I had at Carlisle till I caught another from the same cause. The fire maker had not kindled the stove in time to warm the room. It is a hall like a barn, with eight large windows. I am going back to my old room, which I am sorry I left. I had bought a thermometer for it, and by proper instructions to the attendants had escaped colds.

"My present cold has been as severe as the preceding one except that I have no cough, but my head is much affected and my strength greatly prostrated. I went into court yesterday morning merely to receive a verdict. I adjourned over to Monday to meet in my old room. I am better to-day, but yesterday I lay almost entirely on the bed."

The children of Judge John Bannister and Sarah W. Gibson were as follows:

(1st.) Anne Sarah, born June 13th, 1813, died July 12th, 1813.

(2d.) Margaretta, born November 20th, 1814.

(3d.) Annie Barbara, born December 6th, 1817, died August 28th, 1857.

(4th.) John Bannister, born January 14th, 1820, died January 7th, 1822.

(5th.) John Bannister (2), born November 3d, 1822, died January 15th, 1856.

(6th.) George, born April 5th, 1826, died August 5th, 1888.

(7th.) Francis West, born October 31st, 1828, died March 2d, 1830.

(8th.) Sarah, born October 30th, 1830, died August 11th, 1872.

Margaretta was married November 5th, 1833, to Colonel Charles McClure. Colonel McClure represented the Cumberland county district in Congress, and was secretary of the Commonwealth of Pennsylvania during Governor Porter's term. He was an older brother of the late Judge William B. McClure, of Pittsburgh. Mrs. McClure is at present living in Carlisle. Her husband died in Allegheny City in January, 1846, from the effects of overwork and excitement attending the trial of an important case before the Supreme Court in which he was a counsellor. The remains of Colonel McClure are buried in the Allegheny Cemetery, Pittsburgh.*

---

* Mr. and Mrs. McClure had five children, two of whom died in infancy, prior to 1845. The three surviving children are, (1st.) Colonel Charles McClure, now of the paymaster's department, U. S. A. Colonel McClure served on the staff of various prominent generals through the war in the army of the Potomac,

Annie Barbara Gibson was married to W. Milnor Roberts, January 5th, 1837. Mr. Roberts was a civil engineer, commencing his active life in that profession while a boy of fifteen, in 1825, on the first canal attempted in Pennsylvania. Eventually he became chief engineer of public works in the State service. His name and services were intimately connected with the Portage railroad, Harrisburg & Lancaster, Cumberland Valley, Allegheny Valley, among the earlier works. In 1858 went to Brazil, remaining until 1865, during which period, in company with Mr. Jacob Humbird and other Americans, built the first railroad, the Great Dom Pedro II railroad, in that country; and later he was associate chief engineer St. Louis bridge, chief of the Northern Pacific, charge of Ohio river improvement, under appointment of Secretary of War Stanton, etc.

In 1879, accepting an appointment from the Emperor of Brazil, as chief of the commissioners of hydraulic engineers on the improvement of rivers and harbors in the Brazilian empire, he went to that country for the last time, where he died July 14th, 1881. His remains were brought to this country in the following year and buried in Philadelphia, his native city. Mrs. Roberts died in Carlisle, August

---

participating actively in many severe engagements. He had for several years prior to the war been in the office of his granduncle, General George Gibson, Commissary General, U. S. A. His present address is El Paso, Texas. He was married September 16th, 1869, at Santa Fe, New Mexico, to Annie, a daughter of Brigader General George W. Getty, U. S. A. General Getty was a major-general of volunteers during the war. When retired he was colonel of the fourth artillery, and a major general United States army by brevet. Colonel McClure and wife have seven children. (2d.) George Gibson McClure, late of the Third National Bank, New York, now with the pay department, U. S. A. Not married. (3d.) William McClure, broker in stocks in New York, and recently chairman of the New York Stock Exchange. He married Miss Ella Crane, daughter of the late Theodore Crane, a merchant of New York city; they have no children.

28th, 1857, and is buried in her father's lot in the cemetery at that place.*

John B. Gibson, second, was a strikingly handsome man of six feet three inches in height. He was appointed a lieutenant in the First Artillery, U. S. A., at the breaking out of the Mexican War. He was brevetted for gallant service in that war, and died in 1856, in Carlisle. He never married.

Judge Gibson's son George entered the army in 1853, originally in the quartermaster's department. Before the war he was transferred to an infantry command. At the time of his death, at Las Vegas Springs, New Mexico, he was colonel of the Fifth United States Infantry. He was married November 10th, 1863, to Miss Fannie Hunt, daughter of the late Dr. Henry Hunt, of Washington, D. C. They had no children.

Sarah (Sallie), Judge Gibson's youngest daughter, married,

---

* The children of W. Milnor and Annie Roberts are as follows: (1st.) William Milnor Roberts. At present on his farm "Riverside" on the Potomac river, near Cumberland, Md. He married in 1864 in Brazil, S. A., Elizabeth, a daughter of Jacob Humbird, of Cumberland, Maryland. They have eight children. (2d.) John Bannister Gibson Roberts. Recently chief engineer and superintendent of the West Wisconsin railroad, and connected with other roads in the Northwest and Texas. At present in the engineering department of the Edison Electric Light Company. He is married to Jane, a daughter of Jacob Humbird, Esq., of Cumberland, Maryland. They have one child, a son. (3d.) Thomas Paschall Roberts, civil engineer, connected in past years with various railroads and river improvements in government service. At present chief engineer Monongahela Navigation Company, Pittsburgh. Married June 8th, 1870, to Juliet, a daughter of James M. Christy, Esq., of Pittsburgh; five children living, one dead. (4th.) George Gibson Roberts, assistant engineer on various public works. At present in Carlisle. Unmarried. (5th.) Annie Gibson Roberts. Married Captain George W. Yates, Seventh Cavalry, U. S. A., who lost his life at the side of General Custer, in the battle of the Little Big Horn, Montana, July, 1876. Mrs. Yates has three children, and resides in Carlisle, Pennsylvania. (6th) Richard Anderson Roberts. At present secretary and auditor of the Manufacturers' Natural Gas Company, Pittsburgh. Married Lelia P. Christy, daughter of James M. Christy. (7th) Charles Watts Roberts, died in infancy.

in 1851, Captain R. H. Anderson, of the Second Dragoons, U. S. A. Captain Anderson was the last of the thirty-three officers from South Carolina to resign from the army in 1861. In the Confederate services he rose to the command of a corps. Throughout the war his wife was indefatigable in her efforts to alleviate the sufferings of "Yankee prisoners," visiting the sick among them, and in many instances securing their early exchange. She died in Charleston, South Carolina, August 11th, 1872. General Anderson died a few years later.*

General Anderson was among the first of the prominent army officers of the defunct Confederacy to be pardoned by President Johnson, and this was brought about through the influence of Senator Simon Cameron. In a letter dated Harrisburg, June 12th, 1865, to Colonel, then Captain Charles McClure, U. S. A., who had laid the case of General Anderson before him, he says:

"Your kind letter of the 9th inst. is more than compensation for any kindness I may have rendered your family. I have always believed it the duty of men reaching high positions to use the power delegated to them for good, and when I have done so, I have rarely failed to get a grateful return. Besides, your grandfather, who was among the greatest of our great men, treated me with respect in my early obscurity, and continued my friend till his death, and so it was with his good brother the general. In the case of your aunt, I was made as happy as she could be herself by the ready acquiescence of the secretary."

The allusion to Judge Gibson's brother, General George Gibson, has reference to the general's kindness to him

---

* The only surviving children of General Anderson and his wife are Richard, in business in the South, and Sallie, who recently has married, also in the South.

when he (Cameron) first visited Washington looking for
work in a printing office, and when he was an entire
stranger to General Gibson.   No man in the country has
probably performed more kindly deeds than General Cameron for friendship and for "auld lang syne," and in count-
less cases, no doubt, without the least expectation of a return. The service he did at this time for the daughter of
Judge Gibson, who was both loyal to her country and to
her husband, in "the time that tried men's souls" more
than ever did the revolutionary struggle, is kept in grateful remembrance by Mrs. Anderson's relatives and friends.

Judge Gibson died in the United States Hotel on Chestnut
street, 2 A. M., Tuesday, May 3d, 1853, surrounded by all the
members of his family excepting Mrs. Anderson, who at this
time was with her husband in the army in Texas.   On the
following day his remains were removed to Carlisle, and
buried at noon on the 5th in the old graveyard sometimes
called the " English burial ground." *

Notwithstanding the inclemency of the weather, the day
being very rainy, a large concourse of citizens followed the

---

* The view presented in this ancient burial ground represents Judge Gibson's family lot with his monument in the foreground.   To the right is seen the
Nesbit monument, which he designed in 1824.   In the background are the tombs
of Justice Hugh H. Brackenridge and Thomas Duncan, of the Supreme Court.

"Within a radius of a hundred yards of Gibson's monument lie David
Watts, Samuel Alexander, S. Dunlap Adair, Hugh Gaullager, Wm. M. Biddle,
Hon. John Reed and Hon. James H. Graham, all of whom have argued cases
before him, and some of them had their opinions passed upon by him.   James
Ross, author of the Latin grammar, a fine classical scholar and the instructor of
many an ingenious youth, lies there, and there lies Doctor Alfred Foster, *facile
princeps* of a brilliant circle that has passed away."   (Carlisle newspaper.)

Thickly strewed about are the graves of the veteran officers and soldiers of
every war the Colonies and the United States have engaged in since 1740 ; among
the latter none possess greater interest than the modest slab first erected when
" Decoration Day" came in vogue, which marks the spot where reposes the can-
noneer's wife, " Molly " Pitcher, the heroine of the battle of Princeton.

remains to the grave. The following is the order of the funeral procession :

1st. Members of the Masonic Lodges representing Philadelphia, Carlisle, etc.

2d. The reverend clergy of the borough.

3d. Wm. M. Biddle, Hugh Gaullager, W. H. Miller, J. E. Bonham, Edward M. Biddle, A. B. Sharpe, Wm. M. Penrose and R. M. Henderson, as active pall bearers in the cemetery, and the residue of the members of the Carlisle bar as honorary pall bearers.

4th. The family and relations of the deceased.

5th. The faculty and students of Dickinson College.

6th. The officers of the U. S. army stationed at Carlisle barracks.

7th. The citizens generally.

The burial services of the Episcopal Church were read by the Rev. J. B. Morse of St. John's church.

No one has done more to keep the name of Judge Gibson green than the late Hon. Jeremiah S. Black, and to him Mrs. Gibson and the members of her family were indebted for the inscriptions which fill the panels on the sides of the shaft erected to his memory, and which read as follows :

JOHN BANNISTER GIBSON, LL. D.,

FOR MANY YEARS

CHIEF JUSTICE OF PENNSYLVANIA.

BORN NOVEMBER 8TH, 1780.

DIED MAY 3D, 1853.*

---

* The inscription on the monument reads that he died May 2d, and Mrs. Gibson so wrote it in her family Bible. He died on Tuesday morning, two hours after midnight of the 2d; the mistake, no doubt, originated in considering the

13

IN THE VARIOUS KNOWLEDGE
WHICH FORMS THE PERFECT SCHOLAR
HE HAD NO SUPERIOR.
INDEPENDENT, UPRIGHT AND ABLE
HE HAD ALL THE HIGHEST QUALITIES
OF A GREAT JUDGE.
IN THE DIFFICULT SCIENCE OF JURISPRUDENCE
HE MASTERED EVERY DEPARTMENT,
DISCUSSED ALMOST EVERY QUESTION, AND
TOUCHED NO SUBJECT WHICH HE DID NOT ADORN.

_____

HE WON IN EARLY MANHOOD
AND RETAINED TO THE CLOSE OF HIS LONG LIFE
THE AFFECTION OF HIS BRETHREN ON THE BENCH,
THE RESPECT OF THE BAR,
AND THE CONFIDENCE OF THE PEOPLE.

_____

HIS INTIMATE FRIENDS
FORGOT THE FAME OF HIS JUDICIAL CAREER
IN THE MORE CHERISHED RECOLLECTIONS
OF HIS SOCIAL CHARACTER,
AND HIS BEREAVED FAMILY
DEDICATE THIS STONE
TO THE PERPETUAL MEMORY
OF
THE AFFECTIONATE HUSBAND
AND
THE KIND FATHER.

_____

time the night of the 2d, when in reality it was two hours in the 3d of May. A number of Philadelphia newspapers and other journals of the period in the writer's possession, fully establish the fact as here stated, as does also the official records of the Supreme Court.

MONUMENT TO JUDGE GIBSON.

In the background is the Nisbet monument and the tombs of Judges Brackenridge and Duncan.

PART SECOND.

PROCEEDINGS OF THE SUPREME COURT OF PENNSYLVANIA UPON THE DEATH OF JUDGE GIBSON.

ADDRESS BY THE HON. THADDEUS STEVENS, AND THE EULOGY DELIVERED BY CHIEF JUSTICE JEREMIAH S. BLACK.

REPORTED IN 7 HARRIS, 10.

SUPREME COURT OF PENNSYLVANIA.

HARRISBURG, May 9th, 1853.

The May term of the Supreme Court for the Middle District commenced on Monday, May 9th. Present, the Hon. Chief Justice Black, and Associates Lewis, Lowrie and Woodward, Justices.

Mr. Stevens, of Lancaster, on the meeting of the court, called attention to the death of Mr. Justice Gibson in the following terms:

May it please the Court:

Respect for the memory of your late colleague, the former chief justice of Pennsylvania, seems to require that this court should adjourn without transacting any business on this the first day of its session since his decease. The circumstances of his illness and death are known to you.

Judge Gibson had occupied a seat on the bench for more than forty years, with credit to himself and his native State. Pennsylvania has had many able judges. Chief Justice M'Kean, Tilghman, and many of their contemporaries, would have done honor to the judiciary of any country. But in intellectual power, I doubt if any of them excelled, if they equalled, Judge Gibson. His perception was strong and clear, and he uttered his thoughts in the most forcible and lucid manner. His style, equally removed from dry insipidity and meretricious ornaments, is a model of judicial composition. I do not know by whom it has been surpassed. He analyzed and mastered the most abstruse and difficult questions, and presented them with singular perspicuity. His opinions delight by their admirable brevity. Above all pedantry, all affectation of learning, master of his subject and of the English language, he did not find it necessary to waste pages to express an idea.

He was appointed to the Supreme Court thirty-five years ago. On the death of Chief Justice Tilghman he became his successor, and presided over the deliberations of this court for more than twenty years, with honor to himself and the country. So distinguished was his ability, learning and impartiality, that, after the adoption of the amended Constitution, in 1838, in times of the highest and bitterest party excitement, Governor Ritner, forgetting his personal and party feelings, and looking only to the qualifications necessary for that high office, re-appointed him chief justice of this commonwealth; an act, I may be permitted to say, honorable to both. It taught, in significant language, that however proper it may be to fill the gubernatorial chair, and other executive offices, with politicians, none but able, learned and upright jurists are fit to be indued with judicial robes. It was an example which will be creditable and useful to the people and their rulers, whenever they shall occupy a like elevated position.

Judge Gibson lived to an advanced age; his knowledge increasing with increasing years, while his great intellect remained unimpaired.

Those who believe, as all should believe, that the judiciary is the most important department of government, and that great, wise and pure judges are the chief bulwark and protection of the lives, liberty and rights of the people, will deeply and sincerely regret the loss of Judge Gibson.

This, perhaps, is not the proper place to speak of his private worth and delightful social qualities. They will be sufficiently attested by his numerous mourning friends and acquaintances in every part of the State.

His Honor, the present chief justice, replied as follows, and the court adjourned for the day:

It is unnecessary to say that every surviving member of the court is deeply grieved by the death of Mr. Justice Gibson. In the course of nature it was not to be expected that he could live much longer, for he had attained the ripe age of seventy-six.* But the blow, though not a sudden, was, nevertheless, a severe one. The intimate relations, personal and official, which we all bore to him, would have been sufficient to account for some emotion, even if he had been an ordinary man. But he was the Nestor of the bench, whose wisdom inspired the public mind with confidence in our decisions. By this bereavement the court has

---

* A pardonable error on Judge Black's part. Judge Gibson lived 72 years, 6 months, 25 days.

lost what no time can repair; for we shall never look upon his like again.

We regarded him more as a father than a brother. None of us ever saw the Supreme Court before he was in it; and to some of us his character as a great judge was familiar, even in childhood. The earliest knowledge of the law we had was derived in part from his luminous expositions of it. He was a judge of the Common Pleas before the youngest of us was born, and was a member of this court long before the oldest was admitted to the bar. He sat here with twenty-six different associates, of whom eighteen preceded him to the grave. For nearly a quarter of a century he was chief justice, and when he was nominally superseded by another as the head of the court, his great learning, venerable character and over-shadowing reputation still made him the only chief whom the hearts of the people would know. During the long period of his judicial labors he discussed and decided innumerable questions. His opinions are found in no less than seventy volumes of the regular reports, from 2 Sergeant & Rawle to 7 Harris.

At the time of his death he had been longer in office than any contemporary judge in the world; and in some points of character he had not his equal on the earth. Such vigor, clearness and precision of thought were never before united with the same felicity of diction. Brougham has sketched Lord Stowell justly enough as the greatest judicial writer that England could boast of, for force and beauty of style. He selects a sentence and calls on the reader to admire the remarkable elegance of its structure. I believe that Judge Gibson never wrote an opinion in his life from which a passage might not be

taken, stronger, as well as more graceful in its turn of
expression than this which is selected with so much care by
a most zealous friend from *all* of Lord Stowell's.

His written language was a transcript of his mind. It
gave the world the very form and pressure of his thoughts.
It was accurate, because he knew the exact boundaries of
the principles he discussed. His mental vision took in
the whole outline and all the details of the case, and
with a bold and steady hand he painted what he saw. He
made others understand him because he understood himself.

> "Cui lecta potenter erit res,
> Nec facundia deseret hunc, nec lucidus ordo."

His style was rich, but he never turned out of his way
for figures of speech. He never sacrificed sense to sound,
or preferred ornament to substance. If he reasoned much by
comparison it was not to make his composition brilliant, but
clear. He spoke in metaphors often, not because they were
sought, but because they came to his mind unbidden. The
same vein of happy illustration ran through his conversation
and his private letters. I was most of all struck with it in
a careless memorandum, intended, when it was written, for no
eye but his own. He never thought of display and seemed
totally unconscious that he had the power to make any.

His words were always precisely adapted to the subject.
He said neither more nor less than just the thing he ought.
He had one faculty of a great poet, that of expressing a
thought in language which could never afterwards be para-
phrased. When a legal principle passed through his hands, he
sent it forth clothed in a dress which fitted it so exactly
that nobody ever presumed to give it any other. Almost
universally the syllabus of his opinion is a sentence from

itself, and the most heedless student in looking over Wharton's Digest can select the cases in which Gibson delivered the judgment as readily as he would pick out gold coins from among coppers. For this reason it is that though he was the least voluminous writer of the court, the citations from him at the bar are more numerous than from all the rest put together. Yet the men who shared with him the labors and responsibilties of this tribunal (of course I am not referring to any who are now here) stood among the foremost in the country for learning and ability. To be their equal was an honor which few could attain; to excel them was a most pre-eminent distinction.

The dignity, richness and purity of his written opinions was by no means his highest title to admiration. The movements of his mind were as strong as they were graceful. His periods not only pleased the ear but sunk into the mind. He never wearied the reader, but he always exhausted the subject. An opinion of his was an unbroken chain of logic from beginning to end. His argumentation was always characterized by great power, and sometimes it rose into irresistible energy, dashing opposition to pieces with a force like that of a bat-tering-ram. He never missed the point even of a cause which had been badly argued. He separated the chaff from the wheat almost as soon as he got possession of it. The most complicated entanglement of fact and law would be reduced to harmony under his hands. His arrange-ment was so lucid that the dullest mind could follow him with that intense pleasure which we all feel in being able to comprehend the workings of an intellect so mani-festly superior.

Yet he committed errors. It is wonderful that in the course of his long service he did not commit more. A few were caused by inattention; a few by want of time; a few by preconceived notions which led him astray. When he did throw himself into the wrong side of a cause, he usually made an argument which it was much easier to overrule than to answer. With reference to his erroneous opinions, he might have used the words of Virgil, which he quoted so happily in *Eakin vs. Raub*, 12 Ser. & R., for another purpose.

" Si Pergama dextra
Defendi possent, etiam hac defensa fuissent."

But he was of all men the most devoted and earnest lover of truth for its own sake. When subsequent reflection convinced him that he had been wrong, he took the first opportunity to acknowledge it. He was often the earliest to discover his own mistakes, as well as the foremost to correct them.

He was inflexibly honest. The judicial ermine was as unspotted when he laid it aside for the habiliments of the grave, as it was when he first assumed it. I do not mean to award him merely that common-place integrity which it is no honor to have, but simply a disgrace to want. He was not only incorruptible, but scrupulously, delicately, conscientiously free from all wilful wrong, either in thought, word or deed.

Next, after his wonderful intellectual endowments, the benevolence of his heart was the most marked feature of his character. His was a most genial spirit; affectionate and kind to his friends, and magnanimous to his enemies. Benefits received by him were engraved on his memory as on a tablet of brass; injuries were written in sand. He

14

never let the sun go down on his wrath. A little dash of bitterness in his nature would, perhaps, have given a more consistent tone to his character, and greater activity to his mind. He lacked the quality which Dr. Johnson admired; he was not a good hater.

His accomplishments were very extraordinary. He was born a musician, and the natural talent was highly cultivated. He was a connoisseur in painting and sculpture. The whole round of English literature was familiar to him. He was at home among the ancient classics. He had a perfectly clear perception of all the great truths of natural science. He had studied medicine carefully in his youth and understood it well. His mind absorbed all kinds of knowledge with scarcely an effort.

Judge Gibson was well appreciated by his fellow citizens; not so highly as he deserved, for that was scarcely possible, but admiration of his talents and respect for his honesty were universal sentiments. This was strikingly manifested when he was elected, in 1851, with no emphatic political standing, and without manners, habits or associations calculated to make him popular beyond the circle that knew him intimately. With all these disadvantages, it is said, he narrowly escaped what might have been a dangerous distinction — a nomination on both of the opposing tickets. Abroad he has, for very many years, been thought the great glory of his native State.

Doubtless the whole commonwealth will mourn his death; we all have good reason to do so. The profession of the law has lost the ablest of its teachers, this court the brightest of its ornaments, and the people a steadfast defender of their rights, so far as they were capable of being protected by judicial authority. For myself, I know no form of words to express my deep sense of the loss we have suffered. I can most truly say of him what was said long ago, concerning one of the few mortals who were greater than he: "I did love the man, and do honor his memory, on this side idolatry, as much as any."

As a token of respect for the deceased, it is ordered that the court do now adjourn.

PART THIRD.

JOHN BANNISTER GIBSON,

AS A LAWYER, A LEGISLATOR AND A JUDGE.

SELECTIONS FROM JUDGE WILLIAM A. PORTER'S ESSAY.*

At the period of Mr. Gibson's entrance into Dickinson College the presidential chair of the institution was filled by Charles Nisbet, D. D., whose attachment to the American cause had made him an exile from his native land, and whose love of letters and science had given him a just celebrity in the country of his adoption. His pupil retained through life a grateful recollection of the advantages he derived from the instructions of this celebrated teacher. In the seventeenth volume of the "Port Folio" (January, 1824) he published a memoir of his preceptor, equally creditable to the author and to the subject of it. I extract this sentence: "His lectures on criticism and taste are particularly admired by those who are competent

---

* Judge Porter was a son of Governor Porter, and brother of J. Horace Porter, Esq., who prepared a memoir (see Appendix) of Gen. George, Judge Gibson's brother. Judge Porter was born in Huntingdon county, 1821, and died very suddenly at Wissahickon, Philadelphia, June 28th, 1886. It has been well said of him that he was not only "a distinguished jurist but also a Christian gentleman." He was aware that a memoir of Judge Gibson was about to be prepared, but unfortunately for the writer he started his undertaking too late to have the advice and assistance of him who was so well qualified to give it.

to judge of their merit. As a preacher there was nothing
to strike the senses in the character of his eloquence, yet
he never failed to fix the attention of those who could
dispense with the graces of personal exterior and be satisfied with a manly and fervent piety, with sound doctrine,
with strong and original conceptions, and with a masterly
arrangement of argument and matter delivered in a down-
right natural manner, and in a plain but polished style."
At page 327 of the same volume of the "Port Folio"
will be found an engraving of the monument erected to
the memory of Dr. Nisbet in the burial ground at Carlisle, Pa., "for the drawing of which," says the editor,
"we are indebted to the pencil of our friend J. B. Gibson, Esq., one of the judges of the Supreme Court of this
commonwealth."* The drawing appears to evince some

---

* Not only the sketch of this monument, but as well also the inscription and
the design for the sculptor, were original with Judge Gibson. A search in the
libraries of Philadelphia brought to light the volume of the "Port Folio" mentioned by Judge Porter, and we are therefore able to present almost a fac-simile
of the original drawing. The inscription reads as follows:

M. S.
CAROLI NISBET, S.S.T.D.
Qui, unanimi hortatu
Curatorum Academiae Dickinsoniensis,
Ut Primarii ejusdem munia susciperet,
Patria sua, Scotia Relicta,
Ad Carleolum venit, A. D. 1785.
Ibique, per novem decem annos,
Summa cum laude,
Muneri suo incubuit.
Viri, si quis alius, probi piique,
Omni doctrina ornatissimi
Lectione immensa, memoria fideli,
Acumine vero ingenii, facetiis, salibusque
Plane miri, et undique clari.
Nemini vero mortalium, nisi iis, infensi
Qui, cum Philosophiae praetextu, sacra insultant,
Familiae autem suae, amicisque,

THE NISBET MONUMENT, DESIGNED BY JUDGE GIBSON.

artistic merit; and this is a convenient place to observe that Judge Gibson possessed peculiar skill in that department of art. He could at any time sketch by a few dashes of his pen admirable likenesses of both men and things. Many a dull speaker who has been encouraged by the energy with which the judge's pen moved might have found on his notes little more than a most excellent representation of the speaker's face. Occasionally on his forgetting to destroy such efforts they have passed round the bar to the amusement of all but the sketcher and the sketched. His taste also extended to painting, in which he was regarded as a competent critic.

On the completion of his collegiate course, he entered on the study of the law in Carlisle, in the office of Thomas Duncan, with whom he was afterwards to occupy a seat on the bench of the Supreme Court. In this preceptor he was equally fortunate. The name of Judge Duncan occupies a respectable place in our judicial annals.* His manners were

---

Ob mores suaves, benignos, hilares, comesque,
unice dilecti.
Animam placide efflavit 14 mo. Kal. Feb. 1804
Anno aetatis 68.
Abiit noster : proh dolor !
Cui similem haud facile posthac visuri sumus !
At quem terra amisit, lucrifecit Coelum,
Novo splendore
Corporis resuscitati, vitaeque eternae,
Cum Domino Jesu, omnibusque sanctis,
Ovantem rediturum.

* The Rev. Dr. Nevin contributes to the Philadelphia *Times* the following of Judge Duncan : "He was also, it may be noted, remarkably ready in repartee. An instance may be given. His principal competitor in practice was David Watts (father of Hon. Frederick Watts), a distinguished member of the Cumberland county bar. Mr. Watts was a large and athletic gentleman, while Mr. Duncan was of small stature and light weight. On one occasion, during a discussion on a legal question in court, Mr. Watts, in the heat of his argument, made a personal allusion to Mr. Duncan's small stature, and said he 'could put

kind and simple; his habits of investigation, patient and
systematic; his powers of discrimination cultivated by study
and by intercourse with the acutest minds of his day; his
style, both of speaking and writing, easy, natural, graceful
and clear; and his acquirements quite equal to those of
his predecessors on the bench. In that day the learning of
the profession was confined mainly to special pleading and
real estate. The former attracted the attention of students

his opponent in his pocket.' 'Very well,' replied Mr. Duncan, 'if you do so,
you will have more law in your pocket than you have in your head.'"

Judge Gibson, as has already been noticed, had a penchant for writing epi-
taphs, and upon the monument of his friend and preceptor Duncan, in the Carlisle cemetery, is inscribed his graceful, and no doubt, well merited, tribute, which
reads as follows:

Near this spot
is deposited all that was mortal
of THOMAS DUNCAN, Esquire, LL. D.,
born at Carlisle 20 November, 1760; died 16 November, 1827.
Called to Bar at an early age,
he was rapidly borne
by genius, perseverance and integrity
to the pinnacle of his profession;
and in the fullness of his fame
was elevated
to the Bench of the Supreme Court of his native
State,
for which
a sound judgment,
boundless stores of legal science
and a profound reverence of the common law
had peculiarly fitted him.

Of his judicial labours,
the reported cases of the period are the best
eulogy.
As a husband, indulgent;
as a father, kind;
as a friend, sincere;
as a magistrate, incorruptible;
and as a citizen, inestimable;
He was honored by the wise and good,
and wept
by a wide circle of relatives and friends.
Honesta quam splendida.

by its utility in practice, by the profound and intricate nature of its principles, and by the satisfaction which, when mastered, it imparts to the mind. The doctrines of real estate were investigated with care, because in the state of the country, the settlement of titles to land necessarily formed the bulk of every lawyer's business. Of commercial law, we had next to none. No bank had then been chartered by the State to do business exclusively out of the city of Philadelphia, and that city had but three banks within its limits. Partnership, negotiable paper, and insurance were terms whose import differed widely from their import now. The carrying trade of the country was done mainly in the "Conestoga wagon," and as this required in each case, but one wagon and one set of horses and harness, the time had not arrived for that union of capital and labor so essential to the success of large commercial enterprises. Where credit was small, and labor was paid for in cash, or by an exchange of commodities, negotiable instruments were comparatively unnecessary. So little were insurances known out of Philadelphia, that according to the recollection of persons now living, when a bill was introduced into the legislature to incorporate the first life insurance of the State, it was scouted and rejected as a vain effort, if not to affect by pecuniary considerations the length of human life, at least to trifle with that which belongs to the dominion of a Higher Power. In the absence of the usual subjects of commercial decision, we could have little commercial law. The jurisprudence of England, though some centuries older, exhibited almost equal dearth. Lord Holt had here and there laid a foundation stone in such cases as *Coggs vs. Bernard*, 3 Salkeld II, on the liability of common carriers, and these had been improved by Lord

15

Mansfield in many such cases as *Heylyn vs. Adamson*, 2 Burrows, 669, on the steps necessary to fix an endorser, and by Lord Loughborough in such others as *Lickbarrow vs. Mason*, I. H. Blackstone, 357, on the right of stoppage in transits. But all that had then been done will be found to bear feeble comparison with the generous contributions which have since been made to that department of legal science. In this branch, therefore, we must suppose that neither preceptor nor pupil had made any considerable attainments in the outset of his career. I think it might be shown by citations from his opinions, that Judge Duncan's taste inclined more strongly to special pleading than to real estate, and that his accuracy in that department was greater than in the law of property. We shall see that his pupil acquired eminence in the entire three branches; certainly in our Pennsylvania land law; while of our mercantile law, he must be regarded as a chief architect.

On the 8th of March, 1803, on motion of Mr. Duncan, he was admitted to the bar of Cumberland county, and entered on the practice of the law in Carlisle, afterwards for a short time in Beaver, Pennsylvania,* and then in

---

* Judge Gibson used to relate an amusing story of his first appearance at Beaver.

He was approaching the town, riding a very small but powerful little horse, from which his long legs almost touched the ground. A small countryman, riding a fine large white horse from the town, meeting him, proposed an exchange of animals, suggesting to the young disciple of Blackstone that he would look much better mounted on a horse more nearly proportioned to his own size. The idea appeared to him to possess force; he was no doubt mindful of the lasting effect of first appearances, so, after paying the farmer a few dollars "to boot," the exchange was made. A few minutes later he proudly reined his new acquisition before the village tavern, where the landlord meeting him as he dismounted, inquired if he was not afraid to ride a beast which was so evidently stone blind.

Hagerstown, Maryland. It is known to his friends that he always refused to include in the computation of his age the time he spent in Hagerstown. It is related on good authority, that having on one occasion, in the presence of his brethren of the bench, who knew his age exactly, stated it as somewhat less than it really was, and resolutely reaffirmed it, a calculation was proposed, and readily assented to by himself. They started with the date of his admission to the bar, with his stay in Carlisle, and were about to include the time spent at Hagerstown, when the judge with good-humored violence, broke up the count, and refused to let it proceed, inveighing strongly against the injustice of charging him with that item of time, and assigning numerous reasons, which it will not be necessary to chronicle here. At the lapse of two years and a few months, he reopened his office in Carlisle, and continued the practice of his profession in Cumberland and the adjoining counties until his appointment to the bench.

During the period of Mr. Gibson's practice at the bar, and for some years preceding it, the professional field in Pennsylvania had been occupied by a race of lawyers of rare powers. Of those who practiced in the eastern and northeastern portions of the State (excluding Philadelphia), the names of Dick, Sitgreaves, Ross, Ewing, Spering, Pat-

---

Gibson never forgot this lesson, but throughout life never made pretensions to any knowledge of horse flesh.

Having seen in a legal journal the statement that Judge Gibson had been admitted to practice in Common Pleas Court, Allegheny county, as early as September 26th, 1803, an attempt was made to verify it by examination of the record at the Prothonotary's office. The court minutes of that period are no longer in existence. Judge Gibson's name appears as the sixty-second lawyer on the list admitted to practice in Allegheny county. James Ross heads the list, with Judge Hugh H. Brackenridge second, both admitted December 16th, 1788. The late Judge Walter Forward was seventy-third, admitted November 12th, 1806.

terson, Shaw, Pawling, Evans, Wells, Griffin, Dimmick, Cross, Mott, Hall and Graham may be mentioned. The West had Jas. Ross, Brackenbridge, Addison, Lyon, Woods, Mason, James and Parker Campell, Alexander, Mountain, Foster, Steel, Semple, Collins, Simonson, Young, Baldwin and Kennedy. In the counties lying between these extremes there were Shippen, Watts, Duncan, Hale, Yeates, Darlington, Hemphill, Duer, Kittera, Montgomery, Hopkins, George Ross, Hubley, Charles Smith, Jenkins, Passmore, Barton, Elder, Fisher, McLean, Laird, Graydon, Biddle, Spayd, Reed and Bayard. But time would fail me to tell of all. Many of them were men of the very first order of intellect. In professional learning and ability they seem to have imbibed much of the spirit bequeathed to them by Hamilton, and by Francis, the only two lawyers in Pennsylvania whose reputation has survived the lapse of a century. In important land causes throughout the State, they were accustomed to enter the lists with the lawyers of Philadelphia, then enjoying a supremacy of reputation throughout the Union, and they proved themselves the equals of the former in all but the good fortune of making so permanent a record of their fame. They were in the main bold, intrepid, self-reliant men, independent in their thoughts and habits, of strong impulses and understandings, and capable by an eloquence suited to the people and the occasion, by superior knowledge of the country and its customs, of prevailing in many a well contested battle over their more polished visitors. Let not the reader be surprised that these lawyers should be spoken of as learned men. It is true they had few books. In 1800 the only Pennsylvania law books were three volumes of Dallas' Reports. Not a volume of Johnson's Reports, and

not a volume of Massachusetts Reports had been published. Perhaps I ought to say, that with the exception
of Mr. Dallas', not one volume of any regular series of
reports had been published on this side of the Atlantic.
Story had not been admitted to the bar, and the design of
writing a commentary had probably never entered the mind
of Kent. Having few books they studied them well. A
lawyer who was disposed to read must take Bacon and
Coke, and authors of that stamp, or not read at all. In
such companionship he must become saturated with the
very elements of the science; for nothing in the history of
the law is more surprising than to observe how few
sound principles have been originated in the vast publications that have since deluged us. The men of that day
had another characteristic. Their physical labors gave them
a degree of bodily vigor and energy which of itself
was no inconsiderable obstacle in the way of an antag-
onist in the trial of a cause. From 1791 to 1806
there were but five judicial districts in the State,
and there were lawyers who practiced in a number of
them. Now in 1855 we have twenty-five. A county then
was not what a county is now. In 1800 Lycoming
embraced all the territory which lies between the Allegheny river and the western line of Luzerne county,
bounded on the north by the State of New York and on
the south by Northumberland, Mifflin, Huntingdon and
Westmoreland. Its population entitled it to one representative in the legislature. Thirteen entire counties and portions of several others now occupy the same space. Northampton county embraced chiefly what is now Wayne, Pike,
Monroe, Carbon, Lehigh and Northampton. These are illustrations. Dispensing law in a parlor with the assistance of

a well stocked library is difficult enough, but transporting it
in the crown of the hat on horseback over a rough
mountain road must be equally so. I venture to suppose that if a sudden requirement were now made on
the denizens of certain destitute frontier settlements on
Walnut street and its vicinity to mount horse and display
their prowess in this manner a few retainers (if any
such continue to be paid) could not fail to be returned,
with what reluctance soever, to their original possessors.
Of a truth the lawyer of the present day is intrinsically,
and extraneously, physically and mentally, a different man
from the lawyer of fifty years ago. The early life of
Judge Gibson was passed with the latter, and no man's
character can be understood without the light which flows
from the associations that have surrounded his youth.

His success at the bar appears to have been equal to
that of the majority of practitioners in the country at
that period of time. In reading our reports I observe
but three cases in which he appeared before the Supreme
Court. The name occurs in others but I have satisfied
myself that the counsel there referred to was Mr. James
Gibson who is mentioned in flattering terms in the
opinion delivered in *Hobbs vs. Fogg*, 6 Watts, 555. The
first case which Mr. J. B. Gibson is reported as having
argued is that of the *Commonwealth vs. Crevor*, 3 Binney,
121, which involved a question of interest on a sum
of money received by the sheriff, and deposited in bank
under an agreement of the parties, but afterwards with-
drawn by the sheriff without their consent. His opponent
was Mr. Duncan, and his colleague, Mr. Watts, and the
judgment of the Supreme Court was in favor of his client.
In his next case, *Commonwealth vs. Blain*, 4 Binney, 186,

he was not so successful. The point which he raised was curious. The Act of 29 March, 1788, in regard to the births of negro children, directed that an entry should be made in the book of the clerk of the peace of the county in which the master or mistress lived, within six months after the birth of the child, which entry should set forth its age, name and sex, etc., under the penalty of forfeiting all right and title to the child, who it was provided should, in case of the omission of the entry for six months, immediately become free; and the entry was to be verified by the oath of the person who made it. The defendant, on the 26th of June, 1807, made an entry of the birth of the relator in the case, and described him as having been born on the 2d of January, 1808, which of course was impossible. Mr. Gibson contended that the registry was void, and that the negro was free; that the intention of the Act was to provide record evidence of the time of the relator's freedom; that it should be construed most strictly in favor of liberty; and that where the owner made by his own fault a registry which was unintelligible and impossible, it was no registry at all. The court, however, differed from him and remanded the negro to the claimant. The remaining case was that of the *Commonwealth vs. Harkness*, 4 Binney, 194, which decided that in forcible entry and detainer, although the indictment does not set out an offence on the part of the defendant, yet, in the event of an acquittal, the jury may require the prosecutor to pay the costs. His argument, as reported by Mr. Binney, seems to be a conclusive answer to that of Mr. Watts, who was retained on the other side, and the court in an opinion delivered by each judge, sustained him. It is proper to remark that the number of the cases in which he appeared in the Supreme Court is by no means a fair criterion of the extent of his practice, for in that day it was less common than now to carry cases to the court of last resort.

In respect to his deportment to clients, a rumor has prevailed so widely and with such universal credit as to warrant its repetition here. It is said that he had become at this time, as he ever afterwards continued, a votary of music, and that when clients knocked at the front door, the sound was frequently overcome by the strains which proceeded from a violin in the hidden recesses of the office. I am unable to vouch for the entire correctness of the story, or to recommend it as an example for imitation. If true, the instance was unique. Euripides, in his Medea, is careful to tell us of the power of Orpheus over the rocks and the trees, and Plato mentions that when the same personage followed his lost wife to Hades, the charms of his lyre suspended the torments of the damned. This was very well for those times. But neither poet nor philosopher has been bold enough to inform us of the existence of any melody sufficient to satisfy modern clients. I certainly have heard few musical airs rapid enough to accord with their excited emotions, or slow enough to suit their ideas of the march of justice, or sweet enough to purify the turbid and bitter waters which litigation lets loose. Whether or not the rumor respecting these exploits of our young practitioner be true, it may serve to show a popular impression that if he wanted clients, the want was ascribed to other causes than the absence of learning and skill.

The question naturally occurs on taking leave of Mr. Gibson's professional life, whether he was fitted to attain eminence at the bar. Certainly, unless his habits of thought had taken a very different turn, he never would have become a successful advocate. He subsequently studied the law profoundly, and evinced real genius for it. He was master of its nicest distinctions, and as capable as any other man of applying them to the practical affairs of life. But these qualities have never yet made an eminent advocate. A man of good sound intellect, well cultivated by philosophical studies and vigorously applied, may readily acquire them. The test of the success at the bar is the capacity to influence a court and jury, and it may be applied almost indiscriminately.

The style of Judge Gibson was well adapted to the uses to which he put it. It possessed, as we shall see, many of the highest and rarest of characteristics of judicial writing. To every extent in which he had employed such a mode of conveying his thoughts at the bar, he would have signally failed. Other disqualifications may also have existed. He possessed no aptitude for that exhausting physical labor so essential to success in the practice of the law. When well roused, the entire professional mind of the State knows what he was capable of producing; but both his mind and his body seemed incapable of exertion, even to the pitch of writing, unless urged by the excitement of a great subject. Of the practical inconvenience of this, he frequently complained. I resume the narrative.

In 1810 he was elected by the Democratic party of Cumberland county a member of the House of Representatives of Pennsylvania, and served as such in the sessions of 1810–11, and 1811–12. His appearance at this time is recollected by many persons yet on the stage. He was considerably over six feet in height, with a muscular, well proportioned frame, and a countenance expressing strong

16

character and manly beauty. Until the day of his death, although his bearing was mild and unostentatious, so striking was his personal appearance, that few persons to whom he was unknown could have passed him in the street without remark; youth and vigor must have rendered his presence even more commanding. In the business of the house he bore at least a useful part. Besides giving the customary attention to affairs pertaining to his own county, and affecting his own constituents, he originated numerous measures of public importance. The legislature convened on the 4th of December, 1810, and on the 15th of December he moved for the appointment of a committee "to bring in a bill to abolish the right of joint tenants to take by survivorship, and to make real estate held in joint tenancy divisible. The resolution was adopted and throughout the session he seems to have labored for the passage of the bill with unusual diligence. On every occasion it was called up on his motion (pp. 100, 290, 306, &c., of the journal). But he was not successful in passing it until the succeeding session. In the spring of 1811 the impeachment proceedings against Thomas Cooper, then president judge of the eighth judicial district, had begun to occupy a share of public attention, and on the 7th of March Mr. Gibson was appointed one of the committee to consider the complaints against him. On the 27th of March the committee reported the draft of an address to Governor Snyder for the removal of the judge from his office. Against this address and the doctrines which it advocated Mr. Gibson placed on record a written protest.

The independence of the stand which he took in this proceeding may be appreciated by the fact that out of ninety-five members of all parties he was joined in his dissent by only four, Thomas Graham, of Luzerne, Jacob Holgate, of Philadelphia, John W. Cunningham, of Chester, and Matthew Brooke, of Montgomery; so high had the tide of popular sentiment run against the judge.

It was probably the position taken by Mr. Gibson on this occasion that led to the intimacy which afterwards subsisted between himself and Judge Cooper. On the death of the latter in 1840 Judge Gibson furnished to Professor Vethake a sketch of the life of his friend, which will be found in the sixteenth volume of the Encyclopædia Americana. He there passes in review his attainments in the natural sciences, in chemistry, anatomy and medicine; his matriculation at the university of Oxford; his residence at the Inns of Court; his attendance on the circuit; his deputation from one of the Democratic clubs in England to the party of the Gironde in France; Edmund Burke's denunciation of him in the House of Commons and Mr. Cooper's reply; his establishment as a bleacher and calico printer at Manchester; his practice as a lawyer in Northumberland, Pa.; his prosecution under the Sedition Act; his appointment as president judge and the effort at his impeachment; his appointment as professor of chemistry in Dickinson College, afterwards in the University of Pennsylvania, and then as president of Columbia College, South Carolina. The sketch concludes with a notice of his numerous works on law, medicine, politics, metaphysics and divinity. It is the history of a very extraordinary man, concisely and clearly written. In reference to the legislative proceedings against him in 1811, the author remarks, that "becoming obnoxious to some influential men of his own party, a complaint of arbitrary con-

duct was got up against him, and so artfully fomented
before the legislature, that he was removed by legislative
address." But this sentiment must be received with some
grains of allowance for the partiality of the writer. If
Judge Cooper had been guilty of one-tenth of the ridiculous and almost incredible acts proved against him, he was
certainly a most incompetent presiding officer in a court of
justice.

At the session of 1811-12, Mr. Gibson was appointed
chairman of the committee on the judiciary, then, probably,
a better test than it would be now, of advancement in
public estimation. Early in the session, he presented a report from a committee appointed respecting a contested
election in Montgomery county, which displays accuracy and
care in the investigation of the subject. His labors in behalf of the bill to abolish joint tenancy were revived thus:
"On motion of Mr. Gibson and Mr. Anderson, ordered
that an item of unfinished business relative to the laws
respecting joint tenancy and the extending of real estate, be
referred to the committee on the judiciary system." The
bill passed finally on 31st March, 1812, and it has since
been regarded so important a provision in our law of real
estate, as to have remained entirely undisturbed, and to
have led to similar legislation in other States. As chairman of the same committee, he reported a bill "for the
more effectual organization of the courts of common pleas
within this commonwealth." He was also a prominent
member of the committee on roads and inland navigation,
and in that early day threw the weight of his character
in favor of the system of internal improvements, which has
since placed the State among the first in the confederacy.
Without going into more tedious details, these may serve

as illustrations of the services which he performed in legislature.

On the 16th of July, 1813, Mr. Gibson was appointed president judge of the eleventh judicial district, composed of the counties of Tioga, Bradford, Susquehanna and Luzerne. He had now entered a new sphere. The duties and qualifications of a lawyer and of a judge are widely different. The business of a lawyer is to plead a cause; the business of a judge, to be right in his decisions. A lawyer is to undertake a case which fairly appears to be just, to state the facts of it in the most effective manner, and to urge with his utmost power, the reasons and principles which support it; a judge is at the peril of his character to see that by no mischance or design the law is misapplied and injustice wrought to either party. A lawyer who performs his duty faithfully, prepares diligently and presents the cause of his client with clearness, fairness and force, may gain reputation and final consolation in the midst of disaster, because it is no part of his duty to insure success; but a judge who is led aside from the right by sophistry or prejudice, who takes the rule for the exception, or the exception for the rule, and fails to pronounce the law as it has been established, by whatsoever splendor of rhetoric or acuteness of reasoning he may announce the result, but in that degree signalizes the loss of his reputation and attracts plunderers to the wreck. All men admit the necessity of the judicial office in civilized and perhaps in savage life; but how few of its incumbents left to their own reflections without the assistance of forensic discussion, and particularly discussion of the facts, would be capable of reaching a just and satisfactory result. The profession of the law is therefore as necessary as the office of the judge.

Since the dawn of civilization it has existed, and how far soever it may sink, it will exist while the administration of justice shall endure. But all eminent lawyers will not make good judges. It is a fact worthy of observation and susceptible of explanation, that our best judges, both in America and in England, have been furnished in men who were not eminent as practitioners. If the digression were not already too wide, this might be illustrated by reference to individual cases embracing the whole range of the law, and extending very nearly to the present time. The explanation is not difficult. A lawyer hears but one side of a cause, prepares for one side, argues one side; and if it were not for the practice of giving written opinions, it would be next to impossible for any man's intellect to resist the warping influence of such a state of things. On the other hand, a judge ought to be, and usually is, engaged in nothing but that most difficult of all human employments, the ascertainment of truth and the settlement of it by firmer landmarks. To the general fact we shall see that the career of Judge Gibson furnishes no exception.

He remained on the bench of the common pleas somewhat less than three years. Of the manner in which he discharged his duties as a judge of that court it is impossible, after this lapse of time, to speak with accuracy. He has left no monument of his labors. Like the fruits of much of the best ability of the State displayed in the same sphere, they perished on the spot without a record to perpetuate their worth. The few survivors of those who practiced in his court describe him as exhibiting much energy in the transaction of judicial business, but too much impulsiveness in his judgments, both of legal affairs and of human nature. Even at that early day it is admitted that he attracted the attention of learned lawyers throughout the commonwealth, and that his opinions were held by them in high consideration. The same vigor of thought and acuteness of intellect had doubtless begun to display themselves which afterwards shone so conspicuously on every page that received his opinions.

On the 27th of June, 1816, he was brought more prominently before the public by receiving from Governor Snyder the appointment of an associate justice of the Supreme Court in place of Hugh H. Brackenridge, deceased, and he was succeeded in the presidency of the common pleas by Thomas Burnside, whose career on the bench, and in the State and national councils is fresh in the recollection of all. This appointment seems for the first time to have roused his intellect and to have fired his ambition. It withdrew him from companions in the country to whom his warm affections and genial temper had greatly endeared him, and this fact, while it lost him the means of much agreeable relaxation delivered him from numerous temptations to indolence and dissipation.* It withdrew him also from politics, the grave of a vast amount of intellectual force, which, if devoted to the practice of the law,

---

* From the account of his life, elsewhere presented, whilst a resident of Wilkesbarre, there is no reason to suppose that Judge Gibson, for want of legal employment in that place would have grown indolent. Through all his life until age and a great increase of flesh weighted him down, he was vigorous and active in his movements. His fondness of nature gave a vent for his study, particularly of the then, new, science of geology, while no doubt much of his leisure was also devoted to the study of medicine. Nor was there at the period of his life, here referred to by Judge Porter, nor at any after period, cause for apprehension that under any circumstances Judge Gibson would have become dissipated. It is more reasonable to think that for want of sufficient employment in his profession, his attention would have been more and more directed to medicine, and that he might eventually have become a physician. Men of decided genius never stand still, and where their genius is in several directions, as was Judge Gibson's, they will not be long in abandoning any particular path when progress in it seems impossible.

might have at least earned for itself a more respectable
name. In Philadelphia, where the court sat for the
longest period of the year, he mingled much less than at
a subsequent part of his life, in general society, and was
much less known to all classes of its citizens. The reason
or, the result was, that he had become more devoted to
study. He seems at length to have formed the resolution to make himself master of the law as a science.
At some time in his life it is evident that he was a dili-
gent student of Coke. No reader of his opinions can fail
to be struck with the frequent and pointed illustrations which they draw from that author. Doubtless the
quaintness of his style, the careless and disorderly mixture
of things great and small, and those unceasing covert puffs
of Littleton which everywhere meet the reader, amused the
new student as much as they have amused lesser men,
while the grasp of his author's intellect, the severity of his
logic, and the abrupt, direct, forcible, and natural expression of his thoughts, waked strangely agreeable emotions in a mind conscious of the possession of vast but
slumbering power. There have indeed been few lawyers
worthy of the name who have not been familiar with
the commentaries and reports of Coke. Eminent jurists
have advanced the opinion that no student could read
them without catching enough of the author's spirit to
give the reader an important impulse in his professional studies. This is possible, but I apprehend the
effect of his writings may be traced to other causes. They
are the great source of law learning. The natural dread
of every practitioner unacquainted with them, that his
antagonists possess more learning than himself, forces him
back to the fountain head. In a few years he returns

established in a confidence which no assumption of erudition in others can shake. When driven into the lowest depths of legal investigation, he stands like a man in deep water whose feet rest on solid ground. Unless nature has endowed him beyond her usual allotment to mortals, he cannot be sure of his footing until the foundations of the system have been thus exploded. In the case of Judge Gibson's study of Coke, I feel confident from all the evidence I have obtained, that it was mainly pursued within a few years after his elevation to the bench of the Supreme Court.

That court had jogged on from the period of its origin, with but three judges on the bench. It was now to experience important and rapid changes. Under an Act passed by the General Assembly on the 8th of April, 1826, increasing the number of judges to five, Moulton C. Rogers and Charles Houston were respectively commissioned by Governor Schultz on the 15th and 17th of April, 1826. But little more than a year had elapsed, when another change was occasioned by the death of Judge Tilghman. "He continued," says Mr. Binney, "to preside in the Supreme Court with his accustomed dignity and effect, until the succeeding winter, when his constitution finally gave way, and after a short confinement, on Monday, the 30th of April, 1827, he closed his eyes forever." "It will be long," adds his eulogist, "very long, before we shall open ours upon a wiser judge, a sounder lawyer, a riper scholar, a purer man, or a truer gentleman." "Such," he concludes, "is the praise of the late Chief Justice Tilghman. He merited, by his public works and by his private virtues, the respect and affection of his countrymen; and the best wish for his country and his office is, that his mantle may

17

have fallen upon his successor." That successor was the
subject of the present sketch, who had been commissioned
chief justice on the 18th of May, 1827, and whose place
in the ranks of the associates had been supplied by the
appointment of Judge Tod, in the same month. We shall
see that the wish thus expressed by the orator was not
unfulfilled. The powers of the new chief justice seem to
have caught a fresh impulse from the eminence to which
they had conducted him. Even then his style was no mean
vehicle of judicial thought; but it soon acquired infinitely
more massiveness, compactness and polish. His original
style, compared to that in which he now began to write,
was like the sinews of a growing lad compared to the
well-knit muscles of a man. No one who has carefully
studied his productions can have failed to have remarked
the increased power and pith which distinguished them from
this time forward. The gradual and uniform progress of
his mind may be traced in his opinions, with a certainty
and satisfaction which are probably not afforded in the case
of any other judge known to our annals.

In the year following his appointment as chief justice,
the friends of General Jackson, whose cause he advocated with
so much warmth as was consistent with a judicial place,
desirous to secure for their candidate the highest measure
of popular confidence, placed the name of the chief justice
at the head of their electoral ticket for Pennsylvania, and
the ticket thus nominated received in the State an almost
unprecedented majority over the vote cast for any other
candidate.

On the 19th of November, 1838, he resigned his commission of chief justice, and was re-appointed by Governor
Ritner. This act received at the time the censure of a

large portion of the press. The Constitution of 1838, which had then been approved by a vote of the people, provided for a change of the judicial tenure, from that of life to a term of years, and for the gradual extinction, according to a prescribed scale, of the commissions then held by the judges; that is, their commissions were to expire at intervals of three years, in the order of seniority in which they stood on 1st January, 1839. In common with a majority of intelligent citizens in almost every portion of the State, except along its northern boundary, Judge Gibson had been decidedly hostile to the adoption of this instrument, and supposed it the forerunner of disorder and confusion. In this frame of mind, a voluntary suggestion was made by his associates for his re-appointment as chief justice, the effect of which would be to prolong for several years his term of office. The proposal seems to have been made and accepted with slight consideration on either side. It was believed that a judge could resign his office at any moment, and that no right to prevent this existed in the people or in any depository power. It was equally clear that the Executive, when the office had become vacant, had the right to fill it by the appointment of any competent person. The constitutional and legal views of the subject were thus believed free from the difficulty. Hear his own views as expressed in a letter to W. M. Roberts, Esq., of the 13th December, 1838. In the music of his periods there is a sad note which will find its way to the heart of the reader.

"To me, who, for a bare subsistence, had given the flower of my life to the public, instead of my dependent family, a continuance in office of the longest period was a matter of vital importance; but the arrangement of the convention, unintentionally severe to me or any one else, proposed to consign me to penury and want, at a time of life when I could scarcely expect to establish myself in practice, which, under the most favorable circumstances, requires several years. This was known to my brethren, and felt by them as men. The measure, since carried into execution, was proposed by one of them on the western circuit, and with the assent of another, whose term would be shortened by it. The assent of the other, who stood in the same predicament, was cordially given, as soon as it was mentioned to him. Feeling, then, that the personal interest of no one else was concerned; that it was an arrangement which contravened no principle of public duty; and that if any objection lay to it on the ground of public expediency, it would be enforced by the constitutional arbiter, I permitted a personal friend, with whom I have never coincided in party sentiment, to submit it to the Executive for his sanction or rejection.

"No condition, express or implied, was attached to the appointment, nor was it hinted that anything was expected. What could I do for the governor or his friends? Personally I had nothing to offer, for my early retirement from the political arena had left me without influence, and officially I had still less."

And what injunction of the amended constitution, or what presumptive intent of the convention has been frustrated by the arrangement so harshly complained of? To introduce the favorite principle of rotation, it was necessary to point out the manner of its application in the first instance by fixing some rule of procedure; and the rule of seniority was adopted because it was more definite and convenient than any other. It will not be said that it was adopted with a view to personal considerations connected with the present judges. If they, or any of them, had died in the meantime it would have operated exactly in the same way on their successors.

"Had the convention intended that the amendments should fix the destinies of the individuals before the system should go into operation, it would have said so in terms instead of saying the contrary. But no such thing was proposed even in debate. Instead of specifying the day of final adjournment as the criterion, which would have done had the intent been to fix those destinies as of that day, the amendments were left to fix them expressly as of a day not yet come. Is it not clear, then, that the convention did not mean to concern itself about changes in the meantime? Forbid them, it certainly did not. It was sufficient for the system, without regard to the individual, that the commission of a judge would expire every three years, a result that must as certainly follow, notwithstanding the change of place betwixt the judges, as if no such change had been made. That the convention meant not to discriminate on the score of years of vigor is manifest from the actual application of their principle, by which the youngest in years was to go out first; and betwixt myself and my brethren who are to be affected by my re-appointment, the difference in that respect is that one of them is six years my senior and the other one year my junior."

These were the views which influenced his mind in accepting the commission. His motives no man who knew him could doubt. He was too proud to do wrong, if he had been restrained by no better feeling. No man ever admired more sincerely than he, high and elevated sentiment and conduct on every subject, and no man ever more cordially despised evasion, indirectness or duplicity. This seems to have been admitted by common consent on the part of the political press on both sides, by dropping the subject and agreeing not to renew the discussion on subsequent occasions when it might have been rendered prominent in party warfare. But it must be admitted that the act was a mistake and an accident to his fame. As such he afterwards felt it. There was no necessity for it. The people, as we shall see, took the earliest opportunity to re-elect him to his office at a period when the advance of age had rendered his capacity to serve them less complete than at any time after his first appointment to office. The acts of every man, and emphatically every public man, which relate to others, should be right, and consequences should take care of themselves; when they relate to himself, they should not only be right but reasonably clear of the possibility of censure.

In this year he received from the University of Pennsylvania the degree of Doctor of Laws, an honor which is believed to have been rarely granted by that institution. The same degree was subsequently conferred on him by the University of Cambridge, Mass., a spontaneous tribute paid to his worth by the distinguished professors who for so many years directed the law department of that university, and to whom he was known chiefly by the productions of his pen.

In 1848, 1849 and 1850, the principle of an elective judiciary was engrafted on the Constitution of Pennsylvania. On the 11th of June, 1851, a convention of one of the political parties of the State assembled at Harrisburg to nominate five candidates to fill the offices of judges of the Supreme Court. The only member of the then existing court who was placed on that ticket was Judge Gibson. The nomination was an act of high homage to his character. It was the result of that feeling. He was more than seventy years of age, too old, if he had been willing, to accomplish by his own energy anything to promote his nomination, and as unacquainted as a child with partisan politics and with party leaders. In one sense the nomination was a rebuke to himself. He had seldom lost an opportunity to express his want of confidence in popular action, and his disapprobation of every movement designed to enlarge the boundaries of popular power. He took as little pains to conceal his sentiments on this point as on all others, and while he expressed them decorously, he uttered them boldly. It must, therefore, have cost him some surprise, if not compunction, to find that carrying into practical effect the very movement of which he had most horror, the people, through their representatives, chose to retain their hold of him as one of their most important public servants. In yet another respect his nomination was memorable.* For many years a disposition has

---

* Modesty probably forbade Judge Porter speaking of himself in a memoir of another, and of the part which he took in this nominating convention. He waited thirty years to tell the story, and as it concerns as well our late able Chief Justice Mercur, and introduces also a glimpse of Judge Black, it becomes of triple interest, and adds a welcome posthumous leaf to the work in hand from the fertile pen of Gibson's biographer. It is taken from a lengthy letter by Judge Porter on his " Recollections of Black," published in the Philadelphia *Press*, Oct. 16th, 1883.

" When the principle of an elective judiciary was engrafted on the Constitution of Pennsylvania (the heaviest curse which, in my judgment, ever fell upon the people) [here Judge Porter appears to agree with what he had criticised Judge Gibson for thirty years previously], a Democratic convention assembled at Harrisburg in June, 1851, to nominate candidates for judges of the Supreme Court, then five in number. Before it assembled, Judge Black, in reply to a letter from the present writer, said that he was not a candidate, that he had a comfortable home in Somerset, that his district exactly suited him, and that he greatly preferred his then present life to wandering up and down the State, hunting up errors for correction. When the convention assembled, it became evi-

prevailed in Pennsylvania to overthrow rather than to sustain
men of distinguished ability. It has long been the subject of
remark at home and abroad, that it seems only necessary for a
man of more than ordinary capacity to appear in the politics
of that State to be struck at by every other politician, great
and small. For this reason, probably, in the sixty-seven
years which have elapsed since the adoption of the Federal
Constitution we have not sent to Congress one man in ten
years capable of making an impression there, and not more
than three or four who could lay claim to high ability.

---

dent at once that Judge Lewis, Judge Campbell and Judge Black would be
nominated. The doubt was, whether we could nominate Gibson, who did not
belong to the party which had called the convention. I happened to sit in that
convention as a delegate, side by side with the present Chief Justice Mercur,
who was then rising into prominence in the northern part of the State.

In the course of our conference I learned with pleasure that one of his
objects in attending was to nominate Gibson, and we both labored heartily for
that end. Gibson was nominated by a majority of two votes, and Mr. Mercur
and myself, of course, claimed to be the persons who gave those votes. It is a
pleasant recollection to me that, without our votes, certainly without our exer-
tions, the State would have been guilty of passing by in his old days the greatest
judge who ever sat in her courts.

It is not my purpose to speak of Judge Black as a judge of the Supreme
Court of Pennsylvania. His decisions lie open to the world. By them he must
be judged. I cannot, however, omit to state that I was present at such a scene in
the Supreme Court as scarcely ever occurred there before or since, namely, when
his dissenting opinion in *Hole vs. Rittenhouse*, 2 Philadelphia Reports, page
411, was delivered. No one can understand this remark without reading that
opinion. Take for example the concluding paragraph:

'The judgment now about to be given is one of 'death's doings.' No one
can doubt that if Judge Gibson and Judge Coulter had lived, the plaintiff could
not have been thus deprived of his property, and thousands of other men would
have been saved from the imminent danger to which they are now exposed, of
losing the homes they have labored and paid for. But they are dead ; and the
law which should have protected those sacred rights has died with them. It
is a melancholy reflection that the property of a citizen should be held by a tenure
so frail. But 'new lords, new laws,' is the order of the day. Hereafter, if any
man be offered a title which the Supreme Court has decided to be good, let him
not buy if the judges who made this decision are dead ; if they are living, let
him get an insurance on their lives, for ye know not what a day or an hour may
bring forth.

'The majority of this court changes on the average once every nine years,

There is scarcely a congressional district in the State from which a member could be returned for more than two terms. So far is the policy pushed that it is becoming impossible to re-elect any one to an important office within the State, be his ability what it may.

The renomination of such a man as Judge Gibson, even to a judicial office, was a notable exception to our usual course of policy. Happy for our jurisprudence if it remained not an exception.

without counting the chances of death and resignation. If each new set of judges shall consider themselves at liberty to overthrow the doctrines of their predecessors, our system of jurisprudence (if system it can be called) would be the most fickle, uncertain and vicious that the civilized world ever saw. A French constitution, or a South American republic, or a Mexican administration would be an immortal thing in comparison to the short lived principles of Pennsylvania law. The rules of property, which ought to be as steadfast as the hills, will become as unstable as the waves. To avoid this great calamity, I know of no resource but that of *stare decisis*. I claim nothing for the great men who have gone before us on the score of their marked and manifest superiority. But I would stand by their decisions, because they have passed into the law and become a part of it—have been relied on and acted on—and rights have grown up under them which it is unjust and cruel to take away.'

Each of the judges replied to this opinion with as much warmth as the dissenting judge had manifested, and the whole scene cannot be forgotten by those who witnessed it."

NOTE—It might be inferred from the above that Judge Gibson was not considered a Democrat at the time of the meeting of this convention, but there is no evidence to show that he had deserted the party. He had necessarily been out of politics for forty years, but there is every reason to suppose that his sympathies were with the Democrats. General Simon Cameron went to Carlisle about this time, to urge him to do something for himself. The general told him while he would catch all the lawyers' votes, to the people he was almost a stranger, etc., etc., and that he might fail of a majority of the popular suffrage. But to this appeal Judge Gibson replied in effect that he would say or do nothing, or express in any way his preference of party or platforms. If the people were not satisfied with his record as a judge, or knew practically nothing of him or his sphere of duties, in either case, or in any event, he would give no sign that he accorded with partisan methods in filling the office. General Cameron departed promising that in his tour of the State he would endorse him notwithstanding his averments, and nobly he fulfilled his promise.

18

On assuming his seat as an associate justice after his election in 1851 he appeared to take much less interest than formerly in the proceedings of the court, and much less part in its business.* He seemed like a noble bird that had been by some unexpected event thrown into a strange flock, which, whether better or worse, were not his old associates, but, of necessity, widely different and belonging almost to a different age. When occupying his seat on the bench, there was a look of abstraction, which told that his thoughts dealt more with the past than with the present. The powers of his mind however had lost nothing of their ancient vigor. When he wrote at all, he wrote like himself. During the sessions of the court in the country he occupied the bench with his brethren, and delivered an occasional opinion. In Philadelphia he seemed to prefer to hold the Court of Nisi Prius, for this caused him less labor after the usual court hours. In this mode, for the most part, he performed his duties until the occurrence of that last change, which I am to record further on in the narrative.

*   *   *   *   *   *

It is necessary to say something of the manner in which his judgments have been reported. We have occasionally had excellent reporting in Pennsylvania, but a portion of it cannot be described by any but very uncharitable terms. Some of the volumes are hardly written in English. I am looking now at two of them in my library (not of cases in the highest court), which I will present to any one who can show me one page of correct English from the hand of

---

* Not many months after his election Judge Gibson was prostrated with a severe attack of cholera, as is elsewhere noticed. If there was a change in his deportment and appearance, it must be attributed solely to his physical disabilities.

the reporter in the entire two volumes. From such reporting it is as impossible to obtain an intelligible statement of a case as to procure it from a chapter of the Koran. The effect on the opinion of the judge is manifest. A good judicial effort may be caricatured by a reporter, just as a gentleman may be made a harlequin by his tailor. The soundest wisdom that ever emanated from the bench may be converted into its opposite by the statement of the reporter, on which the judge generally does and always should rely. When a single fact is left out, or so stated that nobody can understand it, much more when a mass of facts are omitted, and those which exist are clothed with undue importance, the judge's pen must possess superhuman power if it could adapt its productions to these arbitrary and unanticipated changes. Judge Gibson suffered from this cause more than judges usually do, for the reason that more than all others he relied on the statement of the reporter, and concerned himself only with the principles of the cause. We view many of his writings under this disadvantage.

He delivered his first opinion on the supreme bench in the case of the *Commonwealth vs. Holloway*, 2 S. & R., 305, which decided that birth in Pennsylvania gives freedom to the child of a slave who had absconded from another State before she became pregnant. The style of the opinion is natural and pure, but in conciseness and force it contrasts strongly with that in which he wrote twenty years afterwards.

In *Clow vs. Woods*, 5 S. & R., 275, he established the doctrine that on a private sale of chattels retention of possession by the vendor is fraudulent against creditors and bona fide purchasers. From that time to the present this

has been a leading case, and is much relied on in our
own and other States.   In the excellent note which the
American editors have appended to Twyne's case, in Smith's
collection of leading cases, due prominence is assigned it.
Any one who desires to estimate the value of the decision
which imparted this direction to the law of Pennsylvania
has only to study the difficulties and inconsistencies in
which the courts of the United States, of Virginia, Kentucky, Illinois, Indiana, New Hampshire and South Carolina,
on the one hand, and Massachusetts, Maine, Ohio, Tennessee,
and perhaps Alabama, on the other, have become involved by
adopting different rules.   The forecast which the opinion in
Clow vs. Woods displays was all that saved our own jurisprudence from similar confusion on a topic so fruitful of
litigation.

In *Watson vs. Mercer*, 6 S. & R., 49, he foreshadows that
dissatisfaction with the principles of the common law respecting the rights of married women, which, nearly twenty years
afterwards, was to lead to the adoption of our Act of 11th
April, 1848.*   The passage which I transcribe will afford a
fair specimen of his style at this period of his life:

* More than twenty years after the death of Judge Gibson the Constitutional
Convention of 1873, acting upon hints thrown out in some of his opinions, made
important changes in the instrument it was called together to consider.   A case
in point is cited, where his phraseology was adopted and now forms a very
important clause in the laws determining damages to property by corporations,
etc.   Mention of the fact is made in the case of the Pittsburgh Junction R. R.,
plaintiff in error, vs. Wm. McCutcheon, defendant in error.   Messrs. Johns Mc-
Cleave and W. B. Rodgers, counsel for plaintiff, in their argument, as found in their
paper book, state :

"As to the constitutional provision.   It is conceded that this action could
"not be supported under the law as it stood prior to 1874, but it is supposed that
"Section 8, Art. 16, of the constitution of 1874, has changed the law upon this
"subject, and that this action can be maintained under this provision.   The sec-
"tion referred to provides as follows :

"Municipal and other corporations and individuals, invested with the privilege of taking private property for public use, shall make just compensation for

"In no country where the blessings of the common law are felt and acknowledged are the interest and estates of married women so entirely at the mercy of their husbands as in Pennsylvania. This exposure of those who, from the defenceless state in which even the common law has placed them, are least able to protect themselves, is extenuated by no motive of policy and is by no means credible to our jurisprudence. The subordinate and dependent condition of the wife opens to the husband such an unbounded field to practice on her natural timidity, or to abuse a confidence never sparingly reposed in return for even occasional and insidious kindness, that there is nothing, however unreasonable or unjust, to which he cannot procure her consent. The policy of the law should be, as far as possible, to narrow rather than to widen the field of this controlling influence. In England the courts of equity will

property taken, injured or destroyed, by the construction or enlargement of their works, or improvements, etc."

*   *   *   *   *   *   *   *

"This phraseology, *taken, injured* or *destroyed,* was taken from the opinion of Chief Justice Gibson in *O'Connor vs. City of Pittsburgh,* 18 Pa. St., 190. They are the words of a great lawyer who understood their precise import, etc."

The language in the case cited, of Judge Gibson's, on this point is as follows :

"Yet it must be admitted that, while it is inequitable to injure the property of an individual for the benefit of the many, it would be impossible for a corporation to bear the pressure of successive common law actions for the continuance of a nuisance, each verdict being more severe than the preceding one. The modification of the remedy would be for the legislators, which can turn compensation for a permanent detriment into the price of a prospective license ; but to attain complete justice every damage to private property ought to be compensated by the State or corporation that occasioned it, and a general statutory remedy ought to be provided to assess the value. The constitutional provision for the case of private property *taken* for public use, extends not to the case of property *injured* or *destroyed* ; but it follows not that the omission may not be supplied by ordinary legislation."

The compiler is indebted to R. B. Carnahan, Esq., for references to the above opinion of Judge Gibson.

not assist the husband to obtain possession of his wife's personal property, although it becomes his absolutely on the marriage, before he makes an adequate settlement; here he has the
power to obtain her personal estate, not only without condition
but in some instances by means of the intestate acts, even to
turn her real into personal estate *against* her consent.   In
other countries the wife's dower, that sacred provision which
the law makes for her, in return for the personal property
she brought her husband, and in recompense of a life-time
devoted to him and his children, is put beyond the reach
of every effort which selfishness or profligacy can make to
deprive her of it; in this, it may be swept away by his
debts contracted in the gratification of his vices.   In the
country whence we derive our laws, the wife's land can be
aliened only with her consent, deliberately expressed on a
fair, full and careful separate examination in a court of
record; in this, the examination is considered a matter of
such little importance that it is intrusted to a justice of
the peace, by whom it is sometimes entirely dispensed with
in fact," etc.

     *   *   *   *   *   *

I point the attention of the reader in the next place to
the case of the *Commonwealth vs. Green and others*, 4
Wharton, 531, a case, says Judge Rogers, p. 606, "without
precedent, and presenting some extraordinary features."   It
arose out of the division which occurred in 1837 in the
Presbyterian Church, an institution which for more than
two centuries and a half has served the cause of civil
liberty so well as to have merited better treatment from
the members of her own household.   The case occasioned
intense interest in every part of the Union.   On the trial
at Nisi Prius a verdict was rendered in favor of the

relators, the effect of which, if it had stood, would have been to declare the trustees elected by the New School body, the true, legal and proper trustees of the general assembly of that church. Reasons for a new trial were filed (sixty-five in number), and after argument before the court *in banc*, an opinion was pronounced making the rule for a new trial absolute. If the reader possesses any partisan views of the subject, it is quite probable that in this case, as in others, they will influence his estimate of the result which was reached; but I see not how any one familiar with the best efforts of the human mind in the solution of difficult questions of law or morals can fail to admire the powers of analysis and the condensation which the opinion of Judge Gibson in that case displays. He threads his way with a confidence and skill almost matchless, through constitutions, systems of church polity, plans of union, maxims of ecclesiastical government, books of discipline, rules, orders, motions, debates, synods, presbyteries, congregations and associations, some of them referring to nearly a century of time, and all of them evidently unknown to him before the argument. Any one who has read the case can scarcely be surprised that the opinion of the judge should have had the effect of preventing all other litigation on the subject.

Any memoir of Judge Gibson would be incomplete without some notice of his agency in settling the law of Pennsylvania on the subject of riots. The people of the State, and perhaps of the Union, will not soon forget the popular commotions which prevailed in Philadelphia between the years 1836 and 1846. We had the abolition riots, railroad riots, the negro riots, the weavers' riots, and the Native American riots. Having run short of names, terri-

torial designations were adopted, and we had the Moyamen-
sing, Southwark and Kensington riots. Interspersed with
these were the riots of various fire companies, who seemed
to have achieved little distinction until their members had
been bound over to each successive term of the quarter sessions.   Learned jurists were at work in the meantime.   It
was easily shown that this disorder was all wrong; that the
power to suppress it must exist somewhere; that the sheriff
could employ both civil and military power; that all citizens
were bound to obey his requisition; that peaceable citizens
were more numerous than the disorderly; that the riots could
therefore be put down, and must be put down.   Editors, lawyers, judges and philosophers, all agreed in opinion, and
resolved that there must be no more riots.   This was very
well, but the riots continued.   Good citizens ascertained that
if they disobeyed the sheriff's summons they would be fined,
and if they complied with it their heads would be broken,
and with strange contempt for the law, and unaccountable for-
getfulness of their civil duties, they preferred to encounter the
fine.   The sheriff therefore went to the attack with men
the value of whose assistance may be estimated in proportion
to the price they placed on their own heads, and to whom any
attempt to test the thickness of their skulls was of small consequence, provided they received compensation for turning out.
The writer of these pages saw but one of those bodies of men
so famous in legal treatises under the title of *posse*, and he
hopes to be excused for his want of taste in not desiring to
see another.   The description of Falstaff's regiment renders
any account of it unnecessary.   Their conduct was what every
one but a writer of disquisitions could have predicted.   At
the first discharge of arms by the mob they left the commanding officer with five men out of three hundred.   The military

were next thought of; but when the military arrived, the mob was not there; and when the military had dispersed, the mob, by a singular coincidence, again convened. Thus every theoretical means existed that could have been desired to effect the end, and the practical means were absent to a degree that made all efforts of the kind simply contemptible. In the meantime the character of our city had suffered immensely. Accounts of the disturbances, bad enough if not exaggerated, had been extensively published, both at home and abroad, and one of the most peaceful and peace-loving communities in this sisterhood of States had begun to be known as the city of riots. The commotions of 1844 filled up the measure of our shame. Two churches, a school house, and numerous private dwellings were reduced to ashes. All men felt that the time had come when the law must do something, if it could do anything. Inferior tribunals quailed before the mob spirit, and the mass of the rioters arrested were acquitted and discharged. An opportunity now presented itself to the chief justice to display his powers. The Act of 31st May, 1841, founded on that of George I, authorized the owners of property in the county of Philadelphia, destroyed by this species of violence, to bring suits against the county for the injuries sustained, and numerous suits were brought under the authority of the act. The case of *Donoghue vs. The County*, was the first on the list, and the chief justice held the court. His charge was worthy of the man, and of the occasion. No one who heard it can forget its influence on the case, on the subsequent cases, and on the community. One of the chief defences set up, that armed men had fired on the crowd from the building afterwards burned, was demolished with a boldness, an energy, and an eloquence rarely surpassed in judicial proceedings. He disregarded utterly the

19

distinction which had been taken between defending a dwelling house and a church, and held that a man has the same right to defend and to take life in defence of the place in which he worships God, as of the domicile which shelters his family. He carried the doctrine even further, and applied it to the school contiguous to the church, in which the children were receiving their education. In the meagre scrap of the charge which is reported in 2 Barr, 231, this is sufficiently evident. The result was a verdict in favor of the plaintiff for the whole amount of the property destroyed. A similar result followed in the case of the *Hermits of St. Augustine vs. The County*, Brightly's Reports, 116, and in that of the *St. Michael's Church vs. The County*, Brightly's Reports, 121. Of a different verdict in the first case, on that turning point between the dominion of law and the dominion of violence, no man could have ventured to predict the result. From that time to this we have had no riots. Other causes have contributed to produce this state of things; but no one act tended more directly to restore permanent good order and to re-establish popular confidence in the people themselves, than the manly and patriotic course of Judge Gibson in the case of *Donoghue vs. The County*. Business men began to feel that if they were certainly liable to pay their own proportion of the property thus destroyed, it was their pecuniary interest to require its preservation. Lawless men found that they inflicted no injury on the objects of their violence when the property destroyed was paid for at its highest value. Patriotic men, both at home and abroad, were glad to discover in these proceedings fresh evidence of the power which a wise and benignant system of law administered by an enlightened judge may exert among a free people.

*   *   *   *   *   *

Braddee vs. Brownfield, 2 W. & S., 271, was an instance of lamentable acquiescence in legislative encroachment. In that case the legislature had passed an act directing a judgment to be opened and the defendant let into a defence. The court, on grounds which it is hard to understand, in place of rebuking this usurpation of judicial functions pronounce it "the exercise of a jurisdiction of a remedial character, partly legislative and partly judicial, and not in violation of the constitution." The principle thus announced continued to be the law of Pennsylvania for nearly ten years, and until Judge Gibson upturned it in the case of *De Chastellux vs. Fairchild*. His memory would deserve well of the State if he never had delivered another opinion. I hold these to be words of wisdom:

"If anything is self-evident in the structure of our government, it is that the legislature has no power to order a new trial, or to direct the court to order it, either before or after judgment. The power to order new trials is judicial, but the power of the legislature is not judicial. It is limited to the making of laws; not to the exposition or execution of them. The functions of the several parts of the government are thoroughly separated, and distinctly assigned to the principal branches of it, the legislative, the executive, and the judiciary, which, within their respective departments, are equal and co-ordinate. Each derives its authority, mediately or immediately, from the people, and each is responsible, mediately or immediately, to the people for the exercise of it. When either shall have usurped the powers of one or both of its fellows, then will have been affected a revolution, not in the form of the government, but in its action. Then will there be a concentration of the powers of the government in a single branch of it, which, whatever may be the form of the constitution, will be a despotism, a government of unlimited, irresponsible and arbitrary rule. It is idle to say the authority of each branch is defined and limited in the constitution, if there be not an independent power able and willing to enforce the limitations. Experience proves that it is thoughtlessly but habitually violated; and the sacrifice of individual right is too remotely connected with the objects and contests of the masses to attract their attention.

"From its every position it is apparent that the conservative power is lodged with the judiciary, which in the exercise of its undoubted right is bound to meet every emergency; else causes would be decided not only by the legislature, but, sometimes, without hearing or evidence. The mischief has not yet come to that, for the legislature has gone no farther than to order a rehearing on the merits; but it is not more intolerable in principle to pronounce an arbitrary judgment against a suitor than it is injurious in practice to deprive him of a judgment which is essentially his property, and to subject him to the vexation, risk and expense of another contest.

"It has become the duty of the court to temporize no longer, but to resist temperately, though firmly, any invasion of its province, whether great or small."

After this his opinions were less frequent, and I forbear to trace them. I go back only to notice the peculiarity of expression and illustration to be found in some of them. In *Riddle vs. Welden,* 5 Wharton, 15, in considering whether the goods of a boarder are liable for rent due by the keeper of the boarding house, he supports himself by an authority more frequently referred to at the bar than on the bench: "In fact his (the lodger's) right to enter and use the inn for his accommodation stands on the footing of his legal right to enter and use his own house, which is his castle, and in other respects more highly privileged. It is his own while he uses it, and Falstaff speaks with legal precision when he demands, 'Can I not take mine ease in mine inn?'" In *Gowen vs. The Philadelphia Exchange Co.*, 5 W. & S., 144, he calls Shylock to his aid and speaks of the "hall where merchants most do congregate." In *Logan vs. Mason*, 6 W. & S., 13, he affirms that "the morality of the New Testament is for all times, and that the maxim cannot endure a test so severe, is proof as strong as holy writ that there is something wrong in it," a very just sentiment, which he came very near expressing in the words of Iago, who speaks of "confirmation strong as proofs of holy writ." In *Patterson vs. Poindexter*, 6 W. & S., 227, he declares that "the contract of endorsement is not an independent one, but a parasite, which like the chameleon, takes the hue of the thing with which it is connected." In *Rogers vs. Walker*, 6 Barr, 375, he pronounces certain exceptions, "a reticulated web to catch the crumbs of the cause, and as they contain no point or principle of particular importance, they are dismissed without further remark." In *Hays vs. Harden*, 6 Barr, 413, in discussing the effect of affixing a mark to a legal instrument, he speaks of the "will of a marksman" in terms that would suggest an idea very different from his own, on the Allegheny mountains, or in the territory of Kansas. In *Weiting vs. Nissley*, 1 H., 655, he declares that "the record in this case, as in most others, has exceptions, like the pockets of a billiard table, to catch lucky chances from random strokes of the players; but as they have caught nothing in this instance it is unnecessary to enter into a particular investigation

of them." In *Shannon vs. The Commonwealth*, 2 Harris,
228, in referring to the law of adultery he supposes "the
framers of it knew the futility of attempting to smother
the instincts of our nature, or to cleanse our thoughts by
an Act of Assembly." Other instances of the use of
expressions so novel in judicial opinions might be gleaned
from his writings. In quoting them I have intended only
to present them to the reader.

His manner of reaching his conclusions and writing his
opinions was well known. It is believed that he took little
part in the consultations of the bench, communicating his
views usually in short, detached sentences, sometimes not at
all, but when he did, hitting the exact point, and diffusing
additional light on the principles in question. When
appointed to deliver the opinion, he generally made an
examination of the authorities, and sometimes, it must be
admitted, much too brief an examination. His habit then
was to think chiefly without the aid of his pen, and out
of the reach of books. He did this in his chamber, on
the street, at the table; sometimes, it is feared, on the bench,
during the progress of other causes, and not infrequently in
the public room of the hotel. Persons who approached him
on these occasions were struck with, and sometimes offended
at, his abstracted and careless air. To those who knew
what he was doing, he frequently complained of his difficulty
in determining on what principles to pitch the cause, without
mentioning it particularly. He did all the labor of thought
before he commenced to write, and he never wrote until he
was ready. Before he began, it is believed, the very sentences were formed in his mind, and when he assumed
the pen, he rarely laid it aside until the opinion had been
completed. The bold, beautiful, and legible character of his

hand-writing, and its freedom from erasure, induced those obliged to read his opinions in manuscript, to suppose that he transcribed them, but this was very rarely, if ever done; he had too little time, and too much horror of the pen, to attempt it. Such a method of writing undoubtedly possessed great advantages. It gave his fine logical powers full play. It contributed to that condensation which forms one of the distinctive features of his writings. It enabled him to proceed with directness. right to his conclusion, and to make everything point to it from the first sentence to the last. No repetition occurs. We see each idea but once, and need not count on seeing even the shadow of it, more than once. Having always something to do ahead, the pen spent no more time on the thought in hand than was necessary to complete it. He knew precisely where he was to end before beginning, and he avoided all the difficulties of those writers who begin to write when they begin to think, and sometimes before it, and who produce works resembling, for the most part, the patch-work emblazoned on the best beds of German housekeepers, and giving evidence not to be mistaken, of the exact places at which they have been joined, and of the diverse and heterogeneous materials out of which they have been composed. The most casual reader of Judge Gibson's opinions must have observed how seldom he professes to give any history of the decided cases, from the creation of the world, from the reign of Richard I, or from the assumption of the reins of justice by Chief Justice McKean; and how invariably he puts the decision upon some leading principle of the law, referring but to a few cases for the purpose of illustration, or to show their exception to the general rule, and how all this is done with the ease and skill which betokens the hand of a master.

It must be conceded that rich, powerful, and even graceful as his style was, it had its defects. In common with
Dr. Chalmers he betrayed an unfortunate proneness to the
use of long and unusual words, generally of Latin origin. I
am not sure that the great Scotch divine would ever have
condescended to say *desire* when he could with a show of
propriety have said *desiderate*. So we frequently have Judge
Gibson employing the terms *unilateral, individuate, manipulating* the testimony, *immiscible* as water and oil, *convergen
intent*, etc., etc.* There was also an unnatural stateliness and
dignity in his style. Many of his sentences seem so con-
structed that if placed on a pivot they would remain in perpetual equipoise. Of all this species of writing, the *Rambler*
and the *Idler* are the well known models, and I suppose
there can be little doubt that at some period of his life
those works had made an impression on him. I strongly suspect, however, that the prose writings of Milton had made a
deeper and better impression. But his style had another
defect, it might have unfolded his meaning more rapidly.
To any one thoroughly versed in the subject of his opinion,
or to any one who would take the trouble to read it twice
or thrice, the import of every word or syllable was clear.
But this is not enough, for more than one-half of his readers have not such knowledge or time at their command. It
is not sufficient that the language of a writer when put to
the torture, can be made to yield but one meaning, it should
suggest that meaning at once. Other writings do this, and
all should do it. Those of Calvin and Owen, of Tillotson
and Doddridge, of Hamilton and Calhoun do it, in different
departments, in different ways, and on subjects as difficult as
ever employed human pen. I know of nothing in judicial

---

* Some of these words are now in common use.

station which dispenses its occupant from a like duty. Men are generally not compelled to write, but when they do, it should be borne in mind that one object of writing is to be read ; sometimes, by absolute necessity, to be read rapidly, and always with the loss of as little time as possible. It must be owned that Judge Gibson did not always remember this, or if he did, that he could not command the time to put it into practice. But when this has been said the worst has been said that can be urged in the way of abatement from his eulogy as a judicial writer. In whatever he uttered on any subject he had a meaning, and a very precise and definite meaning, which few men could have expressed in smaller space.* His words were not used to conceal or to dress up and trick out ideas too poor and mean to be presented simply and naturally. The thoughts themselves were great thoughts, struggling to make themselves felt through words, which, however well chosen, but obstructed them, and which were used at all only because better could not then be found. The resemblance which his writings thus assumed to the best productions on the philosophy of the mind, has frequently induced the charge that he was a metaphysical writer. If by this is meant that he was confused or obscure, nothing is further from the truth. Any man who could establish such an accusation against the works of Locke, Reid or Thomas Brown, would be a most successful slanderer. In itself metaphysical science is abstruse enough ; the principles on which it rests have been refined to the purity of gold ; but in the statement of them, precision and

---

* "Crabbe's Synonymes" was Judge Gibson's *vade mecum*. His well preserved copy of this work, Eng. Ed., 1818, is in the possession of the writer, and we have looked in vain through it for marginal notes. He handled books carefully, and at all times the shelves of his library and table presented a neat appearance. His faculty of order must have been well developed.

20

strength have been attained, unsurpassed in any department of literature. These are the great qualities of a judicial style. Of all other men, a judge ought to be able to state the very point of his decision, and so to express it that human ingenuity cannot make it convey more or less than he intended it should. The time of every court is chiefly occupied by efforts to include, under a principle previously promulged, cases which it was never intended to cover, and to exclude from its operation those which have occurred from its literal and faithful observance. Few greater evils therefore can arise than those which result from the obscure and ambiguous expression of judicial determinations. From such defects the decisions of Judge Gibson are exempt to a degree which make them models. So skillfully are his words adapted to his thoughts, that his writings can be made to convey just what his language expresses, and nothing else. On the other hand, his metaphysics were as little adapted to the splitting of hairs "'twixt south and south-west side," or between any other points of the compass. Though his reasoning is often refined, his conclusions are satisfactory, clear, and fitted to work in the practical concerns of life without friction or damage. I am familiar with no writings to which they bear an exact resemblance. He was in the end almost as unlike Johnson as unlike Addison. He was as far from Carlyle as from Irving. The class whom he most resembled were doubtless, as I have intimated, those on the philosophy of the mind. He had less subtlety than many of these writers, but as much of it as any other judge, unless Lord Eldon be the exception. He had points in common with the great author of the "Analogy," but he must be admitted unequal to him in the power of treating a moral theme with so much of the exactness and conclusiveness which belong to demonstrative reasoning. He never wrote so agreeably as Dugald Stewart, but with decidedly more power. The style of President Edwards, whether for philosophic or judicial disquisition, cannot, in my estimation, be compared to that of Judge Gibson. Every student of the "Treatise on the Will" has observed how frequently the finest distinction and the profoundest reflections are there conveyed with a carelessness of expression to be found only in the most ordinary literary composition. If asked to name an author of note whom he most resembled, I would unhesitatingly say John Foster. He certainly had less credulity than that eminent writer, less brilliance of imagination, and quite as slight a dash of poetry in his nature, or no opportunity to show it. Both were alike addicted to the use of words which suited them, whencesoever derived, and were as little afraid of involved and parenthetical sentences. Both exhibited the same depth of thought, the same power of condensation, and the same facility of illustration from unusual sources. I incline to think, however, that in classic beauty, in strength and boldness of illustration, and in opulence of language, Gibson was more than his match. Having already quoted largely from the writings of the latter, it would be unnecessarily burdensome to quote more. The test may be applied to any of his more elaborate written judgments. If the space justified, it would be easy to gather from the *Eclectic Review*, and from the other publications which gained to Foster his world-wide fame, sufficient proof that, after making allowance for the difference of subject, the resemblance of these writings is not imaginary. I refer, for example, to his essays on a man's writing memoirs of himself, and on the application of the epithet romantic; and to his reviews of

Macdiarmid's "British Statesman," of Franklin's "Correspondence," of Fox's "James the Second," etc., etc. It is of course
difficult to make that allowance for the diversity of subject
which has been suggested; but I am sure that the student
of Judge Gibson's writings will see in the performance to
which I have referred, much that will forcibly remind him
of the dead chief. For one, I doubt whether there is any
man known to our literature who, if he had been discoursing on the same themes, would have spoken more nearly
like Foster than the subject of this sketch, and great
though this praise would be regarded by literary men, I
esteem it within those reasonable bounds which a friend
may prescribe to himself in a tribute to departed worth.

It is not unusual to hear the wish expressed by learned
men, that Judge Gibson had employed his powers in a
treatise on some topic of the law, fit to perpetuate his fame
more completely than the usual round of judicial duties
could do it. I doubt not that if he could have been
induced to construct such a work, it would have proved
equal to any which our American law authors have yet produced. There would have been nothing in its style to
interest a general professional reader. It would have possessed the hardness and dryness of flint. To consume an
hour of professional leisure, a page of the differential calcu-
lus would have been about as serviceable. Its only student
would have been the advocate in search of an authority to
insure the success of his cause, and the judge, anxious to
secure a steady light in threading his path through doubt
or error; these students would have paid to it the profoundest homage of their understandings. But the wish is a
vain one. There probably never was a day in his life when
he could have been prevailed on to undertake such a work.

If attempted, it would have died out before the close of the first chapter. The concurrent testimony of those who knew most of his habits is, that he never wrote except under the pressure of absolute necessity. It seemed to require this to bring his powers to the pitch at which alone they could work satisfactorily to himself. When the time came for the delivery of the opinion, he wrote it, and we have seen how he wrote it. On a work whose completion depended on his own volition, he would have been as little capable of severe toil as any writer equally able whose name is known to the reader.

As a jurist, Judge Gibson was ardently attached to the principles of the common law. His love of them beams in his writings, as affection will beam in the human countenance. He not only looked on them with the admiration of an artist, as symmetrical and beautiful parts of a great fabric, but he regarded them as the best rampart which the common sense of mankind has yet thrown up against the despotism of the king or the judge, of the purse or the sword. We shall see hereafter that the last thing he ever wrote for publication was a declaration of his unshaken loyalty to the doctrines of the common law. A part of the language which he applied to Judge Kennedy (4 Barr, 6) might as justly have been uttered of himself; for like Byron in many of his characters, he was probably describing himself without seeing that the world would recognize the portrait. " He clung to the common law as a child to its nurse, and how much he drew from it may be seen in his opinions, which, by their elaborate minuteness, remind us of the over-fullness of Coke." The chief justice was also an admirer of our Pennsylvania system of law, in which the substantial principles of equity are applied under the forms of the common law. The wonder is that in any case they should have been separated. To appoint one judge to execute the law and another to do equity, seems like creating one man all head and another all heart. To execute the law upon a suitor's person or property, and to allow him in the meantime to apply to a court of equity for relief, or to turn him out of the latter because his case has no equity in it, with the assurance that he will have no difficulty in recovering in a court of law; in other words, to permit two different rules of legal duty on the same subject to press on the same man at the same time, is a state of things which the mass of mankind will never understand, if each individual man should rival the patriarchs in the term of his natural life. From the day when Lord Erskine uttered his quiet humor on the subject down to the publication of "Bleak House," the severest sarcasms on this state of things have been flung into the faces of lawyers without the possibility of turning the point of one of them. The Pennsylvania system of law is among the few that have been measurably free from the reproaches which the learned and the unlearned have thus conspired to hurl at the whole science. It is natural that the mind of a man like Judge Gibson, who had done so much to advance this system, and who had witnessed the strides which the legal world seems making towards it, should feel some pride in perpetuating it. With this spirit, it is consistent that when our legislature adopted certain equity remedies, and provided certain equity proceedings, he should endeavor to carry them fairly into practice. An opposite course, if he could have pursued it, would have caused disquiet and disaster. Besides this, whatever he might have thought, he was not a man to set himself up against what seemed to be useful reform. He had seen defects which some of these remedies seemed to supply, and he applied them in the very spirit in which the profession and the legislature had called them into being. So successfully was this done, that, with all his attachment to the common law, it has not been unfrequent to hear from those most devoted to the equity system the admission that he would have made a better chancellor than he was a judge. It is pertinent to remark here, that he had no undue fondness for the civil law. His mind was too liberal, for the mind of a scholar is always liberal in its appreciation of learning, not to admire the beauty, wisdom and simplicity of many parts of that system, and its adaptation to the state of society in which it has grown up; but it must be admitted that he ever and anon cast a suspicious glance on the efforts of Judge Story, and the writers of that school, to infuse its principles into our cherished common law. He could not have denied that many of the branches of our law have been enriched in this mode, but he was alive to the danger of pushing such improvements too far. I need refer the reader only to the opinion delivered in *Lyle vs. Richards*, 9 S. & R., 322, and in *Logan vs. Mason*, 6 W. & S., 9, in proof of the existence of these views in the mind of their author.

Let me here ask whether any one can fail to perceive the effect which the presence on the bench of such intellect as I have been describing must exert on the bar. Doubtless, in this respect, they act and re-act on each other, but I speak only of the effect of the bench on the bar. I suppose that a display of the highest forensic ability before a tribunal incompetent to appreciate it, would be next to impossible. The chief stimulus for preparation would be wanting; and truth, however sound, would fall powerless. The more cultivated men are, the more conscious they are of their own defects, and the more tolerant of the faults of others; and of this a speaker seldom loses his consciousness. The best orator, as a matter of choice, would probably select the most intellectual and refined audience. One of an opposite kind would be little better than an empty apartment. The oration of Demosthenes could not have been delivered in an age less intellectual than that which witnessed them, and some proof of this is, they never were delivered in any other age. Before others than kings and warriors grappling with questions of life and death, Nestor himself would have been nobody; and I cannot, at this moment, recall an instance throughout the entire poem in which he is introduced in any other company. Eloquent speeches to an ignorant jury prove nothing to the contrary, for in such instances they are generally brought out by the presence of the bar and the bench. These speculations might be carried further. I only meant to say, that a bar which aims at the highest standard of excellence, cannot tell what priceless treasures it possesses in a high order of intellect to those who are to decide upon its efforts. If the mere administration of justice were altogether nothing, the profession would be the gainer by keeping the bench at the highest pitch of intellectual power.

In summing up the personal character of Judge Gibson, I do not mean to represent him as faultless, for then he had been more than human. Doubtless he had his defects; whatever they may have been, I do not propose to discuss them. To do so would be to imitate the conduct of some visitor to a gallery of art, who should employ himself in tracing rough images in the dust of the floor instead of contemplating the beautiful conceptions of genius on all sides around him and above him. I speak rather of what Judge Gibson was than of what he was not. His case has been removed to that great appellate court, which, while it administers perfect justice, is governed also by perfect mercy. Jurisdiction having vested there, on the soundest principles of jurisprudence, no allegation should be permitted against him here. He certainly had small faults, which to small eyes were large enough to shut out any perception of his great qualities. He despised the anise and the cumin, and necessarily lost the respect of those valuable members of the state, outside and inside of the bar, who do the least important things first, and the most important last. Frank, generous and confiding, he spoke on the bench and else-where, of persons and of things, with that impulse which none but an honest heart can know; and in doing so he occasionally lost in dignity as much as he gained in the pleasure of giving expression to his real sentiments in his own way. If, as a presiding officer, he had preserved order more rigidly, his court would have been a more solemn place, and if he had attended more directly to what was passing before him, the business would have been more effi-ciently dispatched.* But enough of what he was not. The

---

* These observations of Judge Porter's justify an explanation of a charac-teristic of the Gibson mind, strikingly illustrated in Judge Gibson personally. Simply to say that he was "absent-minded," which he certainly was in a marked degree, would convey a false impression to many. Absent-mindedness is gener-ally conceded to be indicative of mental weakness. Those afflicted with it are constantly mistaking their right for their left hand, or doing other equally absurd things. Their minds, in fact, are absent, or chronically "star gazing" or "wool gathering." This is their normal condition, and persons so afflicted can never be relied upon in emergencies. But a distinction should be drawn between the so-called absent and the abstracted mind (the dictionary does not do this, how-ever). Sometimes the mind, which concentrates itself upon one subject, takes no note of the presence of persons or what they may be doing or saying, except so far

qualities which he possessed were striking and peculiar.
That which most impressed those who knew him best was
the exceeding kindness of his heart. The knowledge of
this was a key to his character. Any newspaper editor or
legislative orator who had abused him might have approached
him with the profoundest confidence, not only that he had
forgiven, but actually forgotten, any calumny, however gross.
In that respect, at least, no man could have reduced to
practice more directly the morality of the New Testament.
He cherished no antipathies, and formed no prejudices, and
this constituted one of his chief excellencies as a judicial
magistrate. Few lawyers would hesitate between presenting
a cause before a judge who had been purchased to do
wrong, and one blinded by prejudice towards a party, or
the subject in dispute, or the principle which it involved.
The former might be restrained by the fear of detection or
the consciousness of guilt, or he might by the force of
argument, and by the plainness of the matter, be hemmed
in and shut up to decide the right. Not so the latter. His
eyeballs are seared; molten lead has been poured into his
ears; he sees only his own foregone conclusions; he hears
only the voice of his own stubborn will; and it were as
reasonable to expect just perceptions from the dead. One
of these characters is totally unknown in our American
courts, but, alas for the weakness of human nature, the other
is probably not without its types. Both the official and

---

us what they say or do chords mentally with the tone whose sound smothers all
other tones in the thinker's mind. This is concentration with abstraction of
mind. The annoying results of this form of absent-mindedness are felt when this
habit of preoccupation of mind is permitted on the streets or in social gatherings,
for then faces pass by unseen, and names are heard to be instantly forgotten.
These observations are pertinent, also, to Judge Porter's remarks referring to
the offense created by Judge Gibson's occasional "abstracted and careless air."
See page 150.

the personal intercourse of Judge Gibson was eminently free from such blemishes. He neither hated nor suspected. In every relation, public and private, he displayed that charity of the heart which makes a man a gentleman despite of early associations, and even of bad manners. In the liveliest sallies of his wit and humor, the last acts on which benevolence exerts its restraining influence, he never allowed himself to trench on the sensibilities of others. When he said anything from the bench approaching severity, as he sometimes did when worn down by a dull and tedious argument, no time was lost in trying, by a remark of a different kind, to wear away its effect both on the speaker and the audience. He was a sound critic in the best sense of the term, and when a harsh observation was made of one whom he knew, he was generally able to relieve its effect by pointing out some excellence which had escaped the attention of others. To the young, and especially to those who were endeavoring to become the architects of their own fortunes, he was kind, affable and indulgent. But the picture requires high coloring. There was something in his magnanimity, in his forgiving temper, in his kindly charity, in his capacity to appreciate excellence of any kind, in any form, which despite his apparent unconcern of manner and sluggishness of body, elicited and compelled affection. There was a true fire of the heart which glowed unceasingly, and cast even the splendor of his intellect into the shade. No man ever more cordially despised a cold, calculating spider-like lawyer, weaving day by day his miserable toils, giving up nothing, retaining his grasp on every victim of chance and folly, and employing his powers only for the production of misery and the practice of oppression. No man ever spoke into being, with so little effort, ardent and permanent friendship. He sat on the supreme bench with twenty-six different judges, none of whom, except Judge Duncan, owed their position to his influence, and almost all of whom, on their accession, were comparative strangers to him, and yet it may be doubted whether the purest and happiest household ever lived in more absolute harmony than he enjoyed in his personal intercourse with his associates. In regard to any body of men long associated together, this fact might be worth repeating; but in that of so many independent men, of strong intellects and wills, employed together in the daily examination of exciting questions, where conscience and duty required each man to stand by his individual judgment, the case is somewhat remarkable. It is quite apparent that in the acceptance of the commission from Governor Ritner, it was the eagerness of his associates and friends to promote his welfare, and to smooth his declining years, that, for the moment, threw his judgment from her balance. His nomination in 1851 was a better directed effort of the same kind. There were in the judicial convention of that year, without his knowledge, more than a score of delegates whose chief business was his renomination. If they had been bone of his bone, they could not have been more anxious for the result. Less friendly exertion in his behalf, and two less votes than the number he received, would have lost to the State the remainder of his life.*

His intellectual acquirements were great, and he had a right to be proud of them; but that would be a poor monument to his fame which should omit to mention those higher and finer qualities of the heart, which placed him

---

* Judge Porter himself and the late Chief Justice Mercur cast the "two votes." See note elsewhere.

so far above the level of ordinary men. Take the following instance of their exercise. During a hot and laborious
session of the Supreme Court, at Harrisburg in 1843, the
idea occurred to Judge Gibson and Judge Rogers, to
place a marble slab over the remains of Joseph Jefferson,
the actor, which, from 1832, had lain in a churchyard in
that town, with nothing to mark their resting place.
The former applied to Mr. Wm. B. Wood, one of the
contemporaries of Jefferson, for some information necessary
in framing an epitaph. [See Appendix.] The information was furnished, the epitaph was written, the slab was
laid, and the facts were, during the present year, thirteen
years after the occurrence, communicated to the public
by Mr. Wood in his "Recollections of the Stage." Here
was the case of a poor actor, who, as the epitaph states,
had closed his career " in calamity and affliction," and, as
it appears, without one other monument to record his
genius than that which was thus erected. The act was
done kindly and quietly, without ostentation, without newspaper notice, and in such a manner as not to connect with
it the names of its authors. Men may differ about the
propriety of erecting a monument to the memory of Mr.
Jefferson, but I should be glad to know whether any man
would have done it but one who had strong sympathies
with human nature. " I knew him well, Horatio," the
epitaph concludes, " a fellow of infinite jest, and most excellent fancy." This was the motive, and the only motive,
except the pleasure of doing a good act without making
parade or exciting suspicion. Mr. Wood justly adds, that
Chief Justice Gibson's sensibilities and taste in the whole
range of the fine arts, music, architecture, painting, statuary,
and the drama, were hardly inferior to his uncommon in-

tellectual parts; and the author, if it had fallen in his way, might have said what I reserved to this place — in that geology,* chemistry and medicine, Judge Gibson's knowledge was probably more extensive and complete than that of any member of the legal profession who survives him.

It was almost unnecessary to speak of him as a man of integrity. I verily believe that the mere force of habit in seeking the truth and finding reasons to support it, would have driven him to the right against every corrupt influence that could have been brought to bear upon him. But the truth is, no idea opposite to that of his utmost purity as a judge, was ever associated with his name. There was something in his character, conversation, manner

---

* This reference to geology reminds the writer that he once, several years ago, came across an extended article on the geology of Niagara Falls and the lake region, by Judge Gibson. It was contained in a bound volume of pamphlets in the library of the late G. L. B. Fetterman, Esq., of Pittsburgh. It had originally been published in Philadelphia in some magazine of which, if the writer is not mistaken, Prof. Silliman was the editor; the date was about 1835. The article was prefaced by a rather depreciatory editorial note, the editor evidently seeking to shirk the responsibility of entertaining the views, as he expressed it, of "his friend," who while he might be learned in other departments, was liable to err in the fields of science, where he had no right to stray. No name being mentioned, it appeared to be an anonymous production. At the time of finding this article the writer was specially interested in the geology of the lake region, of which much was then known, the result of government surveys, etc. "What amusing vaporings concerning the geology of the lake region must have existed in 1835;" and with this reflection we began reading the supposed anonymous article. Having read a few pages in which the author had well opened his subject, and enunciated clear conceptions of the principles of the science in which he dealt, we turned back to make sure that the date was 1835. There was no mistake as to that. Farther along we were struck with the acuteness of his observations, and all through with his conciseness and agreeable style. "Who was this," we kept constantly thinking, "editorially suppressed American Hugh Miller?" "Silliman surely was mistaken, or did not know his friend was far in advance of his times." Thus we read on to the close with interest and considerable profit, but if ever a grandson was not only surprised but gratified, the writer was, when at the end there appeared the signature, J. B. Gibson.

and appearance, which would have crushed such a thought in the bud. A man who had approached him for the purpose of corrupting him, would have been as much disposed to fall down before him in an act of homage as to have attempted to carry out his purpose. After a lifetime devoted to the service of his country, it is surely no mean praise of a public man, that declarations like these can be uttered, with the certainty that they will be credited, not less by the suitors against whom he decided, than by the profession who practiced before him, and the community whose laws he enforced.

There was another feature in his character, which is, though it should not be, worthy of passing notice. I refer to his delicate sense of pecuniary obligation. He remained at the bar for too short a period, if he had been actively employed, to accumulate property. Of the smallness of his salary, during his entire judicial term, the reader is probably aware.* His hospitality through life was so generous

---

* His highest salary was $2,000 per annum, with per diem expenses in addition to this sum, making his salary equivalent to about $2,500 per annum. Judge Porter might have added, "an honest man is the noblest work of God." But while such virtue is possessed, no doubt, by many individuals, it is so concealed as to be seldom appreciated among the living. Nevertheless it is a pleasure to have the fact of its existence demonstrated in our honored dead. Judge Black so spoke of Gibson's character in this respect in his eulogy that it may be permissible, by way of illustration, to quote a paragraph from a letter of Judge Gibson to his wife, written not long before his death. He says: "I have not sent you back the tax paper, as it seems to be according to the return I have made to the assessors; but it has increased my tax fearfully. It is better, however, to deal fairly in these matters." Another to him, from the celebrated Dr. J. T. Sharpless, of Philadelphia, dated May 15, 1844, covers another point referred to by Judge Porter:

"My friend, the Chief Justice, has been rather ahead of the time in paying a bill before it was sent, but it is only in accordance with everything I have had the pleasure to know of him, and I give him my thanks for that, in addition to the thousand obligations heretofore received from him. If all men were such, this would be a delightful world to live in, and the practice of medicine, instead of being a thorny path, would be a garden of flowers."

as to be universally remarked by his friends; and in
respect to all appliances of domestic comfort, his views
partook of the liberality of a man of fortune. Notwithstanding this, it is believed that he was never known to
borrow money, or contract an obligation which he did not
promptly discharge. At his death he bequeathed for the
support of his family no inconsiderable sum, produced
chiefly by the rise of small investments which had been
made from time to time. He had evidently studied on
principle, and studied successfully, the art of living on his
means, however small, and by living very comfortably on
his means. The case contrasts strongly with that of some
of our distinguished public characters. Men who would
have resented indignantly an imputation on their integrity,
have displayed in this respect a recklessness of conduct
which ought to be humiliating to the nation. For the
sake of the public morals, the facts can be referred to
only in the general, but instances have not been rare in
which public men, by contracting debts which they never
intended to discharge, and accepting loans of money which
they never intended to repay, have been content to live
upon the charity of those whose interests their public sta-
tions required them to act, an evil bad enough anywhere,
and one which would be intolerable in those whose duty
it is to urge, on every moral ground, and to enforce by
every legal means, performance of the obligations of others.

I hasten to a close. In *Bash vs. Sommer*, 8 Harris,
159, Judge Gibson delivered his last reported opinion,
which, singularly enough, was the affirmance of a judgment
pronounced by the judge who was to be his successor. In
the March number of the American Law Register for
1853, he published his last essay, in a review of Mr.

Troubat's work on Limited Partnership. It is a compact and elegant specimen of that kind of writing, and will repay perusal. I quote from it the following passage, both for the sake of the subject and the light which it reflects on the taste of the author: "Of all legal mechanism, statutory mechanism is the most imperfect; and this is one of the strongest objections to American codification. It is always adapted to the circumstances of a single case in the mind's eye of the constructor; and when it is required to work on any other, it works badly or not at all. A legislator who has but one model, is like a shoemaker who has but one last. It is this propensity to generalize that leads to perpetual tinkering at the statutes, till they are at last a wretched piece of unintelligible patchwork. This would be prevented by not attempting to do too much, and leaving the rest to the courts. The writer of this article is not a champion of the civil law, nor does he profess to have more than superficial knowledge of it. He was bred in the school of Littleton and Coke, and he would be sorry to see any but common law doctrines taught in it. Water and oil would as readily coalesce, as the technicalities of our law of real property and the simplicity of the Roman law. The principles of the latter require adaptation to the English law of contracts and personal property; but it cannot be denied that when they were adapted to it they enriched it. In France, Italy, Germany, Spain, Scotland, where the Roman law is the basis of the municipal law, it required adaptation to the habitudes of the people; but the English Law Merchant —an unperishable monument of Lord Mansfield's fame— shows what a magnificent structure may be raised upon it, where the ground is not preoccupied."

22

I have said this was his last published essay. The soundness of the great physical and mental machine which had performed its office for so many years was beginning to be affected. While the intellectual fire burned with brightness, the body was yielding to the consuming touch of time, and the pressure of some hidden malady. Early in the spring of 1853* his step became evidently less firm, and his face more haggard. Business began to lose its excitement, and society its charm. The inquiries of acquaintances became more frequent, and the friends who were nearest his heart began to draw more closely to him. In a short time it became necessary to summon about him the immediate members of his family. All that human sympathy and affection have in them to assuage, and all that professional skill and care have in them to alleviate, were vainly exerted to the verge of their power. The silver thread had been spun to its end, and without a murmur or a pain, he gently slept in death. He died in Philadelphia on the third day of May, 1853, in the seventy-third year of his age.

I have probably no more information than the reader, of Judge Gibson's views on that vital subject before which the splendors of human achievement die out in insignificance. He was not a man to say much on such a topic. It is known that he was attached to the doctrines of the Episcopal Church. During his residence in Wilkesbarre, and afterwards in Carlisle, he acted as an officer in that institution, and attended on its worship with regularity. A

---

* Judge Porter seems to have been unaware of the fact that Judge Gibson suffered an attack of cholera in the summer of 1852, whilst at Sunbury, Pa., and from the effects of which he never wholly recovered. His case was so critical at that time that his family was summoned from Carlisle to his bedside.

friend with whom he generally sat in attending church in Philadelphia, testifies to the emotion which he frequently evinced under the preaching of the gospel. On the death of a most estimable lady, at whose house he had been a frequent visitor, he observed in a letter to her son that her vast superiority in intellectual force surprised him less than her unostentatious and orthodox piety pleased him; and adds: "the testimony of a mind so competent to investigate and to judge, overbears, in my opinion, all the cavils of the philosophers." His belief in revealed religion is thus joined to that of all the more eminent men of the present century.* The rest is a question between himself and his final Judge. With it let not the stranger intermeddle. It is enough to hope, that when he laid aside the distinctions of earth he appeared in the spotless robe of imputed righteousness, a guest at the marriage supper.

I have thus concluded the observations I proposed to make on the life of Chief Justice Gibson. No succinct and general summary of his intellectual qualities has been attempted, for that has been already executed in a manner which renders any similar effort unnecessary and undesirable.†
I cannot hope that the reader has coincided in all the conclusions I have thus presented, or in the mode of reaching them. He may know other facts, or entertain different views of those which have been stated, or he may have preferred other selections from Judge Gibson's writings. In that event, I remind him that I have been communi-

---

* Judge Gibson once remarked to the effect that if it were ordered by the Creator, that concerning the divinity of Christianity it was to be left to be tried before a human court of last resort, he believed that applying the rules of law to the evidence concerning it, already known to us, its truth would, no doubt, be demonstrated.

† 7 Harris, 10, Judge Black's Eulogy.

cating my own sentiments, not his; and the truth is best
attained by the free and temperate expression of individual
thought. As an excuse for all that has been written, I
remind him further of what, if an attentive reader of history, he must have before observed—how much more frequently the historian is obliged to rely for his authority on
the fugitive publications of the day in which he writes, and
especially on those of a biographical kind, than on the
more elaborate treatises of preceding authors. Indeed, the
former are the chief means of correcting the errors or misstatements into which the writers of history, beyond all
other men, are liable to betrayal. It seems probable that
Pennsylvania will some day have a history, and somebody
to write it. Considering the character of her early settlements, the size of her territory, her position in the Union,
her exemption, on the one hand, from slavery, and on the
other, from fanaticism in politics and infidelity in religion,
the physical and moral character of her people, her progress
in the useful arts, and the extent to which the advantages
of education are being carried by her direct action as a
State; and comparing her with the ancient republics, with
Switzerland, with Scotland, or with England, there seems no
reason to doubt that she is capable of reaching as high an
elevation as any free State which has preceded her in the
march of nations. In the history that shall mark her rise
and progress, the course of her jurisprudence will form an
important topic; for in a free state, more than any other,
the bench is the great bulwark of civil liberty. In such a
work the name of Judge Gibson must appear. For more
than forty years his influence on that jurisprudence was
such, and the juncture which that period formed in the history of our laws was such, and the character of his indi-

vidual opinions was such, that no historical writer of mere taste, whatever his own opinions or prejudices, could omit his name and labors, unless resolutely bent on suppressing the truth. All this belongs to the future. For the present, I have simply strewn along the road a few facts and considerations, happy if at any time they may be found to serve this or any other useful purpose.

JUDGE BLACK'S NOTICE OF PORTER'S ESSAY.

A copy of Judge Porter's " Essay on the life, character and writings of John B. Gibson, LL. D.," reached the hands of Thomas J. Keenan, Esq., then, and for some years afterwards, editor of the Pittsburgh *Legal Journal*. Mr. Keenan happening to mention the fact to Chief Justice Black, who was in the city at that time, the Judge requested the privilege of writing a notice of it for the *Journal*. While highly laudatory of both Gibson and his biographer, the paper is characteristic of its powerful and profound author. We see him here wearing the editorial disguise, and in the character of the peaceful critic; but as he moves along, the clang, clang, of the weapons of a great judicial warrior are distinctly heard beneath the scanty covering.

From the Pittsburgh *Legal Journal*, 1855.

" Undoubtedly Gibson was the judge whose reputation overshadows all others. His great intellectual superiority gives him a prominence among men of his class, which it is not likely will be attained by anybody else for centuries to come, while his unblemished integrity, the simplicity of his character and the kindness of his heart, have won for him a fervor of affection which is seldom bestowed on any public man.

When he first came on the bench, he was scarcely prepared for his mission. Those who came with him and after him, were as thoroughly furnished as they could be for the work they had to do. But when his powers unfolded themselves, all saw so plainly that no man who sat with him afterwards could pretend to be his equal, without becoming ridiculous. Competition gave up the contest, and rivalry itself conceded to him an undisputed pre-eminence. In saying this, we hope we are free from the slightest disposition to depreciate his associates. Most of them have fairly earned a high character and are justly entitled to their share of distinction. We detract nothing from them when we give his dues to him. They had their virtues and their talents, but when we say that he was their chief, we mean the word in a sense which can never be applied so fitly to another.

> 'He, above all the rest,
> In shape and gesture proudly eminent,
> Stood like a tower.'

The Grecian mythology tells us that in old days there were giants, very large indeed, when compared with ordinary mortals, but small, nevertheless, when they came to be measured by the king of the Titans.

Of such a character, it is fit that the dignity should be vindicated and the value made known. The State can have no better thing to be proud of. In all her store she has no richer jewel to display than the fame of such a son.

Mr. Porter has performed this duty in a manner which entitles him to the thanks of every citizen. He brings to the task a mind deeply impressed with a sense of Gibson's immense intellectual strength. He has examined and analyzed his opinions with great care and much critical skill. His personal habits, modes of thought, and style of expression, are described and illustrated with the utmost felicity. There is, besides, a warmth of personal affection for his subject pervading the whole book which infinitely heightens the interest of the reader. Yet this essay is not an eulogy. The author felt the full force of his obligation to speak no more than the truth. He evidently blames with regret, but he tempers his praise wherever justice requires him to do so.

We think we have detected some slight inaccuracies in Mr. Porter's book. For instance, Mr. Gibson's marriage (page 43) is said to have taken place on the 12th of October, 1812, and his appointment as judge of the eleventh district on the 16th of July, 1813. He was married after he became judge of the common pleas. We make this statement on authority which does not permit us to doubt it. This is very unimportant, to be sure; but there is a graver mistake on page 83, where the writer suffers his Philadelphia education to get the better of him, so far as to endorse a sneer at Judge Gibson's remark in *Logan vs. Mason*, 6 W. & S., 12, on the Land Law of Pennsylvania. Gibson had called it 'a beautiful system founded on principles of general equity.' But the practitioners in the metropolis thought it 'a budget of augers, a collection of sharp points and short corners, having no pretensions to form and comeliness;' and Mr. Porter says it requires *charity* to make one believe that Gibson was right. Now, we take it upon ourselves to assure Mr. Porter that the rules upon which original titles to land are determined in this State, are as simple and clear as the nature of the subject will allow. They are perfectly just and equitable, and they add infinite honor to the wisdom and honesty of the men by whom they were established. They are as well systematized, and quite as consistent with one another, as those which regulate the marine insurance, or the purchase and sale of chattels. We say this with some confidence and without drawing upon anybody's charity, because we have the authority of Gibson, and many others who understand the matter very well, while Mr. Porter, on the other hand, admits that 'the practitioners of the metropolis have almost no acquaintance' with it. We do not expect our metropolitan friends, or anybody else, to admire that which they do not understand. We take leave, however, to suggest that the Land Law may possibly improve in their opinion upon further acquaintance. At all events, they can then speak upon it with a voice more potential. Fielding once wrote a long essay, in which he proved that a person will not be in danger of deciding any question much the more erroneously for knowing a little about it.

But enough of this. When we began this article, nothing was further from our thoughts than finding fault with Mr. Porter's book. We have read it with unmixed pleasure, and so we are sure will every one else who admires Judge Gibson's character, and desires to see it discussed ably and well. We shall only add, as the sum of our opinions on the whole matter, that the greatest American judge has found a writer qualified to do his memory justice.

Mr. Porter has not convinced us that there is much resemblance between Gibson and John Foster. Among the great writers of the English language there is one, and but one, whose mode of enforcing or defending truth will make a fair parallel. We omit the name for the present, simply because we have not time or space to prove it, and the assertion without the proof would hardly be received."*

* This remark naturally excites curiosity to know of whom Judge Black was thinking. Under the date of October 12th, 1883, Judge James J. Mitchell, now on the Supreme Bench, addressed a note of inquiry to Mr. Keenan, directed to this point, at the close remarking: "The judgment of so well read a man in English literature, and himself so great a master of style and language, is in the highest degree interesting, and I should like to make a memorandum of it in my copy of Judge Porter's memoirs."

Mr. Keenan answered, suggesting the name of Calhoun, to which Judge Mitchell replied: "I do not think it was Calhoun that Black referred to; I rather infer that it was some great English writer. Since the receipt of your letter I have had a conversation with Judge Porter, and he told me he had once asked Black the same question—whom he referred to, and Black said, as he had written, 'Well, you won't agree with me, and I haven't time to prove it to you, but some time I will.'"

Upon the receipt of this Mr. Keenan enclosed the correspondence to Lieutenant Governor Chauncey F. Black, thinking that he might know to whom his father referred. A reply came, under date of October 23, 1883, in which the Lieutenant Governor said, "I am very sorry to say that I am unable even to guess to whom my father alluded in that passage referred to by you and by Judge Mitchell." It is therefore probable that Judge Mitchell's question will never be answered.

23

PART FOURTH.

ARTICLE UPON JUDGE GIBSON, FROM THE MERCERSBURG QUARTERLY REVIEW.

REVIEW OF JUDGE PORTER'S ESSAY.

By the Rev. Joseph Clark.

The following review of Judge Porter's essay on Judge Gibson is from the January number, 1856, of the *Mercersburg Quarterly Review*. The author signed himself simply "J. C., Chambersburg, Pa." Throughout his paper, but more particularly in his scholarly comparison of the methods and style of John Foster and Judge Gibson, "J. C." displays a richness and copiousness in his diction with such philosophical treatment, in the very school in which Judge Black, Judge Porter and himself places Judge Gibson, that we leave him with the regret that he had not attempted the larger work which he recommends should be undertaken by the future historian. He seems to have been eminently qualified for such a task.

With the desire to discover his name, as well, also, to learn something of his competency, by personal acquaintance or otherwise, to substantiate the charge he makes against Judge Gibson, to the effect that he indulged in profanity,

the writer referred the matter to his friend, the Hon. John
Stewart, of Chambersburg, and received the following reply
to his communication, under date of February 2d, 1887:

"My belief is that the article referred to was written by
the Rev. Joseph Clark. I can give no other reason for
the belief than that Mr. Clark was a contributor to the
Review, was a gentleman of the highest literary qualifications, and was a resident of Chambersburg. I know of no
one, and I never knew of any one with the initials 'J. C.'
with the necessary qualifications, who could by any possibility
have contributed the article, excepting Mr. Clark.

"He was a Presbyterian clergyman and died about
1864. I am persuaded that he is the author of the article
in question. As to his opportunities of knowing the traits
and peculiarities of Judge Gibson I know but little. He
came originally from Perry county, and I have always
understood that Perry county was the place of Judge Gibson's birth. He could hardly have been himself a personal
acquaintance of Judge Gibson, and could not have spoken
from personal knowledge. Most likely he gave evidence to
the popular rumors he heard as a boy in respect to this
matter."

In regard to this, the writer thinks from J. C.'s evident familiarity with Judge Gibson's early home, that he
came from Perry county, and was, without doubt, acquainted
with Judge Gibson's oldest brother, Francis, for he corrects
misstatements of Judge Porter concerning him. Francis
Gibson was known far and wide through those mountains,
whereas Judge Gibson was only an occasional visitor there
after the death of his mother in 1809.

Mr. Clark's paper is presented entire, excepting his more
extensive quotations from Judge Porter's essay, which can be

referred to in the copious selections made from the essay itself in another part of this Memoir.

In Perry county, Pa., which, until 1820, was a portion of Cumberland county, on one of the old roads leading most of the way along the rugged and shady banks of the Sherman's creek, to Landisburg, one of the oldest settlements of the valley, and the first county-seat, is a place still familiarly known as "Gibson's," because yet occupied by some of the descendants of the family. It is a quiet, romantic nook, formed by the curvature of the towering pine-clad hills, just below a narrow pass which leads out into the more spacious and fruitful valley which lies to the west. A small stone mill, which bears the marks of time and of fire, the ruins of several small out-buildings, a finger-board pointing in several directions on the roads leading out through the ravines, and a tolerably comfortable dwelling, are now the principal artificial features of the place. A little distance below, an immense rock, or pile of rocks, whose base starts at the edge of the water, towers high into the air. About fifty feet from its base the road passes directly through its side, and as the traveler approaches this cut, and casts a suspicious eye towards the beetling crag overhanging him far above, and hears the roaring of the Sherman as it dashes upon the rocks of the deep gorge below, he will be fortunate if he escapes an involuntary shudder. This is known far and near as " Gibson's Rock."

The reader will have already anticipated the purport of this description. The scene itself is worthy of an artist's pencil. On a bright summer afternoon, as the sun declines

to the west, and his beams, flashing on the rippling waters,
catch the eye through the openings in the umbrageous
canopy of leaves, and the huge forms of nature repose in
an almost oppressive silence on every hand, it forms a scene
which would perhaps out-rival many that are more widely
celebrated.   But it has a deeper and better interest to the
initiated.   It marks the birth-place of one of Pennsylvania's
greatest ornaments, of one who, in the language of a competent judge, has been thought, even abroad, to have been
for many years "the great glory of his native State." In
its leading features it resembles the birth-place of James
Buchanan, in the western angle of Franklin county, amid
the same range of mountains, not fifty miles distant, in a
narrow pass known as "the Gap," through which the pack-
horses in "auld lang syne," defiled to "Fort Pitt" and
the "far West."   When John Bannister Gibson, who was
destined to wear, with unapproachable success and honor, the
judicial ermine of Pennsylvania, was about leaving his wild
mountain home on the banks of the Sherman, to enter an
already well known classical institution of his native county,
James Buchanan, who, in another sphere, was destined to
gain the honorable distinction of "Pennsylvania's favorite
son," was prattling with the rough packers in "the Gap,"
and strolling (so says an irresponsible tradition), with a
small bell tied round his neck, in the neighboring woods.
When the history of Pennsylvania comes to be written—
and it must be written some day, for her advantageous
position in the Union, her inexhaustible resources, the blended
and sterling character of her population, alike removed by
constitutional bias from the extremes of headlong and
impracticable impetuosity, and phlegmatic stagnation, necessi-
tate for her a healthy development, a high position, and a

commanding influence—when this history comes to be written, few, if any, names will appear in it with more prominence than those of the boy from the valley of the Sherman, and the bell-boy of the Gap, for the history of a state or a nation is always inseparable from the history of its great men.   *   *   *   *   *   *

A great mind is always a subject of study, generally for admiration. Like Niagara or Vesuvius, its massive grandeur attracts alike the eye of the divine, the statesman, the poet, the philosopher, and the man of ordinary practical intelligence; or, like the giant elm of centuries amid the smaller trees of the forest, it is the "observed of all observers," whilst weaker creatures find shelter and protection within the folds of its mighty arms. Living, productive thought, in any sphere, is a commodity of priceless worth. For these reasons we offer no apology for introducing a paper upon Chief Justice Gibson into this periodical. Theologian, or literary man, in the ordinary acceptation of the term, he was not; but he was a great intellect, and (which is nearer the drift of our review) he was in the organic structure of his mind a great philosopher.

Of the essay by Mr. Porter, we would say here, briefly, that it is a respectable, but by no means an adequate performance. It displays considerable discrimination and accuracy of criticism, and we think touches truthfully upon the strong points of its subject's mind and character; but it is not exhaustive; and the selections from his published opinions give mere glimpses of the workings of his mind. An intellect like Judge Gibson's, and a long life of such eminence as was awarded him, cannot be disposed of in an octavo of 140 pages. We agree with Mr. Porter, that it is remarkable that no more has been written respecting

him since his death, and we hope that the essay before us
may be the forerunner of a comprehensive and complete
life, embodying an extensive selection from his writings.
True, his mind stands sculptured in monumental grandeur
in his published judicial opinions, running through seventy
volumes of the Pennsylvania State Reports, from 2 Sergeant & Rawle to 7 Harris; and no detrition of time,
nor heavings and tossings of the political hemisphere, which
shall span at all the fabric of our jurisprudence, will be
able to destroy it as it there stands.   But in this form it
will be confined to the offices of lawyers; whilst we are
persuaded that the Nestor of the bench, " the only chief
whom the hearts of the people would know," even after
he assumed officially a lower position, ought, in his posthumous influence, to be brought nearer to the people themselves.   We are persuaded that a selection might be made
from Justice Gibson's opinions, and other fugitive writings,
which would be read by that portion of all classes and
professions who are accustomed to seek and peruse the
highest productions of the human mind.

One of the most interesting points in the life of Judge
Gibson is the history of the development of his mind.
As there are certain great classes or types of minds which can
be arranged together with almost generic accuracy, so there
are minds which require peculiar occasions for development.
Other minds seem to have a sort of spontaneity of expansion.
They develop from the free working of their own inher-
ent powers, without the aid of any extraneous stimuli.
But it is not so with all; and it often appears doubtful
whether this other class would develop at all, in any measure correspondent with their native capability, without the
stimuli of occasion and circumstance.   To this latter class

the mind of Gibson belonged. His bodily habit was phlegmatic, and it had its influence upon his mind, and contributed, doubtless, to the lateness of the mature development of his powers, as well as hazarded their development upon the accidents of occasion.* Although, as Mr. Porter says, the burning of Dickinson College destroyed all record of his progress there, yet tradition has preserved some scraps which those who knew him in after life will regard as easily credible. He was called notoriously lazy, and was often almost wholly indifferent about the regular tasks of the course; but his classmates well knew that when he roused himself, under the pressure of a special emergency, he could surpass them all. He was, moreover, the butt of a good deal of innocent ridicule. He was long-legged, raw-boned and awkward, and furnished the point to many a jest, though it is remembered that due care was always exercised, by those who had come to know him, not to carry the fun beyond the point of endurance.† At college, though all the discerning noticed his spasmodic ability, he was generally regarded as a student who had not much "outcome" in him. That he was at first almost wholly unsuccessful at the bar, might be inferred from his numerous and rapid changes, from Carlisle to Beaver, from

---

* Another modern instance of late development is that of Archbishop Hughes. J. C.

† In his letter to John Wallace (see page 25), Judge Gibson says: "Fox hunting, fishing, gunning, rifle shooting, swimming, *wrestling* and *boxing* with the natives of my age, were my exercises and my amusements." At college he must have been six feet or more in height, and with the above mentioned accomplishments previously acquired, he was not likely to suffer much. It is probably the fact, however, that at this age he was awkward, and there can be no doubt that he was a frank, open-hearted young man, of a forgiving nature, of the kind which meaner spirits can, and often do, impose upon for a long time. He was the same kind of a man all his life.

24

Beaver to Hagerstown, from Hagerstown back to Carlisle, all in the space of a little more than two years. We fancy that but few young advocates in such circumstances would not begin to fear that they had missed their calling. He had indeed missed his calling, but he was on the stepping stone to it. He never would have made a successful advocate. The movements of his mind were not rapid enough; he had not patience enough to wade through the wilderness of dry facts which the thoroughly furnished attorney must thread; his profound dealing with the seminal principles of law and justice, had he ever attained to this in the sphere of an advocate, would have been over the heads of most juries; he had little or none of that popular tact for influencing juries, which multitudes even of infinitely inferior men possess; and above all, the profession of attorney would not have afforded stimulus, propulsive force enough, to have driven him onward in the path of development. He would have wasted his powers upon inferior pursuits.   *   *

Doubtless Mr. Gibson's legislative career was instrumental to his first appointment to the bench. He now entered a new sphere, and his true sphere, the aptness of which to develop his best powers, we shall see by and by. It requires no effort of the imagination to suppose that the responsibility of the judgeship resting upon one of his age (he was not quite 33), who doubtless felt the inadequacy of his own attainments, would rouse his mind to unwonted effort, and compel him not only to think but to study. How he discharged his duties we do not know. He began, however, to attract the attention of the eminent in the profession. But tradition is again in character when it reports,

that he exhibited "too much impulsiveness in his judgments, both of legal affairs and of human nature."*

His appointment to the supreme bench as an associate
justice, three years after his first appointment, seems really
to have been the first thing that fully roused his intellect,
and fired his ambition. He now commenced to study in
earnest.† He seemed to have formed the resolution, a resolution the offspring of a mind at length made conscious
of the possession of a vast, but slumbering power, to make
himself master of the law as a science. He resolved to
go down among the lowest foundations of that system,
upon the higher scaffolding of which he was now called to
labor as an architect, that acquainting himself well with
the shape and structure of the whole building, he might
know precisely how to lay on each additional stone.   He
withdrew himself, to a great extent, from general society;
he wore often a look of abstraction and indifference to per-

---

* Mr. Clark's ideas derived from "tradition" are in discord with the statements made by the writer in the *Wilkesbarre True Democrat*. See page 49.

† It is not to be doubted that the powers of Judge Gibson's mind were not
developed to their maximum until long after this period.   His published opinions are witnesses to this fact.   Nevertheless we think that both Judge Porter
and the Rev. Mr. Clark, if they do not overdraw the picture in their actual
statements, present at least an exaggerated contrast to their reader's mind. Thus,
to say that his appointment to the supreme bench was "the first thing that fully
roused his intellect, and fired his ambition," is not exactly correct.   Clark has
pictured him almost a booby at college, yet notwithstanding his peripatetic
experience in Beaver and Hagerstown, he returned to Carlisle to practice law,
and after six years is sent to the legislature (nine years after his graduation),
and at the age of thirty-three we find him appointed a judge.   True, Governor
Snyder, who appointed him, was married to a relative, and this may have had
some influence in the appointment, but there appears, however, to have been no
opposition to his so doing.   In the legislature he was on the judiciary committee,
and it was no doubt his experience there which determined the governor in making
the appointment.   These advancing steps must surely have "fired his ambition"
to a very considerable extent.   But Judge Porter and Mr. Clark are speaking
most probably only in relative terms, but if so, should have qualified the form of
their expressions, to have avoided creating with some of their readers erroneous
impressions.

sons and things around him, and he devoted himself to the
most difficult authors with an assiduity which most astonished those who knew him best.   All the evidence to be
had in the case seems to indicate that his study of the pro-
founder and more difficult principles of the science, was
mainly pursued within a few years after his elevation to
the bench of the Supreme Court.   *   *   *   *

His appointment to the office of chief justice was the
last stimulus that his mind received, which, though not different in kind from that under which he had been moving
for ten years, was different in degree; and from it his
powers seem to have received fresh impulse. He was now
at an age at which many men have reached, if not passed,
the acme of their power, but he was yet far from his.
From this time forward the chief improvement is seen in his
style, and the condensation of thought exhibited in his
opinions. His style now began to assume a massiveness,
compactness and polish, which bespeak unerringly the concentration of mind which his habits of study were acquiring
for him.   *   *   *   *   *   *

To use an expression of his own, in *Lyle vs. Richbards*,
with a different application, it was in his power to lay his
hands on it, and "while it was yet in the gristle, to bend
it and mold it at his pleasure." When Judge Gibson
ascended the bench the compass of our jurisprudence was
vastly narrower than now. All the forms and interests of
society, industrially, politically and legally, were far less
complicated than at present. Questions arose, and decisions
were required during the course of his labors, which could
not possibly have had a precedent. Forty years ago we had
no commercial law. The State had then no chartered bank
out of Philadelphia, and only three in that city. Partner-

ship, negotiable paper, insurance, transportation, and liability
in general, were terms of very different meaning and application then from what they bear now. The two main
departments of the law were those of special pleading and
real estate. Much of the business of the courts consisted
in the settlement of titles of land. With these his studies
chiefly commenced, and he not only completely mastered
them afterwards, but mastered, we might almost say created,
other branches as they arose. It was his thorough understanding of the system, and his confidence in his own perceptions of the beautiful, that emboldened him to declare in
the face of the criticism which he knew it would evoke,
that "he knew no more beautiful system, nor one more
founded on principles of equity, than the land laws of
Pennsylvania." When we remember that such was Pennsylvania jurisprudence then, and glance at what it is now, and
remember that for nearly forty years he was the leading mind
on the bench of its highest tribunal, the one whose opinions
are quoted as authority more frequently than those of all
his contemporaries put together, it will give us a bird's-eye
view of what he has done.   *   *   *   *   *

The other case is that well known as the "Presbyterian Church case." In 1801 a "Plan of Union" was
adopted between the General Assembly of the Presbyterian
Church and the General Association of Connecticut (Con-
gregational), which was designed to secure the co-operation
of these two branches of the Protestant church in their
missionary work in the "new settlements." But like all
unions which grow not out of a community of organic life, it
was found to generate trouble and discord. The effort to
amalgamate principles "as immiscible as water and oil" (to
quote Judge Gibson), only operated to damage both of

them. An element was introduced into the Presbyterian Church which was foreign to its organic life, an element which could not be assimilated and must be thrown off. This was what the Assembly of 1837 did in passing what are known as "the exscinding acts," legislative ordinances by which the "Plan of Union" was dissolved, and the Synods of Utica, Genessee, Geneva and Western Reserve, which grew out of the said plan, declared "to be out of the ecclesiastical connection of the Presbyterian Church of the United States of America," and the Presbyterian elements in said synods ordered "to attach themselves to the nearest presbyteries." These acts formed a party in the Presbyterian Church resolved to assert the prerogatives of the exscinded synods, and the "tug of war" came in the General Assembly of 1838. At this Assembly commissioners from the four synods presented themselves, and the Assembly refusing to acknowledge them, a revolutionary party undertook to seize the reins of ecclesiastical government, organized themselves as the General Assembly, and after retiring to a separate room proceeded to exercise all the supposed functions of the Assembly. Among these was the election of their own trustees to secure the perpetuity of the corporation under the laws of Pennsylvania. The trustees elected by the former Assemblies and by the other Assembly (the Old School) refused to surrender to their rivals "the franchises, offices, privileges and liberties" conferred on them by law "as Trustees of the General Assembly of the Presbyterian Church in the United States of America." Upon this refusal an action of law was brought, and the case tried before Judge Rogers and a special jury at the Nisi Prius for Philadelphia, on the 4th day of March, 1839. The case was one "without precedent and presenting some extraordinary features," and it occasioned intense interest in every part of the Union. The Nisi Prius jury, under the charge of Judge Rogers, found a verdict against the defendants, which, if it had stood, would have had the effect of declaring the trustees elected by the New School body the true, legal and proper trustees of the General Assembly. Sixty-five reasons for a new trial were filed, and the case argued the same month before the court *in banc*, and the Chief Justice pronounced the opinion of the Court. Their decision made the rule for a new trial absolute. Here we quote Mr. Porter: [Omitted, see Porter's Essay, page 142 of this Memoir.]

*   *   *   *   *   *   *

That opinion (see 4 Wharton, page 598) is indeed a masterpiece. Its opening sentence is eminently characteristic, and shows how vigorously his powerful mind had been working through the case: "To extricate the question from the multifarious mass of irrelevant matter in which it is enclosed," etc. The case we believe to have been one eminently suited to his peculiar powers, and none but he could have dealt with it so thoroughly. He shows, with most searching analysis, that the abrogation of the "Plan of Union" as a legislative act of the Assembly was perfectly constitutional and valid; that the commissioners from the exscinded synods were not entitled to seats in the Assembly after the Act of 1837; that the proceedings of the minority in the Assembly of 1838 were in violation of the established order, and hence a forfeiture of constitutional rights and titles; and that their trustees were not trustees of the General Assembly of the Presbyterian Church, which though not itself a corporation, is the reproductive organ of corporate succession, according to its charter.

In this decision and opinion, Judge Gibson rendered a service of incalculable importance to the whole country. The finding of the Nisi Prius jury would have perpetuated a great and most flagrant wrong. It would have put a schismatical and revolutionary branch in possession of the true lineal succession of the Presbyterian Church, so far as that could be done by the civil law. It would have legitimated revolution and disorder, and might have proved the entering wedge to consequences of which it would have been impossible to have foreseen the end.   *   *

He combined to an unusual degree the *perceptive* and the *logical* faculties. His intuitions were clear, strong and comprehensive, and his logical processes from ascertained data were sure and steady, though not characterized by the minute syllogystic method of the mere logician. The perceptive or intuitive faculties of his mind predominated, and hence had his calling lay in that sphere he would have been a philosopher of the Platonic rather than of the Aristotelian school. He grasped, with a far-reaching intuition, great principles or universal facts, and he took in at once all their bearings and relations, and applied them with matchless and almost unerring skill to any particular matter in hand. He had little taste or patience for mere hair-splitting; and though unsurpassed, in his sphere, in the discrimination with which he stated a point, yet he had no fondness for those discriminations which rest on a distinction without a difference. Hence the epithet which most accurately describes his caste of mind and style, is philosophical rather than metaphysical. His mind was well fitted to reflect intelligently on the most elevated subjects of human knowledge, and to represent clearly and coherently the ideas thus attained, whilst at the same time are wanting that overstrained subtlety, fine-spun sophistry, and unintelligible mysticism, which are so common in the department of what is technically called metaphysics. Metaphysics owes its parentage to Aristotle; philosophy is the offspring rather of the antagonistic school. His intellectual processes have been thus described: "His mental vision took in the whole outline and all the details of the case, and with a bold and steady hand he painted what he saw."* This is the highest exercise of a philosophical mind. Mr. Porter, in endeavoring to classify him amongst writers and thinkers, assigns him his place, generically, and correctly enough, among those whose fame rests upon treatises of a philosophical nature; but he finds no little difficulty, as is common in such cases, in naming one with whom he may exactly liken him. He finds points of resemblance in Johnson, Butler and Edwards, but no likeness. This he finds most nearly in John Foster. On this point we think his accuracy may be successfully challenged. There are doubtless points of resemblance, and these may be traced with much plausibility in some of Foster's essays, but there are points of great dissimilarity which can scarcely pass under the plea of allowance for the difference of sphere and of subject. There were elements in the structure of Foster's mind which were wholly wanting in Gibson's, and important elements in Gibson's which were wholly wanting in Foster's. In no sphere could Gibson have been found carefully elaborating such palpable absurdities, magnifying unimportant matters into matters of the first importance, and propounding plausible theories for nobody to adopt, as are to be found here and there in the writings of the great essayist. And though we are a

---

* Chief Justice Black's Eulogy, 7 Harris, page 11.

25

great admirer of Foster, and claim for him no second place among modern writers, in originality and power, yet we are free to assert for the Pennsylvania chief justice a sounder and safer mind in its organic structure.

Such being his intellectual conformation, the reader might almost predict, prior to actual ascertainment, what would be the department of his profession for which his powers were specially adapted, and in which his tastes would most luxuriate. To say that he was strikingly deficient in any of the great branches of the law would be a great mistake, and not in accordance with the universal character of his mind. But he was most at home in the sphere of *constitutional law*. The breadth and comprehensiveness of his views, and his tendency to rely upon the great principles of the science, rather than upon technicalities and decided cases, found here the sphere for their fittest exemplification. "In the fertile and extensive fields of American constitutional law, his powers exhibited to advantage the proportions which nature had given them, and he breathed out his great thoughts with the conscious freedom of a man who is master of the very ground which he occupies."*

He was a champion also of the common law. In speaking of Judge Kennedy he once said: "He clung to the common law as a child to its nurse, and how much he drew from it may be seen in his opinions, which, by their elaborate minuteness remind us of the overfullness of Coke."† Writers of eulogy and biography, as well as poets, sometimes unconsciously draw their own portraits as accurately as those of the departed. In this instance Judge Gibson, leaving out the idea contained in the last member of the sentence, furnished a master stroke for his own portraiture. The com-

---

* Porter's Essay, etc.   † 4 Barr, p. 6.

mon law is the evolution and product of great principles working through successive ages, and it may be called organic, when contrasted with the civil or statutory law, which may be called mechanical. * * * *

His style has often been spoken of as a model of judicial composition. Perhaps as such it has never been excelled. It combines richness, dignity, force, condensation and clearness in a remarkable manner. It abounds in illustrations, comparisons, metaphors and quoted maxims, but none of these seem to have been sought, but to spring up unbidden in the spontaneous workings of his mind, they seem indeed, at all times, to have been a constituent part of his mental processes. He never seemed to choose his language; it was the natural garb in which his thoughts clothed themselves, and the drapery always revealed the exact shape of the body it covered. * * * *

He seemed to use language at all times as the medium and servant of thought, at best an imperfect one, and one which he felt authorized to bend and readjust to suit his purposes. "The thoughts themselves were great thoughts struggling to make themselves felt through words, which, however well chosen, but obstructed them, and which were used at all only because better could not then be found." He had a habit which is always observable in men of original and profound minds, whose power of conception, perception and mental combination being so much superior to the average of the race, makes language as it is found to exist, a meagre and insufficient vehicle of their thoughts, viz., the habit of manufacturing words, and of using words in unusual significations. Mr. Porter has cited a number of these words, as 'unilateral,' 'individuate,' 'manipulating the testimony,' 'convergent intent,' etc. In a very cursory examination of some of his opinions, in search of such words, we picked out the following: 'questionless,' 'rebuttal,' 'inequity,' 'voidable,' 'intactible,' 'retropulsive,' 'remainderman.'* The list might be extended indefinitely.

This habit sometimes gives an undue stateliness to his style, and puts it above the heads of that class of readers who may not be able to resolve his Latin combinations. It suggests, also, that at some time in his life he had read with admiration the writings of Dr. Johnson. But his style is in a high degree artistic. It bears the impress of his æsthetical taste. It is like the creation of an artist whose power lay, not in airy Greek porticoes and Corinthian friezes, but in massive Roman arches, and ponderous domes, and heavy Gothic buttresses and clustered pillars.

We are disposed to receive with some abatement Mr. Porter's statement, a statement very common among certain orders of critical writers, that a writer's meaning should always be apparent at first sight. Clearness is certainly a desirable quality in authorship, but it must be remembered that it is a relative quality, and depends as much upon the power of perception in the reader as upon the language of the writer. "A man who has never seen the sun," says Calderon, "cannot be blamed for thinking that no glory can exceed that of the moon. A man who has seen neither moon nor sun cannot be blamed for talking

* It is curious that both Judge Porter and Mr. Clark consider some of these words strange, or coined. "Unilateral" is a botanical term in common use. "Individuate," "manipulating," "questionless," "voidable," "intactible," "retropulsive," are all in Webster's Dictionary. Judge Porter of course knew that "remainderman" was a law term. However, for the words "inequity" and "rebuttal," neither Webster nor Johnson gives them, and while both are now common words in law practice they are not to be found in Abbott's or Brown's Law Dictionary; it is possible, therefore, that Judge Gibson invented them.

of the unrivalled brightness of the morning star." The mass of readers, accustomed to little else than commonplace thought, will toss aside a masterwork upon the highest subjects of human knowledge in disgust at its obscurity, which, to a mind capable of comprehending it, will be not only sufficiently clear, but a perennial source of intellectual pleasure. We would undertake to find Mr. Porter any number of readers to whose minds the writings of Calvin, Owen, Locke, Tillotson (instances cited by him) would *not* "suggest their meaning at once." Away then with that silly catering to popular ignorance and prejudice (we speak not of Mr. Porter), which would compel every original and powerful thinker and writer to write in terms comprehensible by the unthinking and incapable masses. A great thought stuck out in a form comprehensible by only a few, will by and by reach the masses, in a shape suited for them, by the agency of men who could not have originated it. And if a reader finds the production of a great mind obscure, let him diligently consider whether the fault is in the writer or the reader. The great lights of succeeding ages have been those who were pronounced obscure in their own age.

The condensation of Judge Gibson's style is owing partly to his well known method of preparing his opinions. He had a horror of the pen. He seldom wrote except under the pressure of the most absolute necessity. He did all the needful thinking first. This he did in his chamber, on the street, at the table, on the bench, in the public room of his hotel, any place and every place, and in any attitude which ministered to the sluggishness of his body; and when he seized the pen he rarely laid it aside until the opinion was completed. Such a method, with such a mind as his, doubtless added to the compactness and directness of his style. His bold, beautiful and legible handwriting, free from erasure, induced the belief that he transcribed his opinions, which was rarely, if ever done.

Another feature of Judge Gibson's character, which all the testimony concurs to make prominent, was the benevolence and kindness of his heart. "His was a most genial spirit, affectionate and kind to his friends, and magnanimous to his enemies. Benefits received by him were engraved on his memory as on a tablet of brass; injuries were written in sand."*

We are sorry to be unable to record anything satisfactory respecting the *religious character* of the illustrious subject of the present sketch. In him as a man, a human denizen of earth, there is everything to admire; in him as an heir of immortality, and a subject of the government and gracious dispensations of God, there is much the want of which we mourn. The evidence which Mr. Porter has gathered of a religious element in his nature are very meagre: his attachment to the doctrines of the Episcopal Church, his occasional emotion under the preaching of the gospel, and a letter of condolence to a gentleman who had been bereaved of a most excellent mother. Against these, meagre as they are, the great blemish of his character, *profanity*, also a family heirloom, is a sad offset. We fear that like many of the leading minds of the day, engrossed in other pursuits, he passed the subject of religion *sub silento*.†

---

* Eulogy, 7 Harris, p. 13.

† The writer was born in Judge Gibson's house and lived there much of the time for nearly three years with his brothers and cousins, immediately preceding the judge's decease. He has also traveled on several occasions with the judge over the State in canal boat, stage-coach, and by rail, but under all the vicissitudes, dangers or annoyances in which he was placed, he never heard an oath, or the semblance of an oath, escape his lips. Judge Gibson naturally courted either the society of ladies or his books in his hours of recreation or

We venture a remark in conclusion respecting the principle of an elective judiciary which was engrafted on the
Constitution of Pennsylvania in the years 1848, 1849 and
1850. We shall not attack it on its broadest ground, nor

---

enforced idleness. The contrary is sometimes asserted, as elsewhere alluded to,
the result of confusing him with other persons. He was a regular attendant of
the services of the Protestant Episcopal Church; was baptized in mature years
in that faith, but was not a communicant. To every outward appearance he
was a Christian. Of the fifty or sixty of his private letters in the writer's possession every one breathes the language of a great, loving, tender and sympathetic
nature. In not one of them does he say aught against any of his fellow men. It
must be true of him, as Judge Black said, "Benefits received by him were
engraved on his memory as on a tablet of brass; injuries were written in sand,"
for malice and resentment, in the ordinary acceptation of those words, appeared
to have no abiding place in his nature. If Mr. Clark made a mistake, it came
from the head, scarcely from his heart, and the only serious evil resulting from
such charges is the necessity of replying to them. Judge Gibson probably
believed more in the common law of religion ("on these two things hang all the
law and the prophets") than in the statutory creeds and doctrines which some
men formulate and then use to lash their fellow men, whom they fail to make
agree with them. All this does no harm to those so happily constituted as
never to feel or experience the necessity of such lashings. But the charge of
profanity is something susceptible of argument, and permits of the admission
of testimony. On this point Col. Chas. McClure writes as follows: "I never
heard him swear, and think that 'J. C.,' in the article in the *Mercersburg
Quarterly Review*, must have confounded him in this particular with his brother,
the general, who swore at times, not like the army in Flanders, but like Uncle
Toby in 'Tristram Shandy.' I remember grandmother's indignation at the
statement in the *Quarterly* when she read it first, and she characterized it as
untrue."

Concerning his Christianity, the following may be of interest. In a letter
from Mrs. W. Milnor Roberts to her sister, Mrs. Anderson, the last mentioned of
whom was in Texas at the time of her father's death, Mrs. R. details the scenes
attending her father's last illness and death, and among other things says: "On
Monday afternoon (the day before his death) I asked him if he would not, to
gratify his dear children, see a clergyman. He said, 'What for, dear?' I replied,
'Dear pa, you know if we pray to God for you He will hear us in your behalf.' He
at once consented. I then named Dr. Ducachet, as Mr. Norris, our old pastor,
was very sick at the time. He was perfectly willing to see the doctor, and we at
once dispatched a note requesting him to come as soon as possible. Although pa
could speak but little, still his answers were to the point, and so satisfactory.
His noble intellect never deserted him, and each word he uttered was like a jewel
of inestimable value. Pa said he had no apprehensions concerning or fears of
death; he had thought long and seriously upon the subject, and could trust entirely
for his acceptance with God on the merits of our Saviour."

speak of it as an indication of that radical tendency of the age which has been gradually putting the power more immediately into the hands of the people, and thus changing our republicanism more and more into pure democracy; we shall interrogate it only upon one point—can such a man as Judge Gibson, or any other man, be kept, under this principle, on the supreme bench for thirty-seven years? That the judiciary may produce such men, and the glory of such distinguished attainment be cast upon the ermine of the commonwealth, it is absolutely necessary that a seat upon its bench be not an ephemeral position. Rotation in office would be utterly destructive of any such results. We not only seriously doubt whether Judge Gibson could have been nominated and elected when he was appointed to the supreme bench, but we doubt whether he could have been kept there for a succession of years, when in his highest vigor. The highest qualifications of a judge are of all others those which the people are least able to comprehend or appreciate, and the office is of all others the one which ought to be kept out of the arena of party strife. There is not a political party in this country which would hesitate for a moment to drop the name of such a man as Gibson from its ticket, if in a contest characterized by partisan zeal and clap-trap he did not seem to have the shallow qualification of availability. His nomination in 1851 was the result of strenuous exertion on the part of a few devoted personal friends, and two votes less than he received in convention would have lost to the State the remainder of his life, and this with all the prestige of his unqualified career with which to confront the claims of inferior men. *O tempora! O mores!*

Besides, there seems to be in Pennsylvania, as Mr. Porter remarks, a disposition to overthrow rather than to sustain men of distinguished ability. " It has long been the subject of remark both at home and abroad, that it seems only necessary for a man of more than ordinary capacity to appear in the politics of the State to be struck at by every other politician, both great and small." This narrow jealousy, and green-eyed envy of true greatness, made to bear upon the prejudices of the suspicious multitude, will be perpetually fatal to our production of eminent states- men, and may forever keep us from having a President, unless some medium man should "wake up some morn- ing and find himself famous." As long as this disposi- tion prevails in Pennsylvania it will be most unfit to select its supreme judges, and we shall despair of seeing the repetition of such a career as that of Chief Justice Gib- son. "If the same feeling had prevailed in Virginia and South Carolina, Massachusetts and Kentucky, where then had been the great lights of our firmament ?"

There is as much intellectual material in Pennsylvania as in any other of her sister commonwealths. In her popu- lation she presents as broad a basis as is to be found on this continent. She combines in admirable proportion the two most sterling races which have ever put foot upon these shores—the German and the Scotch-Irish. Nothing but a suicidal policy can dwarf her intellectual devel- opment in the bud. Let us hope for the best, and in the meantime let us be thankful for such a beacon-light as the name of John Bannister Gibson.

J. C.

CHAMBERSBURG, PA., 1856.

26

PART FIFTH.

IN MEMORIAM OF CHIEF JUSTICE GIBSON.

TRIBUTES FROM THE BENCH AND BAR.

The following extracts from the newspaper reports of various bar meetings on the occasion of the death of Judge Gibson are well worth preservation. While entirely eulogistic, the monotone of praise in the burnished sentences of some of Pennsylvania's ablest lawyers, many of whom have passed away never more to be heard before any earthly forum, cannot fail to be interesting.

They form a picture, as it were, of the generals and staff who stand at the bedside of a dying chieftain, fellow soldiers, and part of the history of his time. They represent all political parties, and among them were some of the warmest friends of Judge Gibson; but it is noticeable the infrequence of personal sketch and incident the speakers attempt, which makes it apparent that their subject had outgrown his fellows in the race of life, and fell at last, like the giant tree of the forest, prostrate to earth, dead and shattered, to lie beneath the friendly shade of its successors.

Such is life, and the moments attending the crash in death of the greatest are wisely selected by mankind to pause and pass in review the history so far 'accomplished.

In the court of Nisi Prius in Philadelphia, Judge Lewis presiding, May 3d, 1853, after remarks on Judge Gibson by Chas. B. Penrose, J. M. Read, and others (not reported), Judge Lewis said:

"I have heard with great satisfaction the testimony that has been borne by the gentlemen who have just addressed the court of the great grasp of intellect, the high judicial talents and profound learning that have characterized his distinguished career as a judge, and impressed his name upon the highest pages of the judicial history of the State and Union. Feeling as I do the deepest sorrow for his death, and respect for his memory, sitting as I do, in the seat which he occupied, and holding that branch of the court, in consequence of his sickness, which was peculiarly in his charge, I feel too painfully impressed with the melancholy event to be able to do justice to suitors before me. And in respect to his memory, the court will adjourn until Saturday next."

In Common Pleas, the same day, before Judge Allison, David Paul Brown, following the district attorney, said:

"Chief Justice Gibson occupied a high judicial position for nearly forty years. His intercourse with his brethren and the bar was always characterized by great kindness and courtesy, and in point of ability few occupants of the judicial seat have exhibited higher claims to professional and personal regard. During thirty years of my professional life my relations to him have been of the most friendly and affectionate character, and I cannot, therefore, but feel that this brief expression of regret for his loss, is, on my part, peculiarly appropriate and becoming."

Judge Thompson replied :

"The decisions of the Supreme Court for more than thirty years contain the indelible marks of his brilliant intellect. In extensive legal learning he was second to none, and the more we study his opinions the more deeply are we impressed with his capacity as a lawyer, his soundness and integrity as a judge.

"To the memory of such a man, closing a long life of usefulness and industry, we who have benefited by his labors should be the first to tender the deserved tribute."

It is proper to observe that the reports of the proceedings of both the bars at Philadelphia and Pittsburgh were greatly condensed. The newspapers of to-day on such occasions furnish more amplified reports of addresses.

At the bar meeting in Philadelphia presided over by Justice Grier, of the U. S. Circuit Court, Hon. J. M. Dallas and C. J. Ingersoll, vice presidents; Messrs. Wm. Rawle, J. Randall, Chas. Ingersoll and J. S. Cohen acted as secretaries.

J. Cadwallader, in moving the appointment of the committee to draft resolutions, said: "It was necessary to adopt more than the usual formal expressions of grief upon the decease of one who looked down upon jurisprudence as he did upon the other sciences, while others have to look up."

Speaking to the resolutions, Josiah Randall said :

"His judicial ermine has passed from him unspotted. No one of his day stood before the country in a more felicitous position, for his whole life consisted in devotion to his country. He was a great lawyer, and a great judge. It might be said he was a Hercules in intellect, with such great power of analysis as to make everything clear to the meanest comprehension. No man ever surpassed him in this particular.

"In Great Britain, Lord Holt was considered the clearest mind in his legal views, and Judge Gibson would lose nothing by comparison with him. His opinions were remarkable for their simplicity and force. A single sentence would sometimes contain many of the most potential principles of the laws of Pennsylvania. He had not, like Marshall and Washington, been connected with the courts of the United States, but he shone with equal lustre in the courts of his own State.

"Story and Kent have furnished in their Commentaries a judicial character for Judge Gibson which posterity will never forget. His opinions are oftener quoted by them than are those of any other man in the country. At Westminster, and on the continent, his name, as a judge, is heard with respect and attention.   *   *   *   *   * He was one of the greatest and soundest jurists that ever lived. In testing his merits he had to pass through a trying ordeal, as Chief Justice Tilghman had left a proud product of his labors."

Mr. E. D. Ingraham said, at the close of his remarks:

"He had lived in the same house with him, and had had the benefit of his private instruction. The natural powers of Judge Gibson's mind were strong, and the feelings of his nature were of the kindest character. No man possessed gentler feelings towards his family and friends, and none were more devoted to his country."

The committee appointed to engraft the resolutions and forward them to the family of the deceased was composed of the following named gentlemen: Horace Binney, John R. Kane, T. J. Wharton, G. Mallory, T. S. Bell, Wm. M. Meredith and T. A. Budd.

In the U. S. Court, in Pittsburgh, Hon. Chas. Shaler,* U. S. District Attorney, after reading a telegram announcing the death of Judge Gibson, in the course of his remarks, said:

"No man, sir, filled a higher or more dignified station than Judge Gibson, and no man among us, through a long life of judicial eminence, had acquired in so great a degree the reverence of the members of the bar, and the love and

---

* HON. CHAS. SHALER.—Native of Connecticut (1788). Educated at Yale; went to Ravenna, O., in 1809, as agent for his father's lands at Shalersville, near by; studied law, and was admitted to the bar there; moved to Pittsburgh and was admitted to the bar there in 1813; was recorder of the city (the law judge of the mayor's court) from 1818 to 1821; was judge of common pleas court from June 5, 1824, till May 4, 1835, when he resigned; was associate judge district court from May 6, 1841, till May 20, 1844, when he resigned; was U. S. district attorney for western district of Pennsylvania under President Pierce; died March 5, 1869, aged 81 years. He was a well read and skillful lawyer, and had a very large and lucrative practice, from which he retired several years before his death, because of partial blindness. For some years his partner was Hon. Edwin M. Stanton, afterwards secretary of war during the rebellion. He had been a Federalist, but in the Jackson contests became an ardent Democrat, and remained so for fifty years, till the close of his life. He never sought party nominations, but had them thrust upon him, and then never refused to run, though defeat was certain, asking for himself no man's vote, but defiantly carrying aloft the banner of his party, apparently the more joyous the greater the odds against him. He was a most stirring stump orator, throwing out, in a shrill, clear, penetrating voice, admirable specimens of irony, invective, logic and humor, to the great delight of the multitude. Though passionate and vehement in his impulses, he was a most genial and honorable gentleman. He never shirked responsibility. It was an admirable trait in his character that he would always shelter a young associate from reproach for any mistakes in the management of a case, assuming all blunders as his own. Always generous, he lived up to his large income, and as some one says of another, "Like most great lawyers, he lived well and died poor." T. J. K.

respect of the people. He was one of the greatest men that Pennsylvania ever produced, and no one, either in this or any other State, surpassed him in judicial reputation. His opinions, elaborate and replete with legal eloquence and acumen, are contained in nearly fifty volumes of reports, and are not to be excelled, in this or any other country, for accuracy as regards their construction of law, beauty of expression, and a high sense of justice. In your bosom, sir—in those of the members of the bar, are felt those sentiments of sorrow, to the expression of which I find myself inadequate."

Hon. Wilson McCandless* followed, and said:

"Since I entered this room, the gentleman who preceded me showed me the telegraphic dispatch announcing the melancholy intelligence of the death of one who has occupied so eminent a position in the judicial position in the history of Pennsylvania. I am proud to remember that I have enjoyed the friendship of the deceased ever since I came to the bar. In social life, no gentleman ever possessed qualities better calculated to endear him to his friends; as to his abilities, they were not to be equalled in Pennsylvania; as to his legal learning, all the members of this bar

---

* HON. WILSON MCCANDLESS.—Born in 1810, in Allegheny county, Pa.; educated at the Western University, Pittsburgh; admitted to the bar in 1831; died June 30, 1882, aged 71 years. He practiced for some years in connection with W. W. Fetterman, afterwards with Wm. B. McClure, his brother-in-law, and was judge of the U. S. district court from 1859 till 1876, when he resigned because of ill health. He was an accomplished gentleman, and a model orator; tried many causes of an important character; was very effective with juries, but was in his glory as speaker on great public occasions, especially on the political rostrum. His speeches always glowed with the loftiest sentiments, expressed with sonorous tones in the grandest language. Scholarly, witty, highly appreciative of wit in others, exceedingly social, and with no bitterness in his nature, he was admired by all who knew him. The Democracy several times nominated him for Congress and sent him frequently to their conventions, State and National.   T. J. K.

and the profession throughout the State well know that he stood second to none. When, by the alteration of the constitution, the judiciary became elective, he was chosen by the people again to fill the station which he had adorned, for they had long had confidence in his decisions, and though many came into the Supreme Court, dissatisfied with the proceedings of the court below, they never left it without being satisfied that he had done justice, however it might militate against their interest.

"Sir, this melancholy event was not unexpected. The last time we saw Judge Gibson, in another room in this court house,* those who were acquainted with him perceived that the sands of life were fast wasting away; that his body was worn out by the brilliancy of an intellect which even to the last shone with a resplendent lustre."

The Honorable Judge Irwin† then replied as follows:

"I feel that the tribute of respect to the memory of the lamented Judge Gibson, which has just been paid by the distinguished gentlemen, is a very just one, and that no man deserved it better. The people of this State for forty years have been acquainted with his judicial abilities, and it is due to them that this court should comply with the suggestion which has been made. I know of no man who held a higher place in the respect and in the hearts of the people than the deceased, and I sympathize in their loss."

* The present postoffice and U. S. court building was at this time (1853) in progress of construction, and the U. S. court was held in a room in the county building.

† HON. THOS. IRWIN.—Born in Philadelphia, 1784; son of Col. Matthew Irwin of the Revolution; educated at Franklin college, Lancaster, Pa.; went to Louisiana, 1808, and practiced law; came to Uniontown, Pa., in 1811, and practiced there; elected to legislature in 1824 and 1826, and to congress in 1828; appointed by Jackson, 1830, judge of U. S. district court, western district of Pennsylvania; died, 1870, aged 87; obtained a national reputation by an able opinion in the fugitive slave law of 1850.   T. J. K.

27

On the same day, in the District Court, Judge Shannon*
entered into a review of the life of Judge Gibson, and at
the end of it said:

"During the long period that vast interests were
entrusted to him, what great principles were announced, and
what conflicting points and sophistical arguments were obliged
to pass the grave and searching review of his comprehensive intellect. His opinions are scattered over and run
through about sixty-six volumes of our Reports. Of what
judge in this country, or elsewhere, can so much be said?

"He was materially assisted in laying the foundations
and in building up the superstructure of our jurisprudence.
Some of his legal opinions are masterpieces, which have
justly won admiration, even in the courts of Westminster
hall, and which will remain lasting memorials of his skill
and genius. It would be unnecessary to dilate upon the
fitness of his style, or the purity of his diction; these are
familiar things to the gentlemen of the law, worthy of imitation. His name will properly rank in point of ability
with those of the most eminent judges who ever graced a
bench. If Massachusetts boasts of a Story, and New York
of a Kent, we, as Pennsylvanians, can proudly point to the
great intellectuality and profound legal learning of John
Bannister Gibson."

In the Court of Common Pleas, which was engaged in

---

* HON. PETER C. SHANNON.—A native of Ireland, a man of letters, brought
to this country in his childhood; studied law with Hon. H. D. Foster, in Greensburg, Pa.; was admitted to the bar there in 1845; appointed by Governor Bigler
president judge of district court of Allegheny county in 1852, on occasion of the
death of Judge Walter Forward; afterwards practiced in Pittsburgh till 1869,
when he was appointed chief justice of U. S. courts in Dakota; then moved to
Yankton, D. T.; returned to Pittsburgh in 1886, and is now in practice there. He
is a gentleman of culture, a poet and orator; was twice Democratic candidate for
congress, and since the rebellion is a prominent leader in the Republican party.
T. J. K.

the trial of a case, after a few remarks by the Hon. Wilson McCandless, who announced the news of Judge Gibson's death, Thomas Williams, Esq.,* said :

"If the court please, although I am engaged in the trial of a case, I deem it but proper to yield to an exigency such as this, in order that the court may pay that token of respect which is due to the memory of so great a man as the late chief justice of this State. I concur in the remarks which have just been made by the gentleman, for no man connected with the legal history of Pennsylvania has left a deeper stamp upon its jurisprudence than Judge Gibson. His history, in fact, is a part of its history, and he has done as much as any man in this commonwealth to mold it into its present shape. The opinions of no other judge of this State have been more universally diffused, or characterized by a deeper judicial wisdom."

S. W. Black, Esq.,† counsel on the opposite side of the case before the court, on behalf of himself and the Hon. Cornelius Darragh, colleague, seconded the motion, and could

---

* THOS. WILLIAMS.—Born in Greensburg, Pa., 18—; received an excellent academical education; admitted to the bar in Allegheny county August 7, 1828; obtained a fine practice; participated actively in politics as an acknowledged leader in the old Whig, and after in the Republican party; was some years State senator; again in the house of representatives, Pennsylvania, and in congress during the rebellion, when he was a chief confidential adviser of President Lincoln. He was an admirable classical scholar, and an eloquent speaker and writer. He was quite conspicuous in the legal battles made against the constitutionality of municipal subscriptions to railroads, and wrote acrimonious, yet powerful reviews of the supreme court decisions on that and kindred questions. Died in Allegheny in 187—.   T. J. K.

† SAML. W. BLACK.—Born in Pittsburgh, Pa., September 3, 1816. Educated under the immediate care of his learned father, Rev. John Black, D. D., president of the Western University. Admitted to the bar March 7, 1838. Became foremost in criminal practice; was first colonel in the Mexican war; was governor of Nebraska Territory; was colonel of Sixty-second regiment, Pennsylvania volunteers, in the late civil war. Killed at Gaines' Mill, Va., June 27, 1862. He was a fiery orator, at the same time full of wit and inimitable at repartee.
                                                                        T. J. K.

only say that he cordially joined in the sentiments which had been expressed, and trusted that the court would respond to them promptly.

Hon. William B. McClure* addressed the members of the bar as follows:

"This announcement fills the court with sorrow. He has died full of years and full of honors. His legal decisions are our inheritance, and his fame is his country's. They will endure longer than the marble and the brass, by which men endeavor to perpetuate the memory of a transcendent merit. The intimate family ties existing by marriage between the family of the chief justice and the president judge of this court,† interdict the expressions of admiration and homage due to his overshadowing genius and learning."

The meeting of the bar of Cumberland county was held May 4, and was presided over by the Hon. Frederick Watts, Judge Gibson's next door neighbor, and kinsman by marriage. In early life he, with Sergeant, was a reporter of the Supreme Court; later, the judge of Cumberland

---

* HON. WM. B. MCCLURE.—Born 1807, near Carlisle, Pa.; graduated at Dickinson college in 1827; read law in Pittsburgh, and was admitted to the bar in 1829; had a very large practice in connection with his brother-in-law, Wilson McCandless; was law judge of the courts of common pleas, orphans' court, quarter sessions and oyer and terminer, of Allegheny county, from 1850 to 1859, first by appointment of the governor, and twice afterwards by election; died December 27, 1861, worn out with the enormous amount of labor required of him, and which he faithfully performed in his official position. He was, by nature, kind hearted, but rigid in enforcement of the criminal law for repression of crime. He was famous as a criminal judge, and tried more offenses of the higher grade than any other judge in the State, in the same period of time. He was closely related to Judge Gibson by marriage.   T. J. K.

† Judge McClure here alludes to himself and his relationship through the marriage of his brother, Col. Charles McClure, to Margaretta, eldest daughter of Judge Gibson. The families were closely allied by common residence in Cumberland county.

county; afterwards one of the most successful practitioners of the bar. For years also he was president of the State Agricultural Society, and was appointed by President Grant commissioner of agriculture, which office he held under Grant for both terms.

In concluding a brief sketch of Judge Gibson, Judge Watts said:

"Nothing short of a laborious study of our profession will enable us to fully appreciate those firm foundations and pillars of the law, and especially those just principles of equity which have been so beautifully developed and aptly molded into rules of right by his great mind."

Following the resolutions offered by himself, the Hon. Hugh Gaullager * delivered a fervent and highly eulogistic address, in which he said:

"We are told by Lord Coke that 'law is the perfection of reason,' and we may truly say, in the language of our great master, that these opinions of our late chief justice are the perfection of reason, and products of a powerful and discriminating intellect, schooled and trained by long study, often conference, long experience and continual obser-

---

* Mr. Gaullager spoke always in a deep toned, powerful voice, with guttural intonations amounting to an Irish brogue, peculiar to himself. He lived but three years after Judge Gibson. The writer, though a boy of but thirteen at the time of his death, has a vivid recollection of him, as well as of the style of many others of the Carlisle lawyers of this period, for if sometimes he was a truant from school he could have been found "during court week" occupying a front seat in the sacred hall of justice, with mouth agape perhaps, but certainly with ears more intelligently open than were those of the average Pennsylvania Dutch juryman. It may be appropriate to remark just here, for the benefit of those unacquainted with the Cumberland Valley and other "Dutch" districts, that the Dutch were sensible enough to live in the country and grow rich on their fat limestone farms, leaving the county seats to the aristocratic English, Scotch and Irish, where there being no labor markets open, every person resorted to his wits to gain a living, hence so many lawyers; good ones, too, for many of the "emigrants" driven from home by "over production" achieved distinction elsewhere.

vation. It has often been remarked by members of our profession, that the late chief justice would have made an eminent chancellor. This is true, and although we have no court of chancery, he administered equity principles and under common law forms wherever he could when the justice of the case required it. It is but just to say of him, that in equity science he was as learned and profound as the Harwicks, the Thurlows, the Eldons, the Marshalls, the Washingtons, and Kents."

Mr. William Biddle, who followed, said:

" It can be truly said of him, 'those who knew him best, love him most.' Carlisle will grieve that the last of her distinguished sons that have graced the bench of the Supreme Court, has been taken from us. It is a remarkable fact, and one which her inhabitants may well feel proud of, that our town, with its comparatively small population,* has furnished no less than four of the judges of that court. First, the Honorable Hugh H. Brackenridge, who at his death was succeeded next by the Honorable Thomas Duncan,† and lastly by the Honorable John Kennedy. For a period of more than ten years during which the Supreme Court of Pennsylvania consisted of but three members, two of them, Justices Gibson and Duncan,‡ were distinguished citizens of this town. And after the number was enlarged to five, and Judge Duncan had died, Carlisle could still point with pride to the chief justice and Judge Kennedy."

Following Mr. Biddle came the gifted speaker, J. E. Bonham, who died within a year or two following this meeting, as did also, indeed not long thereafter, the kindly

---

* In 1853 about 4,000; in 1880 about 8,000.

† Mr. Biddle was in error; Judge Gibson preceded Duncan and followed Brackenridge.

‡ He might have added, and from the same law office.

hearted Biddle. In the course of his remarks Mr. Bonham said this of Judge Black:

"At one time I heard the present chief justice say, and he judged by the intuitive knowledge of a kindred spirit, that he was utterly astonished at the freshness and vigor of 'the old chief' in consultation; that his mind appeared imbued with all the elasticity of youth as well as the wisdom of age, and grasped the whole range of legal science. At another and more recent period, when he had known him longer and better, and as his admiration increased, he remarked that he regarded Gibson the greatest mind he had ever met; that, notwithstanding his age, his *vis inertia* of body, and which constantly dragged him down, his intellectual powers were most brilliant and commanding.

"Chancellor Kent ranked him among the first jurists of this age, and it may be said of him, as he truthfully and beautifully said of his late lamented colleague, Justice Kennedy, that 'he clung to the common law as a child to its nurse.' His opinions are as simple and elegant in their style as they are learned and profound. His powers of analysis and condensation were remarkable and peculiar to himself."

Lemuel Todd, then on the threshold of his since achieved fame as an orator, followed and said:

"His duty was almost performed, and the measure of his life almost full, before I entered the profession. He is known to me only as a judge who has impressed upon our jurisprudence the character of his own gigantic intellect, and done more, during his long and distinguished career, to give form, consistency, and strength to our peculiar system, than any man living or dead."

J. B. Parker, Esq.,* closed the addresses, the following being a brief extract from his remarks:

"The characteristic of his reasoning was great power of condensation, of his style, nervousness and perspicuity, with felicity of illustration, choice and apt in the selection of words, peculiarly careful and precise as to their value and meaning, ever emphatically the right word in the right place; his judicial opinions are models for clearness and accuracy of expression, as for cogency of argument. His numerous decisions, which fill and enrich the pages of our Reports, are his best and most enduring monument—a monument of intellect; but his vigorous mind was not restrained within the limits of legal science. It was richly stored with the fruits of research in other domains of science, while in literature and the fine arts his taste was cultivated and refined."

It would serve no good purpose to extend this compilation by adding editorial notices, resolutions of condolence of political and other organizations throughout the State, for while they breathe with expressions, no doubt, of sincere regret at the loss of the deceased jurist, they throw but little additional light upon his character, and none whatever, except in the case of the Wilkesbarre paper, elsewhere noticed, upon his life and domestic habits, particulars of which are always of the greatest interest in any memoir. Historical consistency may, however, justify an exception in the case of the following extract from the pages of a March number (pages 311 and 312, exact year unknown) of

---

* Mr. Parker died recently in Carlisle. He was for many years the law partner of Judge Watts, and was named by Judge Gibson as the executor of his will.

the *United States Law Magazine,* in a sketch of Gibson several years before his death :

"Independently of constant sittings throughout the commonwealth, on the circuits and at Nisi Prius, where some of the ablest opinions have been given without record, the Pennsylvania Reports preserve enduring evidence of his ability, fidelity and learning.

"'The Reports of Pennsylvania,' said the late Charles Chauncey, 'are entitled to the admiration of the lawyer, at home and abroad. They contain decisions which have led the way upon some very interesting subjects, and which have been followed both here and in England.'

"How far and how faithfully Chief Justice Gibson has participated in those labors so honorable to his native State, is attested by upwards of *six thousand cases* in which he has taken part in the final judgment of the court, and more than *twelve hundred* in which he has himself delivered opinions distinguished for their impartiality, learning and conclusive force. Mr. Binney, we are sure, did but speak a sentiment of perfect truth, when on an occasion dictated by respect to the tribunal, where for five and twenty years Chief Justice Gibson has presided, he declared, amidst the enthusiastic response of men of every party, that at no time has the judgment of the court been guided by either favor or resentment; and that in learning, integrity and industry, the judges of the court have never been wanting to themselves, the profession or the country. ' *We all agree,*' said this eminent lawyer, ' that the judges of the Supreme Court have been faithful to the *Constitution* and the *Law ;* faithful to the *State* and to the *Union ;* faithful to the *People* and to the *Bar.*'

28

" In person the chief justice is above the common stature,* and has always been distinguished by extraordinary vigor of health and frame. His temperaments are eminently social, and among all classes of society throughout the State, he is ever greeted as a welcome guest. His hearty health, his fresh and genial tastes, and his devotion to judicial labors, indicate a man on whose vigorous power age has made no mark."

---

* Judge Gibson was six feet three inches in height.

APPENDIX A.

SKETCH OF JOHN GIBSON.*

John Gibson was born at Lancaster, Pennsylvania, May 23d, 1740. He received a classical education, and was an excellent scholar at the age of eighteen, when he entered the service. His first campaign was under General Forbes, in the expedition which resulted in the acquisition of Fort Duquesne, afterward Fort Pitt, from the French. He then settled at Pittsburgh, as a trader. War broke out in 1763 with the Indians, and Gibson was taken prisoner at the mouth of the Beaver, 28 miles below Fort Pitt, with two men who were in his employ. They were, at the time, descending the Ohio in a canoe. One of his men was immediately tortured at the stake, and the other shared the same fate as soon as the party reached the Kanawha. Gibson, however, was preserved by an aged squaw, and adopted by her in the place of a son who had been killed in battle. In 1764 he was given up by the Indians to Col. Boquet, when he again settled at Pittsburgh, resuming his occupation of trading with the Indians.

In 1774 Gibson acted a conspicuous part in the expedition against the Shawnees, under Lord Dunmore (Governor of Virginia), particularly in negotiating the peace which followed. It was upon this occasion, near the waters of the Scioto river, in what is now Pickaway county, Ohio, that Logan, the Mingo chief, made to him the speech so celebrated in history.

At the breaking out of the Revolution Gibson was the western agent of Virginia at Pittsburgh. After the treaty in the fall of 1775, at that place, between the Delawares and the representatives

---

* From the "Washington-Irvine Correspondence," p. 349.

of the Shawnees and Senecas on the one part, and the commissioners of the American congress on the other part, by which the neu-
trality of the first mentioned tribe was secured, he undertook a
tour to the Western Indians in the interests of peace.   Upon his
return he entered the continental service, rising, finally, to the command of the Thirteenth Virginia regiment, at Fort Pitt, in the
summer of 1778, he having previously seen service east of the
mountains.   He remained at that post from that date until the
close of the war, having several times the chief command, though
temporarily, of the fort, and its dependencies.   For his services a
Virginia military land warrant was issued before December 31,
1784.   He remained in the West, and was a member of the convention which framed the constitution of Pennsylvania in 1790 ;
and subsequently was a judge of Allegheny county, that State ;
also a major general of militia.   He was secretary of the territory
of Indiana until it became a State, and, by virtue of his office,
was, at one time, its acting governor.   He died at Braddock's
Field, in Allegheny county, Pa., April 16th, 1822.   At the time
of his death he was a pensioner under the Act of March 18, 1818.

SKETCH BY THE REV. LICHLITER.

Following is an extract from a sketch of "General John
Gibson" read before the Historical Society of Western Pennsylvania by the Rev. M. D. Lichliter, February 13th, 1890 :

"Col. Gibson made Allegheny county his home the remainder
of his life, serving in various positions of honor and trust.   He
was a member of the convention which framed the State constitution in 1790, and subsequently served his country as an associate
judge.   He obtained the rank of a general by being promoted
major general of militia.   In 1801 President Jefferson appointed
him secretary of the Indiana territory, which position he filled until
the territory became a State, of which he was acting governor from
1811 to 1813.   He died at Braddock's Field, April 16th, 1822,
and is buried in Allegheny cemetery.   On a flat stone tablet lying
upon his grave is the following inscription :

In memory of
COL. JOHN GIBSON,
who departed this life on the 16th of April, 1822, in the 82d year of his age.

He was amongst the earliest settlers in the western part of Pennsylvania, and participated in the long struggle for our independence. This testimony of respect and affection is erected by the disconsolate widow.

On another slab is the following:

In memory of
ANN GIBSON,
Relict of
JOHN GIBSON.
Was born at Carlisle, Pa.,
Nov. 15th, 1762,
and died at Pittsburgh,
July 19th, 1835,
in the 73d year of her age.

In the same burial plot are two slabs bearing the names of George Wallace and his wife. Mr. Wallace was one of the pioneers, and at one time owned the historic field where Braddock met his defeat, which tract of 328 acres was conveyed to him by George Thompson, in 1791. Wallace, who was the first judge of common pleas of Allegheny county, erected a beautiful home upon his land, in which he had the honor of entertaining General Lafayette, in 1825, who stopped and took luncheon with him.

At the time Wallace came in possession of the above tract he was Washington's personal friend, and chief of his staff.

An upright stone, more modest in style, yet quite plain, stands within the enclosure of this plot, having on one side the names of the Gibson and Wallace families, the date of their birth and death. On the opposite side are the inscriptions in commemoration of Rev. Z. H. Coston and his wife. The Rev. Coston was a noted pioneer preacher in the Methodist Episcopal Church, whose name is still cherished among many of the older members in Western Pennsylvania. He died May 4th, 1874, aged 80 years. His wife, who was a daughter of George Wallace, was born April 2d, 1787, and died April 9th, 1864. Col. Gibson was the father-in-law of George Wallace." *

* From the above it would appear that General Gibson must have been married to Ann Gibson before 1770, to have had a granddaughter born in 1787. Mr. Lichliter is mistaken, therefore, in the statement in another part of his sketch, not quoted, that in 1774 Gibson's wife was a sister of Logan, the Indian chief.

SPEECH OF LOGAN, THE MINGO CHIEF.

Thomas Jefferson, who probably found the speech, or message, of Logan, in the archives of the State of Virginia, presented it to the public, accompanied with the following prelude :

"I may challenge the whole of the orations of Demosthenes and Cicero, and, indeed, of any more eminent orators, if Europe or the world has furnished more eminent, to produce a single passage superior to the speech of Logan, a Mingo chief, delivered to Lord Dunmore when governor of Virginia. As a testimony of Indian talents in this line, I beg leave to introduce it, by first relating the incidents necessary for understanding it.

"In the spring of the year 1774 a robbery was committed by some Indians upon certain land adventurers on the Ohio river. The whites in that quarter, according to their custom, undertook to punish this outrage in a summary way. Captain Michael Cresap, and one Daniel Greathouse, leading on these parties, surprised, at different times, traveling and hunting parties of the Indians, who had their women and children with them, and murdered many. Among these, unfortunately, were the family of Logan, a chief celebrated in peace and war, and long distinguished as the friend of the whites.

"This unworthy return provoked his vengeance. He accordingly signalized himself in the war which ensued. In the autumn of the same year a decisive battle was fought at the mouth of the Great Kanawha, between the collected forces of the Shawnees, the Mingos, and the Delawares, and a detachment of the Virginia militia. The Indians were defeated and sued for peace. Logan, however, disdained to be seen among the suppliants; but, lest the sincerity of a treaty, from which so distinguished a chief absented himself, should be distrusted, he sent, by a messenger, the following speech to be delivered to Lord Dunmore :

"'I appeal to any white man to say if ever he entered Logan's cabin hungry, and he gave him not meat; if ever he came cold and naked, and he clothed him not. During the course of the last long and bloody war, Logan remained idle in his cabin, an advocate for peace. Such was my love for the whites that my country-men pointed as they passed, and said, ' Logan is the friend of the white men.' I had even thought to live with you, but for the injuries of one man.   Colonel Cresap, last spring, in cold blood, and unprovoked, murdered all the relatives of Logan, not sparing even my women and children. There runs not a drop of my blood in the veins of any living creature. This called on me for revenge. I have sought it. I have killed many.   I have fully glutted my vengeance.   For my country I rejoice at the beams of peace ; but do not harbor a thought that mine is the joy of fear.* Logan never felt fear. He will not turn on his heel to save his life. Who is there to mourn for Logan ? Not one.'"

Mr. William Hamilton, Superintendent of the Parks in Alle-gheny City, and president of the Botanical Society of Western Pennsylvania, has in his possession the originals of the subjoined letters. In referring to the circumstances under which Logan's speech was delivered, Mr. Hamilton says that he heard General William Robinson state that the message was given to Gibson whilst Logan and Gibson were seated on a log, no other person being present. This statement, now revived by Mr. Hamilton, of the manner of the delivery of the message, accords with statements made by General Gibson to several other persons.

The " envoys " referred to in Jefferson's letter to Gibson were most likely Elbridge Gerry, John Marshall and Chas. Pinckney, who were rather coldly received by the French Directory.   When

---

* If Mr. Jefferson had taken the limited vocabulary of the Mingo chief, or for that matter any other Indian tongue, he could scarcely have found an equiva-lent for the expressions, "the joy of fear," "the beams of peace," etc.   Strange, indeed, that the genius of the translator was not taken into some account by him.

Reference was previously made to the fact that Logan came from the Juniata Valley. Mr. R. S. Elliott, in his interesting " Notes Taken in Sixty Years," thus alludes to him :

" The famous Mingo chief had his home at the head of the picturesque gorge called Jack's Narrows (on the Pennsylvania Railroad), where the tumbling Kishacoquillas creek makes its way through Jack's mountain.   *   *   * When game grew scarce Logan moved to a new home on the Ohio river, had all his family murdered by white men, took a fearful revenge, and made (as reported by Jefferson) one of the most pathetic speeches in any tongue."

the demand was made that the United States pay France $250,000 to settle the little war cloud which had arisen between the two countries, came Pinckney's immortal answer: "Millions for defense, but not one cent for tribute," and the country realized the words, building six frigates immediately, in one of which, the "Constellation," Commodore Truxtun defeated a French frigate early in 1799. •

ALLEGHENY CITY, May, 1867.

To JNO. BROWN, JR.,
    President Allegheny Library Society.

    Dear Sir:—Believing that an original document in the handwriting of the author of the Declaration of Independence concerning a tragic event of early times on the Ohio, about forty miles below our city, will be an acceptable relic for preservation amongst the archives of the association over which you preside, I enclose an autograph letter of Thomas Jefferson to General Gibson, expressing a wish to obtain "a minute history" of the murder of Logan's family, the Indian chief, who made a most touching speech concerning the massacre, worthy of the highest culture and civilization, reported in Jefferson's Notes of Virginia, of which General Gibson was an auditor, and perfectly acquainted with the language in which it was delivered, was the interpreter, being for some time a prisoner and afterwards a trader among the Indians.

    Of the authenticity of Logan's speech there is no doubt. More than sixty years ago General Gibson, who was an intimate friend of my father, narrated the circumstances under which Logan's speech was delivered, and affirmed its perfect authenticity and entire correspondence with the original, which he had interpreted at the time of its delivery. The letter referred to was retained by the daughter and only child of General Gibson, with filial care, intermarried with Rev. Z. Coston. She was a most exemplary lady. She died about four years ago in Pittsburgh.

    But this is saying enough, and I remain,

            Your octogenarian friend,

                W. ROBINSON.

PHILADELPHIA, February 12th, '98.

    Dear General:—Your favor of the 2d inst. is received. Should our session be continued to a greater length than I expect, it would be a circumstance of great pleasure to me to see you here, but I do not think we can continue here much longer than the present month, as there is really nothing to do but to receive information from our envoys at Paris. If that wear a peaceful aspect, as I hope it will, we ought not to remain here a week longer for any thing which we have to do. I must, therefore, trouble you to give me, by way of letter, the information respecting Cresap and his party, and the murder of Logan's family. It seems Logan has mistaken the title if not the person. *I wish to get a minute history of the whole transaction* in order to correct or confirm that which has before been given.

We are very anxious to get some information from our envoys in order to know on what ground we are to stand with our former allies. They appear to have established peace with all their continental neighbors and to be collecting all their energies to invade England. Their objects seem to be to republicanize her government, and to bring her power on the ocean within more reasonable and safe limits.

I shall, with great pleasure, make myself useful to you here should anything turn up in which I can do so. I shall thereby be discharging a duty of conscience and at the same time of friendship. I am, with sentiments of great esteem, dear general,

Your most obd. svt.,

TH'S JEFFERSON.

GEN'L GIBSON.

APPENDIX B.

MILITARY SERVICES OF COLONEL GEORGE GIBSON, FATHER OF JOHN BANNISTER GIBSON.

24th Congress, (Rep. No. 345.)
1st Session. Ho. of Reps.
George Gibson,—Representatives of
To accompany Bill H. R. No. 355,
Feb. 17, 1836.

Mr. Muhlenberg, from the Committee on Revolutionary Claims, made the following

REPORT:

The Committee on Revolutionary Claims, to which was referred the petition of the legal representatives of Col. George Gibson, deceased, reports:

Col. Gibson was a brave and meritorious officer. He entered the service of his country at the commencement of the Revolution; enlisted a hundred men at Pittsburgh, then under the jurisdiction of Virginia; marched to Williamsburg, and was commissioned a captain in the Virginia line. Powder and lead becoming scarce, the government of Virginia selected him as a person well qualified to conduct a secret negotiation with the Spanish government for a supply. He was successful in procuring it, not only for the State of Virginia, but engaged a resident merchant of eminence

29

(Oliver Pollock) to ship large quantities to the States in Spanish vessels. On his return he was offered a pecuniary recompense or promotion, and accepted the latter. He was accordingly appointed colonel of the First Virginia Regiment.

With this regiment he continued, and was in all the seven engagements in the North, subsequent to the battle of Germantown, until 1781, when the regiment, being nearly annihilated, was ordered to the South to recruit. He then became a supernumerary, but was shortly afterward ordered to march the prisoners taken with Cornwallis to York, in Pennsylvania, and they remained under his charge until sent to England.

Col. Gibson's services did not, however, close with the Revolutionary war. In 1790 he was appointed by General Washington a colonel of one of the regiments recruiting for General St. Clair's army, and was ordered to the West to assist in the campaign against the northwest Indians. He fell on the fatal 4th of November, 1791, sustaining the character for bravery and coolness which had ever distinguished him.

Col. Gibson's regiment was originally a State regiment. About the 1st of June, 1777, it was ordered to the North, and joined General Washington two days after the battle of Germantown (vide Washington's Letters, vol. 2, p. 180), and was placed on continental establishment, in lieu of Matthews' regiment which was taken by the enemy in that battle, by an act of the Virginia legislature, in these words: "Be it enacted, that the battalion on commonwealth establishment, under the command of Col. George Gibson, and now in the continental service, be continued in the said service instead of the Ninth Virginia Regiment, made prisoners in the battle of Germantown." This Act was never repealed. Col. Matthews' regiment never resumed its place in the line, and Gibson's remained until 1781, when it was ordered home to recruit.

In addition to this proof of the character of the regiment, it is proper to state that the war department decided on the 12th of January, 1830, "that the regiment commanded by Col. George Gibson was a continental regiment from October, 1777." The treasury department also so decided. In consequence of which the benefit of the Act of May 15th, 1828, applicable only to the continental line, was extended to a number of individuals belonging to this regiment. Congress itself has viewed the regiment as continental, having passed an Act allowing to the heirs of an officer belonging to that regiment "five years' full pay, with such interest as would have accrued if a certificate had issued, and been founded under the Act of 1790." (*Vide* Act for the relief of William Vawter's heirs, approved May 25th, 1832.)

By an Act of the State of Virginia of May, 1779, officers of the continental and State line of Virginia were placed upon an equal footing in regard to the bounty of the State, half pay for life, and directed to look for recompense to the State; provided congress did not make some tantamount provision for them. For the State line congress did nothing; but for the continental line it made tantamount provision.

Owing in some measure to Gibson's regiment having been both State and continental, its officers received neither half pay from Virginia nor commutation from the United States. In applying to the State they were referred to the United States; and on applying to the United States they were referred to the State.

By the Act of July 5th, 1832, the claims of the Virginia State line were directed to be liquidated and paid by that State. In that Act the regiment of Col. Gibson was included, and his legal representatives received a certain amount, but not equal to the commutation paid to other officers of the same grade in continental establishment, nor in proportion to what had been paid to subalterns of the same regiment, for whose relief acts have been passed by congress. The most important question in the whole case seems to be, whether the regiment really belonged to the continental line proper. That such was the case the committee have no doubt, and they believe that its colonel should be placed upon an equally favorable footing with his subalterns. They think that justice should be even-handed, and that the petitioners are entitled to the same measure that others have received. A bill is accordingly reported for their relief.*

---

* The above was taken from a printed official copy of the report, in possession of F. W. Gibson.

APPENDIX C.

GENERAL GEORGE GIBSON.

SKETCH OF THE LIFE OF GENERAL GEORGE GIBSON, LATE
COMMISSARY GENERAL OF THE UNITED STATES ARMY,
BROTHER OF JOHN BANNISTER GIBSON—CONDENSED FROM
THE MEMOIR OF S. HORACE PORTER, ESQ., OF LANCASTER,
PA., SON OF THE LATE GOV. PORTER, OF PENNSYLVANIA,
AND BROTHER OF THE HON. WM. A. PORTER.

General Gibson entered the army on the 3d of May, 1808, as
captain in the Fifth Regiment of Infantry.   On the same day
Lieutenant General Winfield Scott was commissioned captain of
light artillery.   The association then formed by these gallant men
resulted in an uninterrupted friendship of over half a century's
duration.

Appointed captain, fifty-three years ago, he recruited part of
his company in this city,* then the seat of government of Pennsylvania.   He was successively promoted to the majority of the
Seventh Infantry, 9th of November, 1811, and to the lieutenant
colonelcy of the Fifth Infantry, 15th of August, 1813.   His services throughout the war of 1812 (so called) are a portion of his
country's history.   Disbanded 15th of June, 1815, on the first
reduction of the army after the treaty of peace, he was commissioned quartermaster general, with the rank of colonel, on the
29th of April, 1816, and assigned to the southern division of the
army under Major General Andrew Jackson, then in the field
against the hostile Indians.   On the 18th of April, 1818, he was
appointed commissary general of subsistence, which position he
held until his death.   (How well he filled it let the army of his
country answer.)   Brevetted brigadier general "for ten years'
faithful services," in the rank of colonel, 29th of April, 1826 ;
he received the additional brevet of major general "for meritorious
conduct, particularly in performing his duties in prosecuting the
war with Mexico," 30th of May, 1848.

---

* Lancaster, Pa.

General Gibson died at Washington City, September 30, 1861, full of years and full of honors, in perfect possession of all his mental powers, and strong to the last in the ruling passion of his soul—love of country. He was in his 87th year. A public funeral was awarded him by command of the Executive.* * *

No officer occupying the same rank in the army held a higher place in the estimation of his fellow officers. It was delightful to see the reverence with which they approached him, and the courteous yet familiar manner with which he made every man feel "at home" with him. The senior exhibited the respect of a younger brother, and the junior felt for him filial affection. There was a charm in his manner that pleased both. He was the safe counsellor of the one, while he was the ready adviser of the other in every trouble or difficulty. His judgment was law, and his opinion, unless disregarded, never failed to benefit those who sought and obtained it.

Conducting for upwards of forty years one of the most responsible departments of the army, the commissariat, he felt that the soldiers of that army were his children, and he provided as the father of a family for their necessities. The slightest complaint of the quality of their rations met at once an examination, and if found just, was soon remedied. He knew what they required and what was best for them, and it afforded him satisfaction to properly gratify their wants. No government ever had a more perfect system for provisioning an army (scattered, too, as it necessarily was over so wide a territory) than he inaugurated and successfully carried into effect. It was always in order, and its operations were as regular as the habits of its chief.

Possessing extraordinary executive capacity, combined with a rare judgment and sense of justice in the settlement of accounts, which enabled him more promptly to discriminate between right and wrong, he resembled, in many powers of mind, his eminent brother, the late John Bannister Gibson, for so many years the chief justice of Pennsylvania, and her brightest legal ornament.

* President Lincoln came himself early to the house, and spoke feelingly of the veteran soldier. General Gibson was the oldest officer in the United States army at the time of his death, being several years older than General Scott, who survived him.

His modesty was akin with his other great qualities, and all uniting together, formed the model officer, and the honest and firm administrator.

The attachment felt for him and the confidence reposed in him, by his old commander, General Jackson ("he who never gave up a friend"), was fully reciprocated, and it was as brothers that they communed together, during the eventful eight years that the "stern old patriot" was president. No matter how much the chief magistrate of the Union was engaged with business, the moment that his old staff officer's name was announced in the ante-chamber, the major general who turned the tide of England's victory at New Orleans was ready to receive and take by the hand his fellow soldier and well-beloved friend. He often recurred to those happy days, and regretted that when the "Old Hero" left for his home in Tennessee, the strongest link in friendship's chain was severed, for they never met again. No longer was the Executive mansion to him the cheerful "half-way house," with the "latch string out" smiling a ready welcome, but the residence of the constitutional commander in chief of the army of the United States.

But it was in the devotion of the brother and the uncle that the fullness of his heart found vent. His two brothers, Frank, his senior, and Bannister, his junior (for by these familiar names he loved to speak of them), were his joy and his pride. It was his melancholy duty to lay them both in the tomb, and although it was granted them all to exceed the years allotted to man by the Psalmist, yet to the last moment of their lives, they were as dear to one another as when their heroic father fell fighting in defence of his country's banner, and they gathered weeping around their fond and widowed mother's knee. To the children and grandchildren of these brothers, he was all that a human heart pulsating with love and kindness could be.

Following is a copy of an autograph letter of General Jackson's to General Gibson. Readers of Jackson's letters almost invariably look for "Oll Korrect" in them. This letter is given *verbatim* and will be found " O. K." with the exceptions of the words "cartridges," "addition," "women" and "hostility," the first of which he spells, as most of the veterans of the war of 1812 pronounced it, viz., "catridges;" "addition" simply lacks one "d;" and "until" has two "l's." Many official and private letters of Jackson to his friend General Gibson conclusively disprove the popular belief that he was illiterate.

HEADQUARTERS BEFORE ST. MARKS.

APRIL 9, 1818.

Dear Colonel:—I wrote you yesterday, sending duplicates, one by a runner, the other by Capt. McKeever, to which I refer you. In adition to the supply of fifty thousand rations and corn ordered, in mine of yesterday I wish you to send one hundred thousand catridges, if to be spared from the defense of Ft. Gadsden, Colonel Lindsey has been ordered to accompany the supplies ordered with the company of artillerists, brought on by himself, if he has not received it you will communicate the order to him, to accompany these supplies, and to reach St. Marks with his command as early as possible, leaving Peters and Colls companies to garrison Ft. Gadsden. If you have not sent for the 4,000 bushels of corn to New Orleans, or ordered, you will take the earliest opportunity, to have it at Ft. Gadsden, by the period of our return to that post.

This is carried by one of those deluded wretches who have asked for peace and it is granted them, seventeen men, eighteen weomen and thirty children have surrendered, they ask permission to pass by water to Ft. Gadsden. This is granted them and they will remain here untill the runner returns by whom you will write to the commanding officer of St. Marks, Capt. Vashon, under what badge you will know them. I shall be happy to hear from you by return of the runner. I hope that the campaign is approaching a happy termination, I march to-day for the Seewaney, and I hope with the smiles of heaven to put a close to Indian and negro hostillity in this quarter.

I can hear nothing of Colonel Dyer, I wish him up, at this period of the campaign he would be of very great service.

I am yours respectfully,

ANDREW JACKSON.

COL. G. GIBSON,

Q. M. General S. D.,

Fort Gadsden.

P. S.—You will cause the runner who hands you this to return as speedily as you can despatch him, we have got in store a good supply of powder and balls and lead, we want nothing but catridges or catridge paper. A. J.

APPENDIX D.

THE TOMB OF JOSEPH JEFFERSON.

EXTRACT FROM WOOD'S "PERSONAL RECOLLECTIONS OF THE
STAGE," WITH JUDGE GIBSON'S LETTER TO WOOD, AND
THE EPITAPH ON THE TOMB OF JOSEPH JEFFERSON.

" His grave remained for many years unmarked by the slightest
memorial. The visitor to those grounds has often since been
attracted by a tasteful monument to his memory, without at all, it
is likely, knowing the history of its erection.

It is a source of great pleasure for me indeed to have an opportunity of recording an act of humanity and feeling, which its
unostentatious author, I am sure, never recorded for himself. It
will be found in the following letter to me, by the late Chief Justice Gibson, of Pennsylvania, a man whose great power of intellect, and whose vast service in the administration of the judicial
affairs of Pennsylvania for more than thirty years, have received
the homage of the profession everywhere throughout that State,
and along with his amiable, winning disposition in private and
social life, have very recently been the subject of one of the most
true, beautiful and eloquent effusions, 'warm, pure, and fresh,' by
his successor in office, that it has been my happiness to read.
Chief Justice Gibson's sensibilities and taste in the whole range
of the fine arts, music, architecture, painting, statuary, and the
drama, were hardly inferior to his uncommon intellectual parts.
He took the most lively interest in dramatic literature, and dramatic representations generally, and as far as the requirements of
his high judicial station made it decorous, was a patron of our
theatrical representations, in those days of propriety and order,
when the theatre was a place through which even the judicial
ermine might pass, without the suspicion of having brought away
a soil or spot. His letter is as follows :

HARRISBURG, June 25, 1843.

My Dear Sir :—My brother Judge Rogers and myself design to lay a marble
slab over the remains of the late Mr. Jefferson in the Episcopal churchyard, at
this place, and we stand in need of information in respect of one or two particu-

lars. Below you will find a copy of the contemplated inscription sketched by me this morning. Might I request that you would note whatever is amiss in it, and suggest any amendment of which it is susceptible. I think I am accurate in Mr. Jefferson's baptismal name, but I am at a loss for the year of his death. His son, or his daughter, Mrs. Chapman, if she still lives, could supply the deficiency, but I know not where either of them are to be found.

I look back with great pleasure on the days when my relish for theatricals had the freshness of youth, and when the stage was a classic source of its gratification. To the memory of Mr. Jefferson, who, with others, beguiled Judge Rogers, myself, and the play-going public of many a heavy moment, we owe a debt of gratitude which we are anxious to repay. I am aware that he and you were separated in feeling at the close of his life. I am confident, however, that you will aid us with whatever materials you possess.

I shall leave this place on Thursday, and will be thankful for your answer in the meantime.

Very truly, dear sir,
Your friend and servant,
JOHN BANNISTER GIBSON.

WILLIAM B. WOOD, ESQ.

Beneath this marble
are deposited the ashes of

JOSEPH JEFFERSON,

an actor whose unrivaled powers
took in the whole range of comic character,
from pathos to soul-shaking mirth.
His coloring of the part was that of nature, warm, pure and fresh; but of nature
enriched with the finest conceptions of genius.
He was a member of the Chestnut street theatre, Philadelphia,
in its most high and palmy days,
and the compeer
of Cooper, Wood, Warren, Francis,
and a long list of worthies,
who,
like himself,
are remembered with admiration and praise.
He was a native of England.
With an unblemished reputation as a man,
he closed a career of professional success,
in calamity and affliction,
at this place,
in the year 1832.

" I knew him, Horatio; a fellow of infinite jest, and most excellent fancy."

30

I must here correct with the reader an idea which a mistaken impression of the chief justice gives as to a fact. I did so at once to him. There was never at any time, on any subject, the least estrangement between Mr. Jefferson and myself. On the contrary, our personal not less than our professional intercourse was, for thirty years or more, an unbroken circle of regard and pleasure. It remained so to the end of it."

Mr. Wood, on page 467 of his book, gives a very interesting account of his last appearance and farewell address before the public at the Walnut Street Theatre, Philadelphia, in November, 1846. Mr. Wood was then seventy years old, and the patrons of this memorable farewell were among the most highly esteemed and distinguished citizens of Philadelphia. Of the hundred and more of the committee who signed the call, we find the names of the Hon. George M. Dallas, president, and the vice presidents were Chief Justice Gibson, Hon. J. R. Ingersoll, William Peters, Commodore Charles Stewart, U. S. N., and William M. Meredith. On the committee appear the names of Pierce Butler, Henry C. Baird, David Paul Brown, Gen. George Cadwallader, Henry C. Carey, Robert Hare, M. D., Hon. C. J. Ingersoll, Morton McMichael, Hon. E. Joy Morris, Josiah Randall, William Rawle, and those of many other distinguished gentlemen. The next morning Judge Gibson remarked to the retired actor, " Wood, you may consider the exhibition last evening an unanimous certificate of good character from the citizens of Philadelphia."

Apropos of Judge Gibson's interest in the drama generally, and great actors personally, his son, Col. George Gibson, Fifth Infantry, U. S. A., a few months before his death sent to the writer the following characteristic story:

" Messrs. Michael and Patrick Ward (formerly caterers for the old United States Hotel in Philadelphia, during the proprietorship of that very estimable gentleman Pope Mitchell, and who afterwards became the proprietors of the La Pierre House on Broad street) used to relate with considerable gusto the following in relation to Chief Justice Gibson:

" ' The old chief,' as he was familiarly referred to by his acquaintances, had been for many years the guest of the United States Hotel during the sessions of the Supreme Court held in that city, and it was while stopping there that he became acquainted with so many prominent actors.

"One stormy winter night, the chief justice having returned from the theatre, according to his custom seated himself in the office near a large stove for the purpose of warming himself before retiring, and was soon surrounded by quite a party of young lawyers from the rural districts, to whom he was well known, and with them he engaged in conversation. The subject of his remarks naturally turned to the play which he had just witnessed, and during the course of his remarks he expatiated at some length upon the drama generally, and on various distinguished actors, both living and dead, whom it had been his good fortune to see, some of whom he had known personally, and of whom he related several anecdotes in his most felicitous style. Finally, warming with the subject, he exclaimed :

"'But, gentlemen, there is one actor of the present day whose fame is world wide, who as a delineator of *Falstaff* has had no superior since the days of the English actor Warren, and yet I have never had the pleasure of seeing him. I mean, of course, our distinguished Hackett.'

"At this moment the Chestnut street door opened with a bang, and in stalked a tall figure, his feet encased in huge buffalo overshoes, his body wrapped to the throat in a shaggy overcoat, his head covered with a muskrat-skin cap, and several yards of red worsted comfort wound around his neck. A boarder on the opposite side of the circle from the judge happened to notice the entrance of the new-comer, and nodding his head as he approached, saying : 'How do do, Hackett?' and resumed the attitude of listening. Immediately the chief justice rose to his feet, and turning quickly around exclaimed: 'Can it be possible that I have at length the pleasure of being face to face with Mr. Hackett?'

"Vainly endeavoring to get hold of the hand of the new-comer, who commenced backing away from him in the most awkward manner, bowing and scraping his right foot, as well as tugging away at his forelock, the chief justice added, 'Permit me to introduce myself, sir; I am Chief Justice Gibson; have I not the pleasure of addressing Mr. Hackett of the stage ?'   Whereupon the apparition in woolen replied :   ' May it plaze yer Honor, not adzactly Mr. Hackett of the stage, but Mr. Hackett of the omnibus.   I drive omnibus on Chestnut street, and its many a time I have driven you to the old Independence Hall to hould the Supreme Court ; I gist stopped in a bit to get a little warrum.'

"A hearty roar greeted this remark, in which the judge joined after he fairly realized the situation, but which left him in no frame of mind to discourse on Shakespeare and the delineators of his characters."

APPENDIX E.

JUDGE GIBSON'S POEM.

Some time after the preparation of the remarks prefacing the poem attributed to Judge Gibson, authoritative information was received from Mr. John Bannister Gibson Roberts which removes every doubt as to its authorship.

Among Judge Gibson's lady friends was the accomplished and beautiful Anna Rickey, second wife of the late Solomon W. Roberts (a distant relative of the late W. Milnor Roberts), formerly superintendent and chief engineer of the Ohio and Pennsylvania railroad (now the Pittsburgh, Fort Wayne and Chicago railroad), and later of the North Pennsylvania railroad.

Mrs. Solomon W. Roberts II will no doubt be remembered by many in Pittsburgh, as well as by many in Philadelphia. Her beauty was something remarkable, her bearing distinguished, and her movements the embodiment of grace, while her manner had that charming *naivete* to which her accent added a suggestion of the French.   Owing, however, to the retiring disposition of her husband, her life in the "Collonade," or Robinson Row, on Federal street, Allegheny, was quite secluded, for seldom did her presence grace the social gatherings of those who would liked to have become her intimate friends.   She really had but one intimate in Pittsburgh, and that one was Judge Gibson's daughter, Mrs. W. Milnor Roberts.   Late in 1851, shortly before her marriage to Solomon Roberts, Miss Rickey published a volume of poems of 150 pages, entitled " Forest Flowers of the West," and marked one copy: " Presented to Chief Justice Gibson by the Author, 1852." Immediately after his marriage to Miss Rickey, Mr. Roberts bought up the entire edition and destroyed it, a very few copies, which had been presented by the authoress before her marriage, alone escaping his vigilant search.

It was in compliance with the request of the poetess, Mrs. Anna Rickey Roberts, that Judge Gibson made his first and last attempt in rhyme.

In 1854, the year following the judge's death, Mrs. S. W., in calling on her friend, Mrs. W. Milnor Roberts, on Stockton avenue, Allegheny, was shown by the latter the volume of her poems she had given the judge. Picking it up she wrote under her original dedicatory note the following touching lines to the memory of her deceased friend:

> " This book goes from my hand again,
>   But not to thee, oh, not to thee,
> And I recall with bitter pain
>   That thou art but a memory.
>
> " But still a memory so sweet,
>   Of kindly looks and words of cheer,
> The living glances that I meet
>   Are not more cherished, not more dear."

The poetess has long been dead, so also is her husband " but a memory," but a sense of justice, not simply poetic justice, but in equity, it is demanded, that what she did for the judge after his death should be done for her after her death through the agency of a descendant, in fact a namesake of the jurist. Judge Gibson marked " fine " at the end of one of her poems; it is therefore selected for reproduction, though not specially indicative of her style.

A VISION.

When the cooling breeze of even waved the branches to and fro,
And the stars, like guardian angels, watched the sleeping world below,
I leaned upon the casement, with my head upon my hand,
And sent my restless spirit to the realms of fancy-land.

*   *   *   *   *   *   *   *   *

Upon the thick and moveless air rolled a deep funereal bell,
Till the firm rocks heaved and trembled with the thunder of its knell;
Keeping time to its solemn tolling, a ghastly train went by,
Of shadowy forms, that slowly passed before my straining eye.

And my wondering spirit recognized its half-forgotten dead,
With the dust of the tomb upon each brow, whence the living bloom had fled;
And a sudden terror through my soul a fearful shudder sent—
Eternity might ask of me the bright ones time had lent.

One passed me, with her pallid brow encircled by a wreath,
But a serpent bound her temples the withered leaves beneath;
And one swept proudly by me, her dark eyes bright with ire,
And flung, in anger, at my feet, a broken, chordless lyre.

And one gazed at me mournfully, with eyes all dim and meek,
And with her tresses strove to hide a stain on lip and cheek;
One hand clasped a fair rose-bud, but she pressed the leaves apart,
And I saw a fearful canker feeding on the withering heart.

And some went empty-handed, with listless step and slow,
Murmuring over idle thoughts, with voices faint and low;
Thoughts that crushed their young lives recklessly with their gift of glorious
            powers—
Oh, never may my soul again behold its murdered hours.

With hands clasped close together, in vain I strove to speak,
But the effort only ended in an agonizing shriek;
Then fading from my vision, rolled the strange and shadowy land—
I was leaning on the casement, with my head upon my hand.

APPENDIX F.

AN UNPUBLISHED OPINION.

The manuscript of the following opinion by Judge Gibson has been contributed by George Gibson McClure, a grandson of the deceased jurist. It was found among some letters of his grandfather's. It is in Judge Gibson's clear, small hand, occupying less than three and a half pages of unruled foolscap, on which was left a blank border measuring almost two inches wide. It is endorsed on the back: *"Patton vs. Newell, use of Rankin.* Opinion of J. B. G. 24 June, 1822. Gibson delivered opinion of the court." Beneath is written in a strange hand, "Not reported."

A peculiarity of Judge Gibson's writing is that the i's are very rarely dotted; the only exception in this lengthy paper is in the case of names of persons, such as Miller, Brailey, etc. Nevertheless his writing is easily read. Another peculiarity is the straightness and parallelism of his lines. If by chance his first line was not parallel with the sheet he never attempted to rectify the alignment. At a later period his handwriting became even more perfect, and rarely did he erase or interline, and never copied his writing. But to the last he neglected to dot his i's.

Patton vs. Newell, use of Rankin.

It is necessary to inquire what was the mischief intended to be remedied by this particular provision of the Act of 1810. In all the preceding Acts on the subject, although the jurisdiction of the common law courts was preserved, there was an evident desire to draw all the business that was indifferently cognizable by either jurisdiction to that of the justices of the peace; and it was accordingly enacted that any person who should bring suit in court for a demand cognizable by a justice of the peace should recover no costs, unless, before the issuing of the writ, he had filed an affidavit with the prothonotary, that his demand exceeded the jurisdiction of the justice.

But before the passing of the present Act it had been held in *Brailey vs. Miller*, (a) 2 Dall., 74, that a plaintiff in court, whose demand had been reduced to an amount within the limit of a justice's jurisdiction, by *set off*, was nevertheless entitled to costs; and for this satisfactory reason: He could not sue before a justice because the defendant might, by refusing to set off his cross demand, oust the justice of the jurisdiction; and he could not make the set off in the defendant's favor *nolens volens* so as to bind him in another suit; while on the other hand he could swear with a safe conscience that his demand was *beyond* the jurisdiction of a justice; because in equity and good conscience only the balance is demandable as the debt actually due.

What, then, was he to do? The courts were compelled to treat the case as an exception, and to allow the costs. This point was more fully considered in *Sadler vs. Slobaugh*, (b) 3 Sergt. & Rawle, 383, to which I refer those who are desirous of pursuing the mat-

ter further.　The legislature, with the decision in Brailey and
Miller before them when they came to pass the Act of 1810, provide that "A defendant who shall neglect or refuse in *any* case to
set off his demand, whether founded on bond, note, penal or single
bill, writing obligatory, book account, or damages on assumption
against a plaintiff, which shall not exceed the sum of one hundred
dollars, before a justice of the peace, shall be, and is hereby forever barred from recovering against the party plaintiff by any after
suit."

Now I recollect that the chief aim in this provision was to
remove every pretext for resorting to the ordinary courts in the
first instance, by compelling the defendant to set off his demand
at all events.　But still a plaintiff could not sue with safety before
a justice for a demand exceeding a hundred dollars if the defendant might, after the suit was brought, and before the trial, avoid
the set off by assigning his counter claim to a third person; he
would experience the old embarrassment in making choice of the
proper tribunal, and the advantage of being able to proceed without hazard on either hand, would not, as intended, be secured to
him.　It would be of little practical importance that the defendant should be bound to default what continued to be matter of
cross demand till the time of the trial, if he were not bound to
default what was a cross demand *when the plaintiff made his election
of the tribunal;* for it is in reference only to the latter that the
right to exact a set off is of the least value.　The indorsee of a
defendant after suit brought would, therefore, hold the note subject
to the right of the plaintiff, which attached to the service of the
writ, and would be barred unless the indorser had some other
cross demand remaining in his hands sufficient to extinguish the
plaintiff's claims, and to which right of set off attached.　How far
the case might be affected by want of notice to the assignee is not
the question; nor am I at present prepared to decide it, if it
were.

Where the plaintiff's demand exceeds the jurisdiction of a justice, these considerations, I think, will appear conclusive as to the
true construction of this part of the Act.　It does not appear from
the record whether Patton's demand in the suit against Irvine was

for more than a hundred dollars or not ; and as the judge laid
down as a rule applicable to all cases, that a defendant may rightly
assign at any time before the trial, the direction was erroneous on
the ground just stated. But I am far from thinking that any distinction was intended where the plaintiff's demand should be
originally cognizable by a justice. The language of the section
is positive and general ; and it would, therefore, require a strong
reason to justify a particular construction of it as applicable to
one case, and a different construction as applicable to another. No
such reason, however, exists. It could not have escaped the notice
of the legislature, that nothing operates more powerfully as a pre-
disposing cause of litigiousness than the providing of ready means
for its gratification. They intended to render justice more easy of
access, but not to foster a spirit of litigation. While suitors were,
on the one hand, relieved from the hardship of being obliged
either to pursue for a small demand, under the burden of great
delay and considerable expense, or abandon it altogether, they were,
on the other, required to settle their disputes under the jurisdiction
provided, with as much dispatch, as little vexation, and as few
suits as possible.

This requisition would be attended with but little practical
effect, if a defendant who should be disposed to reserve his demand
for purposes of annoyance in a second action, were permitted to
assign it after the writ had been served on him. A defendant is
not permitted to set off a demand which he has acquired after the
commencement of the suit; and I see no reason why the converse
should not hold with respect to his supposed power to evade the
right of the plaintiff to exact it where the set off may be made.
No hardship results from this construction. A defendant's property cannot be locked up in his possession by it either to any considerable amount, or for any considerable time. If the demand
which he has against the plaintiff exceeds the jurisdiction of the
justice, he is not bound to reserve it at all. If he has a variety of
demands, each of which is within the jurisdiction of the justice,
he is bound to reserve only as much as is sufficient to extinguish
the plaintiff's claim ; and an assignee of the rest will hold it discharged, and succeed against the plaintiff in a suit on such cause

31

of action, if he can show that the assignor had enough in his
hands at the time of his trial to have extinguished the plaintiff's
claim, if he had chosen to default it; for the law will make the
application against the assignor rather than against the assignee for
a valuable consideration, who has an equity against the assignor in
this respect.

Whether, therefore, a defendant having enough in his hands to
extinguish the plaintiff's claim, uses it as a set off or not, is imma-
terial; the law makes the application for him, and the claim of
each is respectively an extinguishment of that of the other. Then,
as respects the sum actually reserved, the time during which it is
thus locked up is inconsiderable; law suits before justices being,
in the usual course, determined within a few days from their
commencement; so that the inconvenience can, in any view,
scarcely be felt as a hardship.

It is said, however, that Irvine himself being an indorsee could
not have set off this note in the action before Justice Moore, there
having been no previous dealings directly between the parties, and
therefore no mutuality. I see no force in that. The question does
not arise on the Defalcation Act (if happily the argument would be
available if it did) but on the Act giving jurisdiction to justices
for demands not exceeding one hundred dollars, the words of which
are very large, and embrace every demand, " founded on bond, *note*,
penal or single bill, writing obligatory, book account, or damages
on assumption." Now, the indorsee of a note certainly has a
demand *founded on it*. But even if the case did not fall within
the express letter, yet as the Act is remedial in this respect, I
would be disposed to construe it liberally in advancement of the
remedy. Judgment reversed, and a *venire de novo* awarded.

INDEX.

www.ingramcontent.com/pod-product-compliance
Lightning Source LLC
Chambersburg PA
CBHW031405020726
47499CB00005B/1472